"Rafe, you're a he...

She paused until he turned to face her. "Not just because you saved those orphaned children, but because in the middle of a war, you took time to write to kids you didn't know. And you didn't use your letters to tell us how brave you were or how tough. Instead, you talked to the kids from your heart."

His hand came up to cover hers. It felt strong and steady, unlike her heart that was beating so fast and loud that she was certain he could hear it.

"I'm not a hero, Abby. But here, with you and the kids, I almost believe I could be one."

"Believe," she whispered. "Because I do."

Dear Reader,

Welcome to Silhouette **Special Edition**...welcome to romance.

Fall is in full swing and so are some of your favorite authors, who have some delightful and romantic stories in store.

Our THAT SPECIAL WOMAN! title for the month is *Babies on Board*, by Gina Ferris. On a dangerous assignment, an independent heroine becomes an instant mom to three orphans in need of her help.

Also in store for you in October is the beginning of LOVE LETTERS, an exciting new series from Lisa Jackson. These emotional stories have a hint of mystery, as well...and it all begins in *A Is for Always*.

Rounding out the month are *Bachelor Dad* by Carole Halston, *An Interrupted Marriage* by Laurey Bright and *Hesitant Hero* by Christina Dair. Sandra Moore makes her Silhouette debut with her book, *High Country Cowboy*, as **Special Edition**'s PREMIERE author.

I hope you enjoy this book, and all of the stories to come!

Sincerely,

Tara Gavin
Senior Editor
Silhouette Books

Please address questions and book requests to:
Silhouette Reader Service
U.S.: 3010 Walden Ave., P.O. Box 1325, Buffalo, NY 14269
Canadian: P.O. Box 609, Fort Erie, Ont. L2A 5X3

CHRISTINA
DAIR
HESITANT HERO

Silhouette®

SPECIAL EDITION®

Published by Silhouette Books
America's Publisher of Contemporary Romance

For the servicemen and women who taught America's
children that soldiers are real, not just faces on the evening
news. For Marines Lance Corporal Hector Escalante
and Chief Warrant Officer Tom Nunes who wrote
to my children during Operation Desert Storm.
For Kerry Carney-Flores, an extraordinary teacher,
and all the fifth and sixth graders in her 1990-91 class.

 SILHOUETTE BOOKS

ISBN 0-373-09917-7

HESITANT HERO

Copyright © 1994 by Louzana Kaku

Printed in U.S.A.

Books by Christina Dair

Silhouette Special Edition

A Will of Her Own #666
Hesitant Hero #917

CHRISTINA DAIR

began her adult life as a high school English teacher. It wasn't until she "retired" from teaching to raise her own family that she found time and nerve to pursue her first love: writing. Though she misses the challenge of working with young people, she appreciates the fact that her computer doesn't talk back to her and she will never have to read another essay about anyone's summer vacation.

Christina's first book was published in 1984; she has written novels of romance and romantic suspense. *Hesitant Hero* is her second Silhouette Special Edition.

Christina resides with her husband and their two teenage daughters in Cerritos, California, where she is active with school and community groups. She is a member of the Romance Writers of America and the Authors Guild.

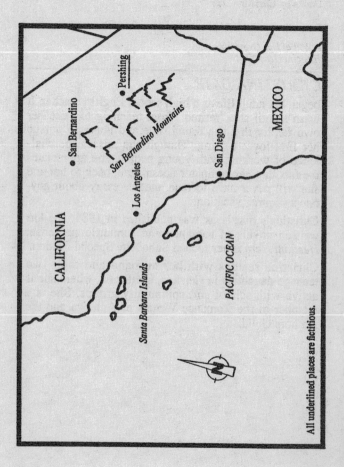

CALIFORNIA

San Bernardino

Pershing

San Bernardino Mountains

Los Angeles

San Diego

MEXICO

Santa Barbara Islands

PACIFIC OCEAN

All underlined places are fictitious.

Prologue

December 1

To any serviceman or servicewoman,
Hi, my name is Kevin Scott. I'm a fourth grader at
Pershing Elementary School in Pershing, California. I like baseball. My favorite team is the Dodg-
ers. I like football, too. But not as much.

My teacher Mrs. Dixon is making our class write
these letters. She says it's a good way to learn to write
friendly letters. I never thought about writing an
unfriendly letter, but I guess people do it. She says
we should write to you because you're going to be
away from home for Christmas. She says you'll be
lonely. Is that true? Are you lonely? Do you miss
your family? She also says you're going to get shot
at. Is that true? Are people shooting at you? If they
are, you'd better wear your helmet.

Well, I guess that's all for now. I hope you'll write back to me. If you do, I'll write to you again.

Your friend,
Kevin Scott

P.S. I just thought I'd tell you that you don't have to be away from home to be lonely. Since my dad isn't here anymore, I get lonely for him a lot. Sometimes I can be in the middle of a great big crowd and still feel lonely. I just thought you should know that.

Christmas Day
San Miguel Island

Dear Kevin Scott,
Thank you for your Christmas card addressed to any serviceman. I especially liked your drawing of the Christmas tree with all the presents under it. We have been deployed just outside the capital city since December 15. It doesn't feel much like the holidays here, but I've hung your drawing over my bunk. It helps to make the place look more like Christmas.

My name is Rafael Calderon. I'm a gunnery sergeant from the Second Marine Division out of Camp Lejeune, North Carolina. Gunnery sergeant doesn't mean I work with guns. That's my rank. I work on the trucks and other vehicles we use to move the soldiers and equipment. It's important work, but it's not as dangerous as a lot of other jobs.

Gunnery Sergeant Rafael Calderon
USMC

P.S. I know you don't have to be away from home to be lonely. But you don't have to be lonely when

tion, when Sergeant Calderon had reminded her he didn't want any of "that hero stuff."

Then she'd remembered the expectant faces of the children who'd been writing to him for the past eighteen months—first when he'd been deployed to the island of San Miguel off the South American coast as part of the peacekeeping force, and later when he'd spent months in the hospital and convalescence. They'd been fourth graders when they received the soldier's first letter. They were fifth graders now, only a few days from becoming sixth graders. And so she'd kept silent. Her students had been dreaming about meeting their pen pal for a long time, and they'd spent the past six weeks planning today's festivities. They deserved the opportunity to show Rafael Calderon just how much he meant to them.

Though she was certain that the program of patriotic songs, speeches and poetry the students had put together was enough to make any grizzled war veteran want to turn tail and run, she'd simply told the sergeant that since he'd survived the San Miguel Crisis, she was certain he could survive a day at Pershing Elementary School. She only hoped she was right.

"Martin. Leo." Despite the smile on her face, Abigail used her best teacher-wants-your-attention voice on the two boys who were still high-fiving in the back of the room.

"Yes, Mrs. Dixon," they answered in unison.

"Please be seated. Doreen," she cautioned the little girl in the front row. Once the diminutive redhead started giggling, there was no stopping her. And her giggles were of the contagious variety; not even Abigail was immune.

Abigail waited until she was certain every eye in the room was on her. "Now everyone knows his or her job. Mr. Williams will escort Sergeant Calderon to the auditorium in fifteen minutes. If everyone stays on task as we practiced, that will be time enough for us to get ready.

"When I count to five, I want each of you with a specific job to hop to it. The rest of you will line up quietly at the door. One. Two. Three." Abigail stopped and nailed the two boys in the back with her most ferocious scowl. They smiled back at her. "Four," she continued once the youngsters were quiet. "Five."

She watched in satisfaction as the ten- and eleven-year-olds went quietly to work. Several of the students slipped out the door to alert the classrooms up and down the hall. Others took their musical instruments and headed for the band room. Still others draped sashes made of red or blue calico over their white shirts and went to join the choir in the auditorium. The flag monitors picked up their bags of small hand-size American flags, the keeper of the book collected the scrapbook the class had assembled and the two students who'd been elected to present the plaque argued in whispers over who should carry it.

Abigail smiled and placed her hand over her stomach to quiet the butterflies. It was too late to go back to the small classroom ceremony she'd envisioned. Too late to cancel the extravaganza the entire school had become involved with. The tide of excitement over Sergeant Calderon's proposed visit had swept from her classroom to the school to the entire town of Pershing. At least she'd been able to politely decline the offer of the high school marching band.

She only hoped the children wouldn't see how nervous she was, because she suddenly realized that it didn't matter that they'd practiced this umpteen times, including three dress rehearsals. All she could think of were the possibilities for disaster. She was no general; what had made her think she could marshal four hundred exuberant children into an organized welcoming committee? Too late to chicken out now, she told herself sternly. Whatever happened, she would congratulate her small army on a job well done.

And if Gunnery Sergeant Rafael Calderon wasn't suitably appreciative of their efforts, she'd make him regret surviving the San Miguel Crisis.

Rafe Calderon folded his six-foot-one-inch frame into the chair that Doug Williams gestured to and thought of all the times he'd visited the principal's office when he'd been in school. None of those men had ever smiled at him or been so effusively glad to see him.

"Can I offer you a cup of coffee?" Mr. Williams asked as he crossed to the corner of the room where an electric coffeemaker sat on a shaky aluminum TV tray. It was obvious that Pershing Elementary, which was located only a few miles from the resort town of Palm Springs, did not operate on a lavish budget.

"No, sir." Rafe resisted the urge to squirm under the principal's scrutiny as he'd done all those years ago. "But you go right ahead and have some," he suggested as the other man looked longingly at the dark liquid. "I don't care for the stuff when the temperature tops eighty."

Doug Williams was at the door in three long strides. "Ethel," he called as he stuck his head into the outer office. "Get Sergeant Calderon a cold drink. And be sure to bring some ice."

While the principal of Pershing Elementary waited for his secretary to return with the soda, Rafe took the time to look over the diplomas and awards hanging on the wall behind the man's desk. He studied the oversize books in the bookcase and remembered how he'd hated elementary school. As he recalled, there'd been little enough to like.

How many students had taunted him about his ragged clothes and unkempt appearance? How many times had he been told he was nothing but trouble? How many teachers had told him he'd never amount to anything? How many demerits had he earned? How many hours of detention had he spent in the office? In a neighborhood filled with poverty, he'd been the poorest of the poor. In an area where struggling, hopeful mothers still slicked their children's hair and mended their clothes, he'd been the one they looked down on.

He could almost feel himself break out in a cold sweat when he thought about it. It had been a mistake to come here. A mistake to dredge up old memories. He had to fight the impulse to get up and walk out the door. If not for the kids, he would.

He'd resisted coming as long as he could. He'd held out against the children's entreaties. Held out against his own desire to meet the kids who'd cared about him and encouraged him when he was ready to give up. Held out against Mrs. Abigail Dixon's calm, rational voice on the phone. He'd thought he could hold out against anything until he received the letter from little Kevin Scott, confiding that he didn't have long to live—and that he didn't want to die without meeting his best friend, Rafael Calderon. Life might have made Rafe tough, but even he couldn't deny a dying child's wish.

Rafe rubbed his leg. The dull ache was a sure sign that he'd put too much stress on it today. And that he was too tense.

He sat up straighter, reminding himself he was a U.S. Marine now. Elementary-school principals no longer had the power to intimidate him. Even more important, he wouldn't do anything that might make the kids think less of him. In their eyes, at least, he'd be a hero.

After offering Rafe the cold soda, Doug Williams slipped into the chair behind the desk. He smiled. He discussed the weather. Then he got down to the subject that everyone wanted to ask Rafe about—The Crisis, as the occupation of San Miguel had come to be called. Not a war or even an invasion, but a crisis. As far as Rafe was concerned, that was the politicians' cowardly term for disguising the fighting that has cost close to two hundred American lives and more than twice that many wounded. The nine months on San Miguel hadn't felt like a simple crisis; it had been the darkest time in Rafe's troubled life.

Doug Williams took another sip of coffee. "So how is that leg coming along?"

"It's getting stronger." Rafe fought the urge to rub the area around the scar that curved from the inside of his knee up to his hipbone. "Almost as good as new." He only wished the scar on his soul would heal as quickly.

"That was a brave thing you did, rescuing those children."

Rafe shrugged. That kind of talk always made him uneasy. "You would have done the same."

"I like to think so." The principal stared into his coffee cup. "But I'm not so sure."

Rafe shrugged again and steered the conversation in another direction. Even talking about the weather was preferable to discussing his role in The Crisis. Rafe had almost run out of small talk when Doug Williams checked his watch and sprang from his chair.

"I'll bet the students are anxious to meet you," the principal told him. Rafe wondered why that thought hadn't occurred to the man fifteen minutes ago.

It was a relief to follow the principal out of the office and down the hall toward Mrs. Dixon's classroom. Though the heat outside reminded him of the time he'd spent on the barren island of San Miguel, the long, dim hallway was cool. At the end of the corridor was a wall made of glass blocks; the June sunlight streamed through, almost blinding him. He squinted against the glare and concentrated on not limping. And on blocking out his own school days.

If these halls didn't seem as massive as the ones in his elementary school, he told himself it was because he'd grown up. If these walls didn't seem as much like a prison, he told himself it was because he'd tasted freedom. But nothing could explain the eerie stillness that permeated the building. He couldn't imagine a school full of children being this silent. On San Miguel this kind of quiet would have had him looking over his shoulder or around corners for an ambush.

The silence was so overwhelming that Rafe didn't see her until he was only a few feet away. Against the bright sunlight streaming in through the glass, she was merely a slim, still silhouette. He could see that she was dressed in white, and he wondered if that might be why he hadn't noticed her at first. To overlook someone in such close proximity under different circumstances could have cost him his life.

He couldn't take his eyes off the diminutive form standing in the wash of light. If this was Mrs. Abigail Dixon, she was younger than he'd expected. And smaller. He wondered how anyone so tiny could keep control of a roomful of active kids. The brilliance shimmering around her dark, curly hair made Rafe think of a halo, and the slight pouf of her sleeves almost looked like angel wings. How strange, he thought, for a man who'd lost his faith in heaven to suddenly be seeing angels. He wasn't absolutely sure she was real until he saw her green eyes. He didn't think angels would have eyes that made a man think of satin sheets and sultry summer nights.

Abigail studied Gunnery Sergeant Rafael Calderon as he marched down the hallway. And yes, marched was the right word, for his gait was even and he looked neither left nor right. He was a big man—probably a shade over six feet—made to seem even bigger by the way he held his body and shoulders straight. She didn't have to be told that he wasn't pleased to be here. His face—at least what she could see of it beneath the shadow cast by the brim of his hat—was expressionless. And there was a tension about him, as though he was walking into a fight rather than a welcoming committee. But, bless him, he'd worn his uniform. That, she knew, would delight the students.

"Sergeant Calderon," she said when he halted a few feet away. Taking a step forward, she held out her hand. "I'm Abigail Dixon. We spoke on the phone," she reminded him as he reluctantly took her hand. She'd never felt so tiny as she did now, with her hand engulfed by his much larger one. "I'm delighted you could come for a visit."

"I appreciate the invitation, ma'am." He might as well have been reading from the phone book for all the emotion he put into it. "And I've appreciated all the cards and letters, too."

His eyes. There was something dark and dangerous in the brown depths, Abigail decided, now that she could see them beneath the brim of his hat. Some enigmatic anger directed at her. Then, as quickly as she'd seen it, it was gone, replaced by a cool gaze that was completely impersonal.

"As I told you in the letters I wrote and in our phone conversations, the children have come to think of you as a very dear friend." She tried to keep the censure from her voice, but weeks of begging and cajoling had taken a toll on her normally even temper. She still didn't understand why he'd been so reluctant to visit. Now she was forced to admit that if he didn't show the students any more warmth than he was showing now, all her work would have been in vain. "The students are excited to finally meet you."

"I'm anxious to meet them, too."

Abigail sighed. He was *anxious* to meet them. Not delighted or excited, but anxious. During all the planning and preparation, this was one problem she'd never anticipated. Who would have thought the man who'd written such warm, encouraging letters would turn out to be so cold? She could only hope the students would be so excited they wouldn't notice their hero was as stiff as the collar on his uniform.

Abigail bestowed one of her sweetest smiles on Rafael Calderon, but she couldn't detect even the slightest softening in his expression. He reminded her of a balloon with too much air in it. She wished she could give him one quick jab in the stomach, just to see if she could let some of that stiffness out. What she did instead was glance from the soldier to the principal and back again.

"Why don't we join the students, Sergeant Calderon," she suggested. "I'm sure they're getting impatient."

"I'd like that. And please, call me Rafe." He smiled then, though it was gone almost as quickly as it had appeared. "The way you say *sergeant* puts me in mind of a general who's about to start issuing orders."

She noticed that the principal smiled at that, though he quickly coughed into his hand in an effort to cover the fact. Doug had told her on more than one occasion that she tended to be a "bossy little thing." She supposed that came from being five feet nothing and teaching elementary-school students who were starting to pass her up.

She smiled at the big man again. "Please follow me, Rafe."

Then, just as they'd practiced, with her on the marine's left and Doug on his right, they led him down the corridor toward the big double doors that opened into the auditorium. With perfect timing, she and Doug threw open the doors simultaneously, so that Gunnery Sergeant Calderon was treated to an unobstructed view of the auditorium festooned in red-white-and-blue crepe paper, with four hundred silent students—and eight hundred wide eyes—riveted on the big man in his blue dress uniform.

In the moment of absolute silence that greeted his entrance, Abigail watched as the arm of Mrs. Braswell, the band leader, started its downstroke. She heard only the first wobbly notes of "The Star-Spangled Banner" before the room erupted into a cheering, flag-waving mass of red, white and blue. When she turned back toward the object of all this adulation, she was satisfied to discover that he looked as if she'd landed that punch right in his solar plexus like she'd wanted.

Stunned. That was the only coherent thought Rafe could manage. He was stunned. He didn't know if he should smile or wave, walk into the frenzy or turn and run. Instead he did the one thing that came as a natural reflex. He raised his right hand and gave a smart salute to the general assembly, causing the crowd to turn up the volume of their cheering—which was probably a good thing, he decided, as he listened to the muted sounds of the band dutifully grinding its way through the final, excruciating notes of the national anthem.

Just as he'd begun to wonder if the screaming and cheering would go on forever, Mrs. Dixon extended her right hand as far above her head as possible. It barely reached the top of his hat, but it settled the crowd into silence. Before he could decide what to do next, two girls materialized beside him wearing blue skirts, white blouses, big red bows at their throat and Uncle Sam hats. He smiled down at them.

"Hello, Doreen," he said to the little redhead. She giggled and blushed. He turned to the brunette. "Hi, Maria."

She blushed like her counterpart, but managed to say, "I'm so glad you're here."

Rafe felt a wave of relief at getting the names right. He was overwhelmingly grateful for the thirty-one Christmas cards the class had sent him this year, each with a photo enclosed. He'd studied those pictures for the last month, so that now, when it really counted, he could call each of the kids by name. He'd been determined that there wouldn't be one child who felt slighted or neglected. He remembered how that felt, and he'd face machine-gun fire before he'd do that to one of these kids. Now all his work was paying off.

When the girls each crooked an elbow toward him, he put his hands through their arms and allowed himself to be led down the aisle toward the stage as the band puffed and thumped its way through "The Marine Hymn." This time the band was joined by the choir, whose members each wore a checkered sash across a white shirt. The singers, in their red or blue sashes, stood all around the front of the auditorium.

Rafe wasn't sure why the display of the national colors and the efforts of a beginning band and youthful choir would have him fighting back tears, he only knew that he was. And he knew whose fault it was. Once Rafe had been led to the stage and seated between Mrs. Dixon and Mr. Williams, he glared down at the tiny woman who was, he was certain, the mastermind behind this entire event.

"I told you I didn't want any hero stuff," he muttered.

Abigail Dixon smiled up at him, completely unfazed by his attempt to intimidate her. "Yes, you did."

Doug Williams planted his elbows on his knees and cast the soldier a sympathetic look. "Abigail rarely takes orders. She likes to give them."

Abigail smoothed a wrinkle from the skirt of her white dress. "Hmph." She shifted her gaze from the two men to the student approaching the microphone and back to the men. The amusement in the principal's expression didn't phase her. Doug Williams was the same age as her older brother. To her brother's delight, Doug had teased her relentlessly throughout her life. The marine's scowl, however, made her want to squirm. She smiled up at him instead. "I know you'll want to give Jeremy your undivided attention."

Rafe was relieved that he recognized Jeremy, too. The boy's blond hair and blue eyes were as perfect in person as they'd appeared in the photograph. Rafe knew, from the letters the boy had written, that Jeremy's father owned the local grocery store and that his mother was the only photographer in town. He was the type of boy who would have made Rafe feel poor and dirty when he'd been that age, before Rafe had shown any indication that he would top six feet or learn to use his fists.

It was hard for Gunnery Sergeant Rafael Calderon to believe that a boy like this was standing at the microphone welcoming him to Pershing. Hard to believe that a boy like this would have anything to do with the boy Rafe had been. But then, he'd made sure the children of Pershing didn't know about his rough childhood. Instead, he'd written to them about a close-knit family and an ideal childhood. In less than twenty-four hours he'd be gone again, and there would be no chance of these kids learning the truth.

The boy cleared his throat. "Gunnery Sergeant Calderon, teachers, students, we are here to welcome a hero."

The "hero" part made Rafe want to squirm. Instead, he sat ramrod straight and hoped no one would figure out that he was a phony.

"We know why the world considers Sergeant Rafael Calderon a hero," Jeremy continued. "After his single-handed rescue of children from the missionary orphanage, the TV and newspapers hailed his actions as heroic. They said he was brave and deserved a medal." Jeremy slanted a quick look at the hero. "They were right. He did deserve a medal. But the students in Mrs. Dixon's class already knew that Sergeant Calderon was a hero. He'd been our hero for nine months by that time, ever since he answered Kevin Scott's letter addressed to any serviceman or woman.

"Gunnery Sergeant Calderon was our hero because he took the time to write to us. Because he took the time to share his life with us. Because he took the time to tell us how important family is. How important it is to study hard in school and try our best. How lucky we are to have a great teacher like Mrs. Dixon to teach us. How much we should appreciate our own parents, and even our little brothers and sisters."

Rafe bit the inside of his cheeks to keep from smiling when Jeremy's fair skin turned pink because of the laughter that followed this remark. When one of the younger students, probably a kindergartner and obviously Jeremy's little brother, stood up and waved his flag until his classmates shushed him and tugged him back into his seat, Rafe couldn't help the chuckle that escaped.

Jeremy gave his sibling a quelling look, then continued. "And so we say welcome to our friend and our hero, Gunnery Sergeant Rafael Calderon."

There was polite applause and then the band and choir broke into "My Country 'Tis of Thee." Next Rachael Nightwind—Rafe recognized her by the thick dark braid and serious brown eyes—asked everyone to rise for the Pledge of Allegiance. Once everyone was seated again, Matt Jackson read a poem he'd written about friendship, and Sally James and Shameka Jackson sang a duet. When the band teacher, who Rafe thought looked old enough to have been around when Beethoven was writing music, took over the drums and started a catchy beat, Rafe couldn't help wondering what was next.

Abigail slanted the soldier a quick glance as the next group of students took the stage. This was it, the moment of truth. They'd managed to surprise a chuckle out of him when Jeremy's little brother stood up and cheered, but now they'd find out if he had a real sense of humor. Staring at his stern profile, Abigail was very much afraid they were about to discover that he didn't have a humorous bone in his body.

Rafe leaned close to her as the students took their places. "That's Kevin Scott, isn't it?"

Abigail nodded. "And Chad Martinez and Andrew Chang."

Rafe studied the trio for a moment. "Kevin looks good, doesn't he?"

Abigail noticed that the boy's shirt was still tucked in and his hair neatly combed. There was no dirt on his face and no milk mustache on his upper lip. It wasn't that he started to school messy; she'd seen him step out of the apartment he shared with his mother and little sister, looking as fresh and neat as a model. Kevin was just one of those kids who never stayed that way. By the time he arrived at school, his shirttail was usually hanging out and his hair standing on end. Dirt was drawn to him like a magnet, and he didn't bother to use his sleeve after lunch, let alone a napkin. But today, bless his heart, he looked like a perfect little angel.

Abigail beamed. "Yes, he looks wonderful."

But her attention was centered on Rafe rather than on the boy. She hoped the soldier would be amused by the rap song Kevin had written. The student had been riding a wave of unusual popularity since he'd convinced the class pen pal to come for a visit. Abigail was delighted by the boy's newfound self-confidence and the fact that he'd quit telling tall tales to get attention. The time and effort he'd put into writing "The Rafael Rap" was icing on the cake. For Kevin's sake, she hoped Rafe had the sense of humor to enjoy it.

The three boys began swaying to the beat of the drums. Kevin stepped up to the mike. "We're here to honor our good friend Rafe. We're glad he came home sound and safe."

Chad leaned into the microphone. "He sent us lots of letters and cards. We sent him all the love in our hearts."

"We heard soldiers were s'posed to shoot and kill," Andrew rhymed. "But savin' lives gives Rafe a thrill."

The three boys put their hands in the air and swayed from left to right. "Say hey." They swayed left. "Say ho."

They swayed right. "Say hey." The entire audience swayed and sang with them. "Say ho."

Abigail was relieved to see that Rafe was starting to loosen up. Not only was he smiling, but he hadn't thrown her a threatening glance since the trio started. She felt herself relax when she realized that the two men on stage with her were starting to sway with the audience just as she was. She discovered that even the butterflies fluttering around in her stomach were beginning to settle down.

"Now Rafe's our pal. He's our man. He has been since The Crisis began."

"He gives us love and wise advice, without ever thinkin' twice."

"Let's let him know we're glad he's here. Let's all stand up and give a cheer."

The entire audience rose and swayed left. "Say hey," the children sang. They swayed right. "Say ho."

Abigail smiled. One more hey and ho, and Kevin's rap song would be at a successful close.

"Say hey. Say ho."

Abigail was ready to resume her seat when Kevin stepped back to the microphone. "One more time let's let him know we'll still be friends when he must go."

The audience remained on its feet. "Say hey. Say ho. Say hey. Say ho."

Just as Abigail was starting to fear that Kevin would prove as difficult to get offstage as the R & B singer James Brown, Mrs. Braswell brought the rap song to an end with a crescendo on the drums that prompted enthusiastic applause. Abigail was impressed; she would never have guessed the older woman was capable of such a display of showmanship.

Once the audience settled down and the three rappers finished taking their bows, Sylvia Santiago presented Rafe with the scrapbook the students had kept of the San Miguel Crisis and of Rafe's heroic rescue of the missionary children. The band played a thankfully shortened version of "Ode To Joy."

While the choir was singing Bill Wither's "You've Got a Friend," Abigail leaned close to Rafe and whispered, "The students have one more presentation, then you'll have a chance to speak to the assembly." She glanced up at the big clock on the wall. They were running just a few minutes longer than she'd anticipated, probably because of the applause and the impromptu addition to "The Rafael Rap." "You'll want to keep your remarks to about five minutes."

The grip Rafe took on her wrist was almost as intense as the look in his dark eyes. "What do you mean by 'remarks'?"

"You know, remarks," she repeated. "A brief thank-you." She smiled up into the dark eyes that seemed to glitter like shards of glass. "A speech."

"A speech?" His grip tightened. "No one mentioned a speech."

Abigail decided that *speech* had undoubtedly been the wrong word to use. With her free hand, she patted the one gripping her wrist. "A talk. Just a few words of appreciation. Something to let the students know you care."

"You never mentioned a speech before."

For good reason, Abigail decided. "It doesn't really matter what you say—"

"Good. I won't say anything."

"—as much as it matters that you make the effort." He muttered something under his breath that Abigail was glad she couldn't quite make out. "Oh, come now. Anyone who can face bullets and bombs can face an auditorium of young children. How difficult can it be?"

Rafe used his free hand to wipe the sheen of perspiration from his forehead as the choir assured him he had a friend. "I'd rather face bullets," he muttered. "Heck, I'd rather face a tank with machine guns."

Abigail had worried that the students might resist the speeches and poetry, but they had thrown all their creative energy into them. She had also expected Rafe to be slightly anxious to thank the students; instead, he was acting like she'd asked him to face a firing squad.

"You have about three minutes to think of something to say. Even a simple thank-you would delight them." When he continued to glare at her, she added, "Surely a grown man—a man who faced bullets and machine-gun fire—isn't afraid of a few elementary-school students. None of them are carrying guns."

"I'm not scared."

"Good." Abigail relaxed.

"I'm terrified."

She shook her head; she couldn't have heard him right. "What?"

"Terrified."

The music faded and the last two students stepped onto the stage, carrying the large wood-and-brass plaque between them.

Abigail gave him an exasperated look. "You'd better get un-terrified. You're next."

She could barely keep from laughing at the expression on the war hero's face as the two students presented him with the plaque designating him the official hero of Room 23 and containing the name of each student in the class. Rafe rose when they approached him and took it gingerly, much as one would handle a live grenade. The assembled students and teachers rose and cheered as he stood there, holding the symbol of all their love and concern. Abigail felt her emotions make a sudden turn from amused to deeply touched. She was just brushing a tear from her cheek when Rafe set the plaque carefully on his chair. She gave him a watery smile of encouragement just as his hand snaked out to grab her wrist.

"I'm not facing that microphone alone, Teacher." He gave her a smile that showed a slash of white teeth against his dark skin. The smile didn't reach his eyes. "You're going in with me."

Chapter Two

Abigail looked from the big hand that grasped her wrist out into the cheering crowd and then up into Rafael Calderon's dark eyes. "What do you mean, you're not 'going in alone'? This isn't a military operation."

The big man nodded once. "It's much worse. It's talking in front of a crowd. At a microphone."

"So?"

"I need someone there in case I don't know what to say."

Abigail ignored the still-cheering crowd and smiled up at the soldier. This was something she understood. She was used to dealing with students who were scared to speak in front of the class. She'd had six years to perfect her smile and words of encouragement. "Just say what's in your heart."

Rafe shook his head. "I don't want them to know I'm scared speechless."

"You won't be when you get up there."

"That's not a chance I'm willing to take."

Abigail glanced around the auditorium, where students still shouted and waved their miniature American flags. Her smile plastered on her face, she turned her attention back to the stubborn man before her. Through stiffened lips, she said, "For goodness' sake, you could recite the Pledge of Allegiance and they'd think you were brilliant."

"I'm not sure I'd remember it."

"Oh, for heaven's sake." She concentrated on keeping her smile in place. "What do you expect me to do?"

"Just be there for moral support. Or in case my mouth locks up on me." He smiled at her then. "It seems only fair, since you're the one who tricked me into this."

Her mouth fell open. She snapped it back into a smile. "*Tricked* you?"

The big marine nodded. "You told me that the kids just wanted to say hi."

"They do."

"You convinced me the kids were worried that I was hurt worse than I admitted. That I wasn't getting well like I said I was."

"They were."

"I told you I didn't want any of this hero stuff."

She sighed and rose. He had her on that one. "Very well."

"Thanks." He kept his grip on her wrist, as though afraid she'd turn and run, then sighed deeply. "How long do I have?"

"You make it sound like I'm a doctor reading your X rays. This isn't deadly, you know." Abigail checked the big school clock. "You have about three minutes until recess."

"I think I can manage that." He turned and took three quick strides to the microphone, dragging Abigail along so quickly that she was afraid she'd get whiplash.

The cheering died down, but the roomful of smiles was still aimed directly at Sergeant Rafael Calderon—marine, war hero and genuine idol of all four hundred youngsters. The students had never looked at her that way, Abigail realized as she felt Rafe's hand leave her wrist and glide to the small of her back. She'd never had such complete, unwavering attention in all her life. It was amazing. Yet it was unnerving. She understood why the marine's hand trembled against her spine. She felt her own hands grow clammy in the silence.

Rafe cleared his throat and prayed that his voice wouldn't fail him now. "I want to thank everyone for such a wonderful welcome. I never dreamed when I answered Kevin's first letter that his whole class would adopt me. And when I came to visit, I had no idea the whole school would turn out to welcome me." He took the time to smile and take a deep gulp of air. "I can see that your teachers have drilled you on it a lot, and I want each of you to know that you did a terrific job."

"The band was wonderful," he told them, and realized suddenly that he meant it. The songs might have been a little off-key, but he'd never heard music that affected him as much. "And the choir was great." That, again, was the truth; they might have been a little flat in places, but their youthful voices were the only ones that had ever had him fighting back tears. "I feel like the luckiest guy who ever wore a uniform. I only wish that every soldier who returned from San Miguel could have been here today.

"I want to thank Doreen and Maria for making me feel welcome and Jeremy for his greeting." He went on, mentioning each student in turn until he'd worked his way up to the two who'd presented the plaque. He was determined that he wouldn't forget even one of them. "I see lots of other students that I recognize in the band and the choir and out in the audience. Thanks to each of you for making me feel welcome. And thanks to Mrs. Dixon for lying to me."

He smiled down into the disapproving scowl she'd turned on him and hoped she couldn't see the tears that were starting to blur his vision. "I told her I didn't want any hero stuff, and she lied and said not to worry." He looked back at the blurry sea of little faces. "I'm glad she lied, or I might not have shown up. And I would have missed the most important event of my life.

"I also want to thank you for all the cards and letters you sent while I was on San Miguel and when I was in the hospital. And for the teddy bears and the cookies and everything else." Rafe cleared his throat again, hoping to keep the tears from clogging it completely. A bell rang, and though he was certain it signaled recess, not one student moved. He smiled at the crowd. "You'll never know how much I appreciate everything. You helped me through the tough times, and I hope I'm going to get a chance to thank each and every one of you personally."

That was it—as much as he could say without having his voice crack with tears. So he smiled and saluted and stepped back from the mike before gently nudging Mrs. Dixon up to the dreaded thing. For a long, silent minute, he wondered if she would refuse to help him out, then she turned to smile up at him and he could see the tears that fell in glistening tracks down her cheeks. The auditorium erupted into more cheers. It seemed to Rafe that it went on forever before Mrs. Dixon got them quieted down.

"I'm going to dismiss you by section to go to recess," she told them, only to be answered with a disappointed moan from the students. "When the bell signals the end of recess, go back to your individual classes. I hope that Sergeant Calderon will agree to visit my classroom at that time." She turned a questioning glance in his direction and Rafe nodded. "The choir and band are dismissed first."

Rafe stood at attention until the last student had reluctantly exited to recess, then he walked over to the chair where he'd left the plaque. Reverently, he lifted it and read the inscription. "To Gunnery Sergeant Rafael Calderon. For bravery above and beyond the call of duty and for being our friend." Below the inscription were thirty-two names.

Thirty-one children and one teacher who believed he was someone important. A hero. He prayed he could live up to their expectations—at least for the next few hours. He hoped they never found out he was a fake and a phony. That he hadn't felt brave when he'd rescued the missionary orphans. That he'd been terrified. That if he'd really thought about it, he would have "sat tight" and waited for help like his commander had ordered him.

When he really thought about it, it seemed like he'd been scared most of the past two years. Scared when he'd gotten orders to ship to San Miguel. Scared when he got there. Scared when he'd rescued those kids. Scared he'd lose his leg. Scared he'd never walk again. Scared of meeting these kids. And now he was scared he'd let them down. God, what kind of hero was he? Why couldn't he be the man the students thought he was—at least for a few hours?

"You were wonderful."

Rafe whirled to face Abigail Dixon. "No, I'm not."

She smiled and nodded. "For a guy who was terrified of the microphone, you were terrific. Are you sure you don't give speeches all the time?"

Relief flooded him. "Only if you call issuing orders to a bunch of grimy marine mechanics public speaking."

"It must count for something, because you sounded like a pro."

Rafe wasn't sure how to respond. He studied her quickly, just to make sure she wasn't making fun of him.

"It must be the uniform," he said when the silence was beginning to stretch out.

Mrs. Dixon laughed at that. Rafe was surprised to find that her entire attitude lightened up as she did. She was no longer giving him that evil eye that teachers were famous for. No longer pushing him to do something he didn't want to do. She was looking at him like he was clever. Like he was important.

When she smiled up at him, her green eyes danced with laughter. "That's no help, then. I doubt they come in my size."

He studied her for a few seconds. She was a tiny little thing. He'd bet she didn't weigh a hundred pounds. Not even dripping wet. So why did he get the impression she could whip twice her weight in wildcats? Why did he have the feeling she'd take on an entire army without blinking twice? How could someone so tiny be so damn self-assured? And why did he find it so attractive? Mr. Dixon, whoever he was, was one lucky man. He was probably a bank president or a real-estate broker, someone with a cellular phone and clean hands. Rafe looked down at his own hands and saw the plaque.

"This is great," he said with a nod to the object. "It's got everyone's name on it."

"You'd definitely know," Abigail told him. "I was very impressed that you could call the students by name."

"I've been studying the pictures you sent with the Christmas cards." He was grateful his dark skin didn't reveal the heat he felt in his cheeks. "I wrote the names on the back of the pictures and then practiced until I could name each one."

"Like flash cards?"

He shrugged. "I guess so. I was just afraid that the kids might have changed so much that they wouldn't look like their pictures anymore."

"Kids do change quickly at this age. In fact, some of them have changed a lot in the past six months." She looked him straight in the eye. "It didn't throw you at all." She broke eye contact suddenly, as though afraid she'd be unable to. "We'd better head back to the class-room." She started toward the stairs leading down from the stage. "Recess will be over soon." Stopping at the top of the stairs, she looked back at him. "The students loved the photos you sent. It helped them put a face to the let-ters. I'm not sure the pictures did you justice, though. There's a lot about you that a still picture can't capture."

Her words made Rafe feel like he could leap tall build-ings in a single bound. Instead, he tucked the plaque un-der his left arm and hopped down from the stage. He winced as the pain shot up his leg. In all the excitement, he'd forgotten about the wound, forgotten about the pain. Refusing to give in to the urge to swear, he reached up to help the teacher down the stairs. Her hand was tiny in his, but her grasp was firm and sure.

"The pictures I sent weren't very glamorous." He'd sent pictures of his tent and his bunk. Pictures of the motor pool and some of the vehicles he'd worked on.

He'd taken other pictures, too. Ones of the poverty-stricken inhabitants of the small island. Pictures of starving children with swollen bellies and eyes made old by the destruction and violence they'd witnessed. That had been the worst part of being stationed on San Miguel—to look into faces surrounded by dark hair and punctuated with dark eyes so much like his own. To look into them and try not to care. To harden his heart so that their pitiful condition wouldn't tear down the wall he'd so carefully constructed around him.

And that was why he'd answered the first letter from Kevin Scott. Because he'd thought it was safe to care about Kevin. With his light brown hair and blue eyes, he was different from Rafe. He lived in a safe little town in California where Rafe wouldn't have to worry that he'd step on an antipersonnel device or catch a stray bullet. He was far enough away that Rafe wouldn't risk being affected.

At least that was the way Rafe had figured it. What he hadn't counted on was Kevin's entire class adopting him. Or the fact that the letters they wrote would worm their way right into his heart despite the differences and the distance. And he certainly hadn't expected Kevin to get a disease that would cut his young life short—and force Rafe into risking his hard-won isolation by coming to the small town of Pershing to see the dying boy. Why was it, Rafe wondered, that things never went the way he planned?

When Mrs. Dixon was safely on the floor, he dropped her hand, but he couldn't help admiring the sway of her hips as she led the way out of the auditorium and down the hall. He gave in to the limp when she couldn't see him, gave in to the weakness that he'd fought so hard to hide. He couldn't help noticing that she didn't look like any teacher he'd ever had. Yes sir, he decided, that Mr. Dixon was one lucky guy.

"I'm glad you can come back to the classroom." She removed a set of keys from her pocket and unlocked the door. "The students are going to have lots of questions." She flipped on the lights and started bustling around, arranging chairs and picking up books from the floor.

Rafe looked at the small desks and chairs. If he sat in one of them, his knees would come up under his chin.

"Back there is the bulletin board where the students have kept your pictures and most recent letters."

Rafe looked at the big bulletin board covered in white paper, with red and blue stars around the edges. He figured that every picture he'd ever sent was pinned there, along with maps of San Miguel and North Carolina. Camp Lejeune was printed by hand beside a big foil star that marked its location. He walked back and studied it.

"Did we misspell something?"

Rafe turned to see the worried frown that furrowed Mrs. Dixon's brow.

"No." He shook his head and cleared his throat. "It's just that I never expected to have my own bulletin board."

Once he'd said it, he figured it probably sounded pretty stupid. But, hell, if any of his former teachers could see this, they'd have a heart attack. Somehow that amused him. He turned back to study the display. He could hear Mrs. Dixon moving around the room behind him.

"The students will be coming in soon, Sergeant Calderon."

Rafe turned to see that she'd set a regular-size chair in the front of the room. "Call me Rafe, please."

She smiled, a hesitant little smile that Rafe found himself returning. "Only if you'll call me Abigail."

"Not Abby?"

She shrugged. "That's fine." She tapped the chair. "If you'd like to sit here, I'll have the students sit on the rug in front of you."

He nodded.

"I should warn you, they have thousands of questions."

"We're in trouble then."

"Why's that?"

He grinned at her. "I don't know that many answers."

"You can use yes and no as many times as you need."

"That's a relief."

"You also can decline to answer a question. At this age, students sometimes ask inappropriate things. You can tell them that a question is too personal. Or you can just say you aren't answering it."

Rafe was about to ask what kinds of questions Abby considered inappropriate when the bell rang.

"The students line up outside. You just relax while I go get them."

She was almost at the door when Rafe called her name. "Abby?"

She turned around. "Yes?"

"Thanks for sticking by me earlier."

She smiled. "You didn't need me, but you're welcome."

"Don't desert me now, okay?"

"Okay." Her smiled widened. "But you aren't going to need me now, either."

Abigail had never seen her class so excited—or so noisy, and she'd had them for two years. First as their fourth grade teacher and then, when Doug Williams had asked her to move up a grade level, as this year's instructor.

They were the last class to get lined up and the last class to settle down enough to enter the building.

"Remember to sit quietly in the reading circle when you enter the room. Sergeant Calderon will be calling on students who raise their hands in an orderly fashion. And remember to use your inside voices." She could feel the undercurrent of anticipation. She had the awful feeling that they were all going to start screaming the moment they saw Rafe. "You did a wonderful job at the assembly, and I know you want Sergeant Calderon to leave here with a good impression, so be on your very best behavior."

All the way down the hall, she could hear them whispering and feel the excitement building. She understood it; after all, they were going to get Gunnery Sergeant Calderon all to themselves now. They wouldn't have to share him with the other students or with their families, as they would tonight. For now, he was all theirs. Still, she felt it was important to keep things under control.

She stopped just before reaching the room. "Remember to be on your best behavior." As a last-ditch effort to get their attention, this wasn't going well. "And remember that Sergeant Calderon will be calling on students who raise their hands."

She took a deep breath and led them through the doorway. Bedlam ensued as the students shouted Rafe's name and swept into the room to surround him. Abigail closed the door in an effort to keep the noise from drifting through the entire building.

Rafe stood when he saw the tidal wave coming at him. He exchanged high fives with several of the boys and tried to call each student by name as he or she approached. He even returned hugs as best he could while being flooded by the seething mass of small humanity; it was a long way down from his six-one height to the children who surrounded him. At least his long arms allowed him to ruffle their hair when all else failed. Abigail was just giving thought to wading into the crowd and trying to reestablish some control when Rafe took over.

"Everyone take a seat on the floor," he ordered. "Just like Mrs. Dixon told you." Only a few students did as he asked, but when he singled them out for praise, others did the same. In no time, he had them sitting quietly in a semicircle. Before he could even get seated, thirty-one little hands were in the air. He called on Kevin first.

"Do you have a gun?" the boy asked.

"I was issued a 9 mm Beretta on San Miguel. However, all weapons must be left on the base, so I don't have one with me."

"Is this the uniform you wore on San Miguel?"

"No, Maria, this isn't the uniform I wore. This is my dress uniform—I wear it only for special occasions. If you look at the pictures on the bulletin board, you'll see how we dressed there."

Abigail breathed a sigh of relief and went to sit at her desk. Sergeant Rafael Calderon was a genius with children. She sat back and relaxed for the first time all day as the students kept up a steady stream of questions.

"What was San Miguel like?"

"What did you do there?"

"Did you want to go?"

"Were you scared?"

"Did you shoot anybody?"

"Did anybody shoot at you?" This brought a round of teasing from several classmates, who reminded the questioner that Rafe had spent almost eight months in the hospital. Of course he'd been shot at.

"What was the hospital like?"

"What was the food like at the hospital?"

"Does your leg still hurt?"

"What happened to the kids you saved?"

Abigail settled back behind her desk and eased her feet out of the high heels she'd worn. She was just wiggling her toes and congratulating herself on how perfectly everything was going when the first inappropriate question slipped past her.

"Do you have any children of your own?"

Rafe smiled. "No, Maria, I don't."

"Are you married?"

"No."

"Are you dating anyone?"

Abigail rose without bothering to slip back into her shoes. "Chad, I believe we discussed inappropriate questions before Sergeant Calderon arrived." To Rafe she said, "You don't have to answer that."

He smiled. "That's okay. No, Chad, I'm not dating anyone."

Doreen's hand waved furiously in the air. Rafe nodded toward her.

"Do you think Mrs. Dixon is pretty?" the little redhead asked.

Abigail slanted her a warning glance. *"Doreen."*

Rafe grinned. "Yes, Doreen, I do. Of course, redheads are my favorite, but Mrs. Dixon is very pretty for a brunette."

The redheaded Doreen giggled, and Abigail relaxed back into her chair.

Kevin stood up in the middle of the group. "Do you want to date her?"

Abigail jumped to her feet. "Kevin Scott, that is a completely inappropriate question!"

Kevin looked at Rafe. "Well, do you?"

Abigail noticed that Rafe just grinned. "I think Mr. Dixon would have something to say about that, don't you?"

"They're divorced," someone volunteered.

"Yeah, divorced," several others chimed in.

Abigail had the urge to hide under her desk. But she stepped out from behind it and faced her students. She was just about to give them a tongue-lashing they wouldn't soon forget when Rafe spoke up.

"I don't think anyone as pretty as Mrs. Dixon needs you guys to fix her up with a date. Kevin, you've embarrassed your teacher and you owe her an apology."

Kevin hung his head. "Sorry," he mumbled.

"I couldn't hear that," Rafe said.

Kevin glanced up at Rafe and then at his teacher. "Sorry, Mrs. Dixon."

Abigail folded her hands at her waist and smiled at the boy. "Apology accepted."

Rafe swept the students with a scowl. "I believe some other students also owe Mrs. Dixon an apology."

Several students stood up and apologized.

Abigail sighed. "Apologies accepted." She looked at the clock above the blackboard. "We have only a few moments left, so I suggest you stick to important questions." Turning, she slipped back into her chair.

"Just for the record," Rafe told the students before they could ask anything else, "I'd be delighted to date Mrs. Dixon."

Abigail jumped to her feet. "Sergeant Calderon!"

He grinned at her. "Sorry, Mrs. Dixon."

The students' laughter forced her to keep a hold on her temper, but she didn't think Rafael Calderon looked the least bit sorry. Before she could tell him so, the bell signaled the end of school. The look she turned on the students had them remaining seated, waiting for her dismissal. She took her time about it.

"Remember to be back here by seven tonight," she said just before they started to fidget in earnest. "Your parents may drop food off any time after five."

A hand went up in the back. "Yes, Kevin."

"My mom has to work tonight."

Abigail sighed. "Mrs. Burton is going to bring you, and your mother has promised to come by as soon as she gets off."

"The buses are gonna leave," Doreen wailed.

Abigail checked the clock. "The buses won't leave for another four minutes." She swept the class with a glance. "Remember to be on your best behavior tonight and to wear your good clothes." She swept the room with one last glance. "Very well, you're dismissed."

"Do we have to wear shoes tonight?" Kevin asked over the chaos.

Abigail rolled her eyes. "Of course you do."

"You're not wearing any now," the boy called as he headed for the door. "Bye, Rafe. See you tonight."

The other students shouted goodbye as they shuffled and pushed their way out the door. And they all informed their pen pal they'd see him that night, so Abigail was prepared for the question when Rafe turned to her. She just wasn't prepared for the scowl.

"What do they mean, they'll see me tonight?" It seemed to Rafe that since he'd started corresponding with Kevin, all he'd had was surprises.

December 26

Dear Sergeant Calderon,

Hi! It's Kevin Scott again. Remember you got my Christmas card and then you wrote to me? Well, I'm writing back.

Thanks for writing me. Out of all thirty-one kids in my class, I was the first one to get a letter back. And I'm the only one who got a letter from a marine! Doreen got a letter from a guy in the navy, but all he does is ride around San Miguel in a ship to keep supplies from getting in. And Andrew Chang got a letter from a doctor in the army, but I don't think a doctor is a real soldier. They don't carry guns or anything. Most everyone else hasn't heard back from anyone.

So everybody is jealous that I got you for a pen pal.

I had a great Christmas. I got a bike that I wanted. Mom said it was from Santa Claus, but I'm old enough to know the score. And I got you for a pen pal. That's probably the best Christmas present I ever got.

My mom's Aunt Lucy came to visit. She's real old and has hair growing out of her ears, but she always gives me money for Christmas so I guess it's okay. As long as Mom doesn't make me kiss her. Yuck!

I hope you're okay. Please write and tell me how you are.

                                        Your friend,
                                        Kevin Scott

Chapter Three

Abigail sighed. She should have mentioned this during the phone call last night, but he'd been so darned skittish she'd feared it would scare him away. So she'd opted to surprise him. The problem was that she couldn't see herself shouting, "Surprise!" into such a threatening countenance.

Rafe's attention never wavered. "Well?"

"Is that the expression you use on your men when they haven't done what they're supposed to? Well, it won't work on me." She smiled at the startled look he wore now. "I'm made of sterner stuff, you know. I face fifth graders every day. See how many of your men would volunteer for that job."

He gave her a grudging smile, as she'd hoped he would. Then he rubbed his left thigh and dropped into a chair before saying, "Okay. Out with it. What's going on?"

Despite his reluctant smile, she decided she'd better ease into the explanation. "Remember when we spoke last week and you said you'd decided to rent a room at the Pershing Hotel instead of driving to L.A. tonight?"

"Yeah."

"Well, I mentioned it to my room mother, and she suggested that it would be great fun for the families to meet you, too. So she decided to put together an event for tonight. And believe me, when Eleanor Burton decides to put on an event, there's no stopping her. I've tried before, and I just end up feeling like I've been steamrolled. Anyway, I know it'll be great. Lots of—"

"Hold it." Rafe stuck his hand out, palm toward her, to stop her monologue. "What's a room mother?"

It certainly wasn't the question she'd expected. "She's the parent who helps out with parties and special events, like Halloween and birthdays. She brings the cupcakes and the punch. In this case, she's also the one who's hauled around the aluminum cans and newspapers. Anyway, she thought—"

"Hold it." There was that hand held out at her again. "What cans and papers?"

Abigail sighed. She'd never finish with her explanation if he kept interrupting. However, patience was the trait she'd cultivated most in her six years of teaching, so she answered carefully. "The cans and newspapers the students saved and recycled in order to pay for mailing their letters and packages, and to buy your plaque and stuff."

"Stuff?"

Rafe was certainly more detail oriented than she'd expected, and it was becoming annoying. She hadn't really gotten to the important part yet. "Like the little flags and the material for the sashes and the hats the girls wore.

That kind of stuff." She waited, just to see if there would be another question.

Rafe nodded. "Go on."

"As I said, Eleanor loves to put together events. My class has the best parties in the world. For Halloween she puts on a witch costume and brings in a big cauldron filled with dry ice. At Easter she wears a bunny outfit and has colored eggs for everyone."

Abigail knew she was starting to babble, but she just couldn't seem to stop. It would be easier if Rafe's face hadn't settled into an expressionless mask. She supposed that was useful when dealing with generals and wars and things like that, but it was making her nervous. And when she was nervous, she talked. Boy, did she talk.

"I know students who want to be in class with Eleanor's sons just so they can have Eleanor for their room mother. So when she decided to organize a potluck supper so that the families would have a chance to meet you, I said yes." When Rafe didn't say anything, she added, "Eleanor wouldn't have paid any attention if I'd said no, anyway." Then she folded her hands and forced herself to wait for his reaction.

Rafe rubbed the back of his neck. "I thought the school had paid for everything."

Abigail let out a very unladylike snort before she could stop herself. "I've been asking for a new set of math books for the last two years. If we don't have the money for books, I can promise you we don't have the money for this sort of thing."

"And just what sort of thing are we talking about? For tonight, I mean."

"Just a small gathering of my students' families to welcome you to Pershing. Very low-key. Lots of home-cooked food," she added when he didn't look convinced.

"The mayor presenting the key to the city. A couple of songs." She forced herself to silence.

"What do I have to do?"

Abigail shrugged. "Eat. Smile. Say hi to people."

"Anything else?"

Abigail shrugged again.

"Abby." He nailed her with a glance. "Do I have to give a speech?"

Abigail rolled her eyes. "There you go again with that speech thing. You were great today."

"That's a yes, isn't it?"

"Just a short one. Just say thank you—and compliment the cooking. That's all." When he said nothing, she found herself chewing on her bottom lip.

"Where will you be?" he finally asked.

"Here."

"Will you stand up front with me again, like you did today?"

"Oh, really!" She sighed. "You don't need me."

"Will you?"

Unable to believe anyone who had faced men with machine guns could need her support, she studied him carefully. Still, if that was all it took . . .

"Okay." She smiled. "I'll face the firing squad with you."

The smile he gave her was so devastating it had her heart marching double time.

"Oh, I hope it won't be that bad. At least the condemned man will get to eat a hardy meal. It's been a long time since I've had home-cooked food."

Abigail didn't have the heart to tell him that once people started shaking his hand and talking to him, he'd be lucky to get two bites down. Some things were just better learned by experience.

* * *

By four-thirty Abigail had showered, put her hair up in a style she thought added an inch to her height and tried on five different outfits, all of which were now strewn across her bed. Getting dressed for a school function shouldn't be this tough, she told herself once more. This was *his* fault. Gunnery Sergeant Rafael Calderon had a lot to answer for, she decided.

She'd known exactly what she was going to wear until Rafe had asked if he could pick her up this evening. Where he came from, he said, attractive women didn't drive around by themselves at night.

She'd declined his offer, of course. She had to be there early to help set up, and there was no reason he should be in the middle of the chaos. In fact, it was probably better if he never realized what went on behind the scenes. Besides, she'd noticed him favoring his leg. It was more important for him to get some rest.

But just the thought that he found her attractive had her worrying about what to wear. Nothing too matronly, she decided; that had eliminated her white linen suit and the pink dress. Nothing too youthful; that had eliminated the navy blue suit with the split skirt and gold military piping. Nothing too fancy, because that would make her look like she was trying to attract his attention; that eliminated the black backless dress. And nothing too casual, because she'd told her students that she expected to see them in their best clothes; that eliminated her denim dress, even with the hand-tooled boots.

She was still in her slip when the doorbell rang. Pulling on her robe, Abigail let her mother in.

Lisa Alexander gave her daughter an exasperated look. "You said to be here by four forty-five. I broke the land speed record and you're not even dressed."

Abigail gave her mother a quick peck on the cheek. "Hi, Mom."

"Don't 'Hi, Mom,' me. Why aren't you dressed?"

Abigail headed for her bedroom with her mom following in her wake "I can't decide what to wear."

The older woman swept the bed with a disapproving glance. "This isn't like you."

Abigail pulled an emerald green jumpsuit out of the closet and studied it. "I know."

"Is it because the mayor is going to be presenting Sergeant Calderon with a key to the city?"

Abigail put back the jumpsuit and pulled out a multicolored dress with ruffles at the collar and hem. "No."

"Is it because the *Pershing Chronicle* is going to be taking pictures for the Sunday edition?"

She replaced the ruffled dress and considered the flowered skirt with matching sweater. "Hardly."

"Then you've heard about the TV coverage?"

Abigail shook her head and flipped past several hangers to the gray sweater dress. "Too hot," she decided before her mother's words sunk in. With her hand still on the padded hanger, she turned to stare at the other woman. "What TV coverage?"

"You didn't know, then?"

Abigail shook her head. "What TV coverage?" she repeated.

"Eleanor called just before I left. It seems she contacted cable channels out of Palm Springs and Riverside to see if they'd be interested in covering the evening event. Both channels were very enthusiastic."

"Oh my God." Abigail stumbled toward the bed and sank onto the only uncluttered space available. "Eleanor never mentioned this."

Lisa stepped forward to inspect her daughter's closet. "I think she wanted it to be a surprise."

Dropping her head into her hands, Abigail mumbled, "Well then, I think she's been successful." But all she could think of was Rafe confronted with TV cameras and the glare of camera lights. If he'd been uncomfortable talking in front of an auditorium filled with elementary school students, how would he feel tonight?

"I think the red knit will do quite nicely."

Abigail glanced up to find her mother holding the dress Abigail had bought last Christmas. It was a simple shirt-waist with a skirt that hit Abigail about midcalf. It was one of those deceptive little dresses that looked prim and proper on the hanger. "Dad said the slit in that skirt is almost indecent."

"Don't be ridiculous." Lisa removed it from the hanger. "My daughter would never buy anything indecent. Besides, you have great legs. It can't hurt to show them off."

"Mother!"

"Where's the slip that goes with this? You certainly can't wear that one."

"I'm not wearing that dress."

"Of course you are. You've eliminated everything else in your closet, and I've got four dozen deviled eggs in the car that I don't want to go bad. Besides, red looks great on camera."

Wearing only his shorts and a T-shirt, Rafe eased off his bed in the Pershing Hotel and made his way to the bathroom. Looking in the mirror, he decided he needed a shave. He wanted to look squeaky clean for the parents; if they didn't look past the surface spit and polish, he just might get out of Pershing with his hero image intact. Not for himself, but for the kids.

He was relieved to discover that the aspirin he'd taken had eliminated the pain in his leg. If he could just get through the next couple hours, he'd be able to stay off it for almost half a day before heading home. He'd talked his way into a three-week leave by promising the doctors he would get plenty of rest, if he needed it. He had a feeling that by the time he got through this ordeal, he was going to need it bad.

The odd part was that he was actually looking forward to the "event." He glanced to where he'd propped the plaque up on the dresser. Today had been great. He hadn't expected to enjoy it so much. When he thought of all the effort the kids—and Abby—had put into it, he was amazed. He'd never believed that anyone would go to so much trouble for him.

Remembering the music and the speeches and the cheering, he got a big lump in his throat. If any of the guys from his old neighborhood in east L.A. had seen him, they wouldn't have believed it. Hell, *he* could hardly believe it. But there was something about all those young, earnest faces looking up at him that caught him right in the gut . . . and in the heart.

Then there was Abby. She'd had an effect on him, too. She might not be much taller than her students, but his reaction to her hadn't been heroic. It had been all too human—and male. Under other circumstances, he'd make certain that she knew it, too. But he was here in Pershing as a hero. As an example to the kids who had written to him. As the answer to a wish from a dying boy. It wouldn't do to try to put the moves on the teacher, even if she was the cutest thing he'd seen in a long time. Even if he'd gotten a glimpse of great legs beneath her billowing skirt. Even if she did have him thinking like a teenager again.

He rubbed a hand over his chin. A shower first, he decided. Then a nice, close shave.

"I wish you'd discussed it with me first," Abigail said again to the human tornado whirling through the school cafeteria, issuing orders like a four-star general.

Eleanor Burton stopped long enough to twitch the red tablecloth a little farther to the left. "I don't know what you're so upset about. I think the publicity will be great for the school."

"Publicity?" Abigail followed Eleanor through the maze of tables and the other mothers who had volunteered to help. "Why does the school need publicity?"

"The public always hears about how bad things are in the schools." Eleanor stopped at the dessert table. She moved the coconut cake a bit to the left and the cherry pie to the right so that her own chocolate-fudge creation was highlighted in the center of the table. "I think the public has a right to know when something good happens, too."

Abigail closed her eyes and prayed for patience. "I'm sure you're right about that." She opened her eyes to discover that Eleanor was two tables away, peeking under the foil to check on the casseroles that were to be the main course. "But I think the newspaper coverage would have been ample."

"I don't. I think the children deserve more credit for what they've done." Eleanor tucked the foil firmly around the baking dish and turned to face Abigail. "I think you deserve more credit."

"I don't want credit. I want the evening to be one that the students and Sergeant Calderon will always remember."

Eleanor favored Abigail with a bright smile. "Exactly my point. Don't you think that the children will find it even more memorable if they see themselves on television?"

Abigail rolled her eyes. She recognized a steamroller when she'd been flattened by one. "I suppose. I just don't want the TV cameras to detract from the evening."

"Don't worry. I'll handle it." The certainty in Eleanor's voice almost made Abigail believe her. "Now why don't you go to the auditorium and mingle while I handle the food."

Abigail checked her watch as she entered the auditorium. It was only six-fifteen and already the place was filling up with students and their families. She was delighted to see that the students had taken her seriously and come in their Sunday best. She was equally pleased to see that the parents were as excited as their children.

There was a definite hum of anticipation by the time Rafe arrived—and still not a TV camera in sight. As she made her way through the crowded auditorium to greet the guest of honor, Abigail said a silent prayer that the TV crews wouldn't show at all.

Rafe stood in the doorway and wondered if it was too late to retreat. He'd never anticipated such a large crowd or all this attention directed at him. By the time Abby made her way to his side, he'd already made polite conversation with three different families—and he didn't remember a thing he'd said.

Grabbing hold of her elbow, he pulled her closer. "I thought you said it would be a small group."

"Small is a relative term."

Rafe shook his head. "Not to me. Small is no more than twenty-five."

"There were thirty-one students. How could there be fewer people tonight?"

"Everyone didn't have to come."

Abby turned a shocked look upon him. "And just how would we decide who to leave out?" Her voice was low and angry. "Draw straws? See whose mother bakes the best cake?"

He tightened his grip on her elbow. "That's not what I meant. I just thought that most people wouldn't bother to show up."

"Don't be ridiculous. This is the biggest event since last month's ice-cream social."

Ice-cream social? Rafe could hardly believe what he was hearing. In his neighborhood parents prayed for their kids to make it to and from school safely, then made them stay indoors where they weren't likely to get hit by a stray bullet. The thought that this many people would show up at school for a nighttime event was unthinkable. Having grown up in the midst of urban poverty and violence, he was unprepared for a place like Pershing. Truth was, he hadn't believed there was any place on earth that still had this kind of Mayberry mentality.

Abigail stepped even closer to him before speaking under her breath. "Here comes the mayor. Smile and don't stare at his tie."

There was no question in Rafe's mind who Abby was referring to. He studied the little man who was working his way through the room. There wasn't a father's hand he didn't shake or a mother he didn't compliment. Rafe decided the only reason he didn't kiss a baby was that he couldn't find one. It wasn't until he stopped to talk to a sour-looking man in a gray suit that Rafe got a good look at the tie. It was an abstract swirl of puce and mustard and was undoubtedly the ugliest piece of clothing he'd ever laid eyes on.

"He's color-blind, isn't he?"

Abigail shook her head. "He just has lousy taste in ties." She smiled at the man, who was a couple of inches taller than her. "Mayor Driscoll, I'd like to introduce you to Gunnery Sergeant Calderon."

The older man was energetically pumping Rafe's hand when the commotion started at the door. His head snapped up like a coyote scenting dinner.

"TV coverage." The mayor savored the words like a master chef discussing his prize creation. "Abigail, you didn't tell me there'd be TV coverage." He smoothed his tie over his stomach and brushed back the thinning hair at his temples. "How do I look?"

"Very... impressive."

He turned to Rafe. "What do you think?"

"Like a four-star general."

The little man appeared to puff up before Rafe's eyes. "Then I think I'll see if I can be of assistance to the press. If you'll excuse me." He gave them a final nod. "It's an election year, you know."

Rafe waited until the mayor was out of earshot before he spoke. "You didn't tell me there'd be TV coverage, either. Did it slip your mind?"

"I would have told you if I'd known."

"Abby..."

"Honest." Her green eyes were big and round. With her right hand she made an X over her chest. "Cross my heart and hope to die. Stick a needle in my eye."

"What?" Rafe hoped his eyes weren't bulging. He could hardly believe that a woman wearing one of the sexiest red dresses he'd ever laid eyes on could be reciting a children's rhyme. "What did you say?"

Abby laughed. "Sorry. That's the kind of thing I pick up from the students. An occupational hazard, I guess."

"It's okay." He smiled, knowing that it wasn't the kind of thing she would have picked up where he'd gone to elementary school. There she would have heard four-letter words or seen fists flying. "But I'd still like to hear about the TV coverage."

"Eleanor Burton arranged it."

"The room mother?"

Abby nodded. "She said she wanted to surprise us."

"I'd say her mission was successful, then."

"She did promise to keep them out of the way." Abby nodded toward a woman who burst through the door and descended upon the camera crew. "That's her now."

Rafe watched as she stepped in front of the mayor and began waving her arms like a plane director on an aircraft carrier. The mayor was unceremoniously shoved aside in the excitement.

"She doesn't have a lot of respect for elected officials, does she?"

"The mayor is her brother. Since you have brothers and a sister, you probably understand how that works. I know I'd do the same to my brothers if I could."

Rafe studied the woman. She was probably close to six feet tall, with the kind of build he generally associated with opera stars. The thought of her in a bunny suit brought an honest-to-goodness smile to his face. The mayor shuffled around behind her but didn't succeed in drawing anyone's attention.

"They're brother and sister?"

Abby nodded. "She took after her father's side of the family."

"And him?"

"We're not sure. Eleanor told me he bears a startling resemblance to the mailman."

Rafe stared down at the woman beside him. "You're joking?"

"Of course I'm joking. He looks just like his aunt Eugenia. That's just small-town humor—don't take it so seriously."

Satisfied that Pershing was still like Mayberry and not Peyton Place, Rafe looked back to where Abby's room mother was doing battle with the TV crew. Before they could mount an offensive onto the stage, the woman had them pinned down in the corner of the room. Once this was accomplished, she turned them over to her brother. Rafe realized the camera crew hadn't stood a chance.

When the indomitable Eleanor Burton had relegated the next television crew to another corner, she sailed toward a seat she'd reserved in the front row, taking time to tell Abby as she passed, "Let's get this show on the road. Those casseroles won't stay warm forever, you know."

And before Rafe could even give it a second thought, Abby led him to a chair set up on the stage. When he saw the choir file in behind him and the orchestra take seats to the side of the stage, he realized he'd been suckered in again. The lights from the two camera crews plus the whir of numerous private video cameras made him realize that Eleanor Burton's idea of a low-key event was probably on a scale with the San Miguel invasion.

Rafe wondered if there would ever be a time when he'd be able to forget the dark days on San Miguel. Even now, as the band and choir performed "The Marine Hymn" Rafe could conjure up the sights and sounds of war. Even here he couldn't shake the memories—or the knowledge that the letters from Pershing had been his lifeline....

January 10

Dear Kevin,
It was nice to get your letter. It came on a particularly bad day when the forces under General Reyes

shelled our positions and forced us to take cover in the bunkers we'd dug. Our navy planes managed to silence them in a short time, but not before they'd destroyed several vehicles, including three of the trucks my men were repairing. Luckily, none of my men were hurt.

I'm glad you had a great Christmas. I understand that you think Pershing is quiet and you'd like to do something exciting for New Years, because I remember being your age. However, I find myself wishing that the only fireworks we could plan on were firecrackers. Unfortunately, that isn't the case on San Miguel.

I'm glad you got a bike for Christmas. I remember when I was your age that was what I wanted. There's nothing like a shiny new bike. But you be sure to take good care of it so it won't get stolen like mine did. My dad told me to take care of it, but I forgot to put it away one night. I remember crying and crying when I discovered it was gone. Be sure to lock yours up whenever you go someplace and be sure to bring it in at night. That's your responsibility now.

I realize January will be almost over by the time you get this letter, but I wish you a happy new year anyway. Please write when you get a chance. You'd be surprised how much I look forward to hearing from you.

Your friend,
Rafael Calderon
USMC

Chapter Four

Two hours later as Rafe glanced around the sparsely populated room, he was forced to admit that "the event" had gone smoothly. Luckily, the daytime ceremony had prepared him for this one. He'd been able to control the emotions that had threatened him at the school assembly. He'd kept the tears from pooling in his eyes and the lump from closing his throat. And the few times he hadn't been completely under control... well, he'd been prepared with a quick swipe at the tears and a fake cough to cover the cracking of his voice.

And when all else failed, there'd been Abby. She'd been at his side most of the evening—introducing parents, suggesting they sit once in a while, which had been a big help when his leg began to throb, graciously coping with the long-winded parents and gently drawing in the shy ones. She might be a small package, but she was quite a woman.

Now that almost everyone had gone home and only a few stragglers remained with the parents who were cleaning up, Rafe was willing to declare the evening a success. Even the TV crews hadn't been intrusive; that Eleanor Burton was a formidable commander. Rafe decided there were several military men who could take a few lessons from her.

Only two things had kept the evening from being perfect. First, no matter that Eleanor had filled three different plates for him, Rafe hadn't managed more than ten bites the entire evening; it was impossible to eat when shaking hands and talking. And second, Kevin Scott's mother still hadn't appeared. That, even more than the hollow feeling in his stomach, had him worried.

When Abby went off to help with the cleanup, she'd assigned Kevin to keep him company. The boy was doing a great job, but Rafe noticed that his glance kept going to the door. He was obviously searching for his mother. And he was looking more disappointed each time the door opened only to reveal members of the cleanup crew.

"It was a real pleasure to meet you," Jim Stafford said for at least the fifth time. The Staffords were the only family remaining and Rafe wondered if they would ever leave. "It's easy to see why Jeremy has enjoyed writing to you."

Since Kevin didn't have the same knack that Abby did for moving people along, Rafe resigned himself to a few more minutes of conversation. "It's been a pleasure for me to meet everyone, too. It's been great to finally meet all the kids who took time to write me. I looked forward to Jeremy's letters." Rafe turned his attention to Mary Stafford. "I appreciate you making pictures of the kids to send me at Christmas. It was real nice of you."

The woman's smile revealed perfect white teeth and lighted up the blue eyes that were so much like her son's. "I'd be happy to make your portrait while you're here."

"That's very kind, but—"

"No charge," she added. "I'd feel like I'd completed the set then. Besides, I owe you after you wrote to Jeremy about being kind to his little brother." Her voice dropped. "I was very sorry to hear that your own brother died when he was only thirteen, but your story certainly made Jeremy think about how he'd miss Mikey if something happened."

Rafe fought the dark wave of anger that always swamped him at the mention of his younger brother. Frank had been only thirteen when his life was cut short in a drive-by shooting. It was a stupid, meaningless way to die. Though Rafe had never come to terms with the loss, he forced himself to smile at Mary Stafford. "If I'm still here next week, I'll drop by."

"Wonderful. My studio is located on Main Street between Royce's Insurance and The Koffee Kup."

Kevin's hand came up to grip Rafe's. "That's where my mom works."

"I know." With his other hand, Rafe ruffled the boy's hair. To the woman he said, "I'll contact you if I'm in town next week."

Once Jeremy's family said goodbye, Rafe eased into a chair and stretched his leg out before him. When Kevin hesitated, as if wondering whether he should leave, Rafe patted the chair beside him.

"I'm glad we have some time to talk while we wait for your mom."

Kevin remained on his feet, looking like he was considering bolting out the door. "She'll be here."

"I know that." Rafe patted the chair again. "I just thought we could talk for a while. You don't mind if I sit down, do you? My leg is starting to ache."

"Nah, that's fine." Still the boy shuffled from one foot to the other. "Do you want something to drink? Or an aspirin or something?"

"I'd love something cold."

"I'll get it. Anything else?"

"That aspirin would be great if you can find one."

"I'll ask Mrs. Dixon. She keeps some in her desk in case she gets a headache."

Rafe smiled as the boy took off, but couldn't help wondering if Kevin was one of the reasons Abby needed the aspirin close at hand. Closing his eyes, he wondered for the thousandth time what he should say to Kevin. It had been so much easier to put his thoughts on paper, but he knew that it was important to talk face-to-face with Kevin. He'd been wanting—and dreading—some time alone with the boy. The problem was that Rafe had no idea what to say to a child who was dying.

"I brought you some punch." Rafe opened his eyes and stared into Kevin's. "And Mrs. Dixon's bottle of headache stuff."

Rafe took the aspirin bottle and poured out two tablets, then used the punch to wash them down. All the while he kept wondering what to say. How to say it. He slipped the bottle into his pocket and patted the chair beside him again. This time Kevin slid into the seat.

"How are things going in the kitchen?"

"Mrs. Burton says they're almost through. She said if Mom isn't here soon, she'll take me home."

The boy's disappointment was obvious, and Rafe wondered how the mother of a sick child could deny him something he wanted so much.

"We'll see." He ruffled the boy's hair again and wondered how the kid had gotten so messy during the evening. Kevin's shirttail was hanging out and he had a punch mustache. Rafe couldn't even begin to identify the stains on his white shirt. Rafe had to smile; he figured the phrase "all boy" had been invented to describe just such a kid.

"How are you feeling?" he finally asked.

The boy's eyes went wide and he looked around to see if anyone else could hear them. "Pretty good."

"I was wondering if all this running around is good for you. Are you supposed to stay in bed or anything?"

"Oh, no. It's okay."

"You're sure?"

"Oh, yeah." Kevin fidgeted in his chair. "As long as I'm feeling good, the doctor says I should...that it's all right if I just act, you know, like a normal kid."

"That's great." Rafe gave Kevin a reassuring smile. "But I know that even with my leg, I have to sit down and rest when I'm tired. I bet it would be a good idea for you, too."

"Yeah, I do that. It's just that sometimes the doctor gives me a shot to make me better."

Rafe wasn't certain what disease Kevin had—he'd never asked and the boy hadn't volunteered the information— but he wondered what kind of shot the doctor gave him. Not a painkiller, he hoped. The doctors had tried to keep Rafe on pain pills until he'd finally refused any more. He hated to think of a kid taking that stuff. Of course, he also hated to think of a kid in pain.

"A shot?"

"Yeah." Kevin nodded. "And medicine."

"And then what happens?"

"I feel a lot better for a while."

"And then?"

Kevin glanced toward the door. "Do we have to talk about this?"

"No. Not if you don't want to."

"Well, it's just that if Mom shows up, it'll make her real unhappy. She cries, you know." The boy shrugged. "And then I don't know what to do."

"Tears do that to a guy." Rafe reached out and put his hand on the boy's shoulder. "But I want you to know that I'm here if you want to talk. And I promise I won't cry." He only hoped that was a promise he could keep.

"Thanks." Kevin's face turned an interesting shade of pink. "I'm glad you came to visit."

Rafe ruffled the boy's hair again. "Yeah. Me, too."

He wanted to say more. To tell Kevin how important their friendship was. To tell him that he would never forget him. But before he could figure out how to say that without sounding mushy, the door opened.

"Mom!" Kevin jumped out of his chair and ran toward his mother. Throwing his arms around her waist, he hugged her tightly. "I told Rafe that you'd be here." Grabbing hold of her hand, he dragged her forward. "Mom, this is Rafe. Rafe, this is my mom." He cast her a quick glance. "Finally."

Rafe rose. "I'm glad to meet you, Mrs. Scott."

"I'm sorry I'm late." She brushed back a strand of hair that had escaped from her ponytail. "One of the other waitresses didn't show up and I had to work late."

"Ah, Mom."

She put an arm around her son's shoulders. "Kevin doesn't understand, but when you're the sole support of two kids, you can't afford to turn down the extra hours."

"I'm glad you could make it." Rafe was silent for a moment as he studied the tired-looking woman before him. She had brown hair and blue eyes very much like her son's, and a sweet smile. Though he guessed she wasn't much older than Abby, Rafe noticed the crow's-feet around her eyes and the grooves along her cheeks. "You've got a terrific kid here."

"Usually." She smiled down at her son. Noticing the punch stains, she tried to wipe them from his mouth.

Kevin turned his face aside. "Ah, Mom."

"I felt very lucky to have him for a pen pal. He writes great letters."

His mother smiled. "Now if we could only get him to do his math homework."

Rafe smiled back. "Since tomorrow is Saturday, I was hoping you'd let me take him out to breakfast."

Kevin's smile was instantaneous. "Oh, please, Mom. Can I?"

"Kevin, you know you have to take care of your sister."

"Ah, Mom."

"I work the early shift tomorrow," Mrs. Scott explained. "I get home around one-thirty."

Rafe thought for a moment. "Maybe lunch then?"

Kevin nodded eagerly.

Mrs. Scott shook her head. "Kevin has a baseball game at two."

"Ah, Mom, couldn't I skip it just this once?"

"No. Remember, we had a long discussion about responsibility when you signed up to play. You know the rule. Once you've made the commitment, you have to stand by it. The only legitimate excuse for missing a game is injury or illness."

Rafe nodded. "Your mom's right. Once you've given your word, you're honor bound to keep it."

Kevin's grin faded and his chin dropped. Rafe wished he'd talked to Kevin's mother before asking the boy; he could have saved him the disappointment that way.

Kevin's head snapped up. "I've got an idea. Why don't you come to my game?"

"Well..."

"Oh, please," Kevin begged. "You'd know a lot of the other guys, too."

Rafe shook his head. "I don't know."

"Kevin..." Mrs. Scott's voice had a cautioning note to it. "Perhaps Sergeant Calderon has other plans."

Rafe had planned to leave Pershing in the early afternoon and head to Los Angeles, but the droop in Kevin's shoulders had him changing his mind. "No, I don't have any other plans. I'd love to see your game."

"That's great!" Kevin hopped up and down in excitement. "Wait till I tell Jeremy and the guys."

"Which means," Mrs. Scott cut in smoothly, "that you need to get to bed so you can play your best tomorrow."

"Ah, Mom."

She brushed the hair back from her son's brow. "Go tell Mrs. Burton that I'm taking you home now. Go on."

Once the boy was out the door, she turned to Rafe. "I want to thank you for all you've done for Kevin."

"Me? I think you have it turned around, Mrs. Scott."

"Sherry, please."

Rafe smiled at her. "I think you have it turned around, Sherry. I have a lot to thank Kevin for. His letters cheered me up. It was Kevin who kept me going when things got really rough."

The woman shook her head. "You don't realize what a profound effect you've had on my son. When his father walked out on me four years ago, he left a hole in his son's life. There's been no man to serve as a strong role model for Kevin.'' She gave Rafe a wistful smile. ''I tried. Like signing him up for baseball and soccer. But no one ever got to him like you did.''

''Ma'am, I just wrote some letters. You're the one who's raised him.''

Sherry Scott glanced over her shoulder, then back at Rafe. ''You wrote to him about values and responsibility. You said a lot of the same things I'd been saying, but when you said them he paid attention. He really hates watching his little sister, and I understand that a boy doesn't want to be saddled with a girl four years younger. But sometimes I need him to help out. Child care is real expensive when you're living on a waitress's salary. But then you wrote and told him how you'd taken care of your own little sister. About how he should be good to her and really try to set an example for her.'' She shook her head and smiled. ''When I said it, he'd just complain. When you said it, he listened. I really do appreciate it.''

Kevin came running back into the room and skidded to a stop less than a foot away from his mother and Rafe. He looked up at his mom. ''Mrs. Burton says fine.'' He looked at Rafe. ''Mrs. Dixon says they're almost finished in the kitchen, and she says not to leave until she's talked to you.''

''We'd better go get your sister from the sitter's.''

''Okay.'' He looked back at Rafe. ''I promised to read her a bedtime story.''

Rafe smiled at the boy. ''That's great.''

''Yeah, she really likes it when I read to her. Doesn't she, Mom?''

Sherry nodded. ''She loves it, and so do I. I love to listen to you, too. And to see the two of you down on the floor with your heads bent over a book....'' She reached out to cup her son's cheek. "It makes your mother very happy."

Kevin turned a bright pink. "Ah, Mom," he complained. But Rafe noticed that he didn't pull away from his mother's touch.

"I'll see you at the park, then," Rafe said as he followed them toward the door.

"It's the only one in town," Sherry told him. "Just ask anyone for directions."

Rafe nodded and held the door open for them. Kevin stopped and looked up at Rafe as he stepped over the threshold.

"I'm really glad you could come for a visit."

Rafe fought the lump in his throat. "So am I, kid. So am I."

Only Abby and Eleanor remained in the kitchen when Rafe got there. Through a back door, Rafe could see a sensible minivan with the two Burton boys sound asleep in it. One was sprawled across the middle bench and the other was curled up in the passenger seat.

"Can I help you ladies?" Rafe asked when he saw they were both starting to lift big cardboard boxes.

Eleanor smiled at him. "That would be wonderful."

"You just tell me what you want where, ma'am."

Eleanor had him carry the largest one out first. She opened the back of the van as gently as possible to avoid waking her sons and had him slip it in where the back seats had been moved aside. When Rafe carried the next two boxes out, the delicious smells had his mouth watering. Leftovers, he realized. He tried not to drool. The last box was by far the biggest, and the tantalizing scent of food almost made him cry. He wondered if there was a restaurant in this small town that was open late at night.

He realized for the first time that he was genuinely hungry, and he knew that he wouldn't get any sleep until his belly was good and full. But it wouldn't be home-cooked food, he mused. He would be lucky to find a fast-food hamburger.

"Oh, no."

Rafe turned to find Abby at his elbow. She shook her head as she gazed into the back of the minivan.

"I didn't know your back seat was folded aside," Abby told the other woman in a whisper.

"There's still plenty of room," Eleanor whispered back.

"But the boys are both asleep."

"We'll just scoot little Burt over."

"But we'll wake him."

"Abby, I promised your mother that I'd get you home, and I will."

Rafe looked from one woman to the other. "Is there a problem, ladies?"

Abby placed a finger over her lips. "Shh."

"Abigail's mother left earlier," Eleanor explained in a whisper. "And I promised her that I'd give Abigail a ride home."

"But the boys are sound asleep," Abby continued. "And I hate to wake them up before you get home."

Eleanor sighed. "That's not a problem."

Abby slanted the other woman a warning glance. "They'll be cranky."

"You mean they'll whine."

"I'll just walk home. It's not that far."

Eleanor pointed toward the last box Rafe had loaded in her vehicle. "What about your goodies?"

"You can take them home."

"Absolutely not. I packed them up for you. You live alone—I know you don't eat good."

"You could drop them on my porch."

"I don't know." Eleanor shook her head. "I promised your mother."

"Oh, for heaven's sake," Abby huffed, placing her hands on her hips. "I've been out on my own for quite some time now. I don't need my mother arranging my life."

Eleanor looked equally put out and glared down at Abby. "Maybe not, but—"

"Hold it, ladies." Rafe thought he'd better intervene or they'd be standing here arguing in whispers until he faded away from hunger. "Why don't I give Abby a lift home? My rental car is just over there." He nodded toward a beige domestic sedan.

Eleanor slanted him a look. "You?"

"Yes, ma'am. I think if the U.S. Marine Corp trusts me with several million dollars worth of equipment and twenty-five men, you can trust me with one little bitty schoolteacher."

"Well, of course I can trust you," Eleanor said out loud. When one of the boys murmured and thrashed around in his sleep, she dropped her voice back to a whisper. "Well, of course I can trust you. But it's out of your way."

"Ma'am, no offense, but this town isn't big enough for it to be very far out of my way."

Abby looked up at him. "You're sure you don't mind?"

Rafe hefted the box out of the van. "Not at all."

"Good." She smiled at the other woman. "I'll see you tomorrow, Eleanor. Thanks for everything." Rafe watched as she gave her friend one of those quick woman hugs.

Rafe nodded. "Thank you for all the work you've done. I've never attended a nicer event, ma'am. It was very kind of you."

"Oh, it was nothing." Rafe wondered if the formidable Eleanor Burton could possibly be blushing. "I was glad that everyone could finally meet you."

Rafe smiled at her, then nodded toward the door to the kitchen. "Do you need to lock up?" he asked Abby.

"The janitor is still there."

He nodded toward the other woman and started for his car. He wanted to get the box locked in the trunk as quickly as possible. If he didn't get away from the smell of food, he couldn't be held accountable for his actions.

Rafe drove through the small town, making left and right turns as Abby directed. But it wasn't the route that occupied his mind, or even the woman at his side. It was the town. There were no tract houses. Bigger homes were set right alongside smaller ones, and each had its own unique character. None of them had bars over the windows or doors, and the walls and fences weren't covered with graffiti. The lawns were neat and the houses well maintained.

Some of the houses were already dark. He thought about the occupants safely tucked into bed with the shades drawn. In other homes the windows remained uncovered, so that Rafe could look in. He could see families watching TV or talking. He could see toddlers scampering down hallways in their pajamas or teenagers sitting out on the porch with their friends.

No one worried about a car cruising the streets, driven by embittered youths with guns. No one worried that a stray bullet might put an end to an innocent's life. Knots of tough street kids didn't stand on corners; residents actually strolled along the sidewalks. Rafe didn't even see a single police cruiser on the short drive to Abby's. The town of Pershing was as different—and unexpected—as taking a left turn and ending up in Never-Never Land.

Rafe couldn't help wondering what it would be like to grow up in a town like this. To live in a normal household where people cared about each other. To have the kind of parent who wanted to know where you were and what you were doing. To attend a school where students weren't carrying weapons and teachers really cared about their students. To be the kind of child whose mother brought cookies and punch to school. He imagined people here probably had backyard barbecues and went to the park on the Fourth of July.

He was as out of place as a cactus in a rose garden.

"This is it." Abby pointed to a small white house with wicker furniture on the porch and an honest-to-goodness white fence. "You can just pull into the driveway."

"This is your place?"

She nodded. "It's small, but it's home."

He studied it in the soft glow of moonlight. It was a simple white home with blue shutters and frilly curtains in the windows. Bright flowers lined the walkway and there were even roses clinging to the fence. It was the kind of setting he would expect in one of those black-and-white movies that had been colorized. He practically had to pinch himself to make sure it was real.

"I appreciate the ride. Little Burt has a habit of whining when he's sleepy. After the long day, I didn't think I could stand it."

Rafe cut the motor. "No problem. I'm glad for the chance to thank you for everything you did. The whole day was great."

She smiled at him. "Even though you had to suffer through all that 'hero stuff'?"

He had the grace to look shamefaced. "I'll admit I was upset at first."

"Upset? You were furious."

Rafe noticed that when Abby laughed, her green eyes sparkled in the dim light.

"I was..." He searched for the right word, then decided he shouldn't use it in front of a teacher. "I was not happy about it."

Not happy was a gross understatement. "You glared at me," she informed him. "If you'd treated the kids like that, I was going to kick you in the shins."

"There was no way I could stay angry when I looked into those kids' faces. I can hardly believe all the work you all went to for me."

"You deserved it," she said simply.

Rafe shook his head and turned to stare out the windshield into the darkness. "There were a lot of soldiers who deserved it, but I wasn't one of them. When I was sitting up on that stage, listening to the speeches and stuff, I told myself it was in honor of all the guys who served on San Miguel. That made it easier for me to accept."

Abigail wondered why it was so difficult for Rafe to acknowledge that he was a hero. Why he didn't want to admit that everything that was good and heroic was there inside him. Why he tried to keep everyone at arm's length with his angry countenance, while inside there ticked the heart of a brave and caring man. Well, she wouldn't let him get away with that—at least not while he was in Pershing.

"Rafe." She waited until he turned to face her. "You're a hero not just because you saved those orphans, but because in the middle of a war, you took time to write to kids you didn't know. And you didn't use your letters to tell us how brave you were or how tough. Instead, you talked to the kids from your heart." She reached out to touch his cheek. His skin was warm. "You can't fool kids. They know when someone is for real. And they knew right away that you were a hero. You would have been a hero to them even if you hadn't saved all those children."

His hand came up to cover hers. It felt strong and steady, unlike her heart, which was beating so fast and loud that she was certain he could hear it.

"I'm not a hero, Abby. But here, with you and the kids, I almost believe I could be one."

"Believe," she whispered. "Because I do."

The silence stretched between them, but Abigail didn't find it uncomfortable. And she didn't protest when Rafe held her hand steady and turned his head so that he could place a gentle kiss in her open palm. She would have been content to sit like that forever if she hadn't heard the loud rumbling of his stomach. He was the one who broke the spell by dropping his gaze and releasing her hand.

Abigail couldn't help smiling. "Is that your stomach growling?"

Rafe nodded. "I didn't really get a chance to eat this evening."

"I have all that food that Eleanor packed up for me."

"Cold casserole in my hotel room doesn't sound all that appealing."

Abigail reached for the door handle. "That's not what I'm suggesting. I didn't get to eat, either. So if you'll carry the box in, I'll heat up the food."

Rafe glanced from her to the house and back again. If she knew the truth about him, she would never issue that kind of invitation. Hell, if she knew the truth, the city fathers would never have let him past the city limits. He'd

Chapter Five

An hour and a half later, Rafe pushed away from the table, wondering if he would ever eat again. Actually, he wondered if he would ever move. He'd never felt so relaxed and content in his life, and the thought of going back to his lonely room made him shudder. But now that he'd eaten, there seemed to be no other reason to stay.

Abby smiled at him across the table. "Would you like some coffee?"

The last thing he needed was coffee, Rafe thought. It would keep him awake so that he'd end up staring at the four walls of a hotel room and then watching some ancient movie on TV.

He smiled. "I'd love some." The restlessness he'd endure later was a small price to pay for a little more time in Abby's spotless, homey kitchen.

The room was done in pale blue and white. The wallpaper reminded him of blue-and-white mattress ticking.

Around the top of the room a wide wallpaper border made it look like flowers and herbs had been hung to dry. White lacy curtains hung at the windows and blue frilly cushions adorned the wooden chairs. There was a cookie jar and potted flowers in the garden window over the sink. He wasn't sure how a room could make him feel out of place yet content at the same time. Kind of like the lady herself, he thought.

He watched her efficient movements as she got the coffeemaker going and began clearing the table.

"Would you like to relax in the living room while I do this?"

Rafe started to rise. "I did my share of eating, so I'll help clean up."

"You will not." Abby placed her hand on his shoulder and nudged him back into his chair. He felt her gentle touch like a punch in the gut and could only stare, helplessly, into her green eyes as his good leg buckled under him. Rafe had never known it was possible to stare into a woman's eyes for so long that time seemed suspended. He was just considering raising his hand to cover hers when she pulled away like someone who'd been hit by a jolt of electricity.

Abby took one step back. "I know your leg must be hurting you."

"What makes you think that?"

"You've been kneading it."

Rafe willed his hand to stop the movement he hadn't even been aware of. "An old habit."

"Earlier this evening, you tried to keep all your weight on the other leg."

He blinked. "I didn't know it was so obvious."

"I doubt that anyone else noticed."

But she had, Rafe realized. He remembered the times she'd said her feet were killing her and had asked if he minded sitting down. It hadn't been for her, he realized, but for him that she'd done it. He couldn't ever remember anyone else being so aware of his pain or his comfort before.

She swept up the plates nearest to her and carried them to the sink. "You go sit in the big chair and elevate that leg on the ottoman. I'll bring dessert in as soon as the coffee's ready."

Rafe groaned. "Dessert?"

"Dessert," Abby said with a nod. "If I have to admit to Eleanor that you didn't have any of her killer fudge cake, she'll never forgive me." She swept a few more plates from the table and gave Rafe what he could only call a schoolteacher scowl. "Go on now. The remote control is on the table beside the big chair."

Rafe was honest enough to admit that his leg really was beginning to ache, and he had the good sense to know when he was outgunned. Deciding that a strategic retreat was his best move, he rose and tested his leg by slowly putting his weight on it. Convinced that it was going to hold, he favored the busy little lady with a smile.

"Why don't you just call me when the coffee's ready? I think I can manage the walk back to the kitchen. At least for Eleanor's killer fudge cake."

Abby turned from where she was working at the sink and smiled as he strolled through the doorway into the living room.

Their trip through the living room earlier in the evening had been quick. Rafe had had time only for a brief impression of a woman's room, done in blue and pink with frills and lace. Now he took the time to study it.

He wasn't really sure where the "big chair" was because the whole room seemed small and delicate, just like
Abby. The bottom half of the walls were covered in the
same blue-and-white wallpaper as the kitchen. The top
half had a paler blue background with big pink roses
scattered over it. A narrow band of whitewashed wood
acted as a border between the two wallpapers. The sofa
was white wicker with plump flowered pillows. A wooden
rocker sat on one side of the fireplace with a blanket
hanging over the back and a basket of yarn beside it. A
wooden churn sat on the brick hearth, and a picture of
women in old-fashioned white gowns hung over the fireplace.

Across the room was a plump blue chair with a delicate bamboo table beside it. The coffee table in the middle of the room was stacked with books as well as several
potted flowers in bright pinks and yellows. What looked
like a spinning wheel stood in one corner. On a round
wooden table was an old-fashioned Victrola, the kind that
the little dog sat and listened to in old RCA ads. Only this
one was fancy, with flowers painted on the polished wood.
Blue-and-white plates hung from ribbons on both sides of
the front window. On a low bookcase were more books
and flowers and a small TV. Definitely a woman's room.
Abby's room.

With a sigh of contentment, Rafe eased into the "big
chair" and picked up the remote control. He slid his leg
onto the ottoman, flipped through the channels till he
found one with a high-speed car chase and settled down
to wait for Abby to call him for dessert. His last conscious thought was that a marine shouldn't feel so comfortable among all these ruffles and flounces.

* * *

Abby had the kitchen cleared in only a few minutes. She stored the few leftovers in the refrigerator and put the plates in the dishwasher in record time. When the coffee was ready, she set to work uncovering the desserts. Aside from a piece of Eleanor's cake, she didn't know what else Rafe might want. He'd certainly eaten like a starving man. She wondered if that meant he was too stuffed to sample several sweets or if he was simply a big eater and would want to try a little of everything.

She also wondered about her reaction to sharing a meal with him in the intimacy of her little kitchen. It had been comfortable and unsettling at the same time. She didn't understand how she could feel so at ease with someone she'd just met, nor could she explain how a look from him could set her nerves on end. Above all, she didn't understand how one touch could hit her like lightning. Upon careful reflection, she decided that the prudent move was to serve dessert in the living room, where she could sit across the room from Rafe rather than sharing the table in her small kitchen.

That decision made, Abigail stepped into the living room to ask Rafe what he wanted, only to have his name die on her lips when she saw him. His big frame filled the wicker chair where she usually curled up with her legs tucked under her. His injured leg was set upon the ottoman, while the good one was stretched out before him on the floor, almost to the coffee table. His big hands hung down from the wide wicker arms of the chair and the top of his shirt hung open where he'd unbuttoned it earlier. His head lolled against the cushion. His breathing was even and his lashes formed a dark crescent against his cheeks.

Abigail smiled. He was sleeping through an intense TV gun battle, and he looked suddenly younger and more vulnerable than he had before. She took the time to really look him over. His short hair might be dictated by the military, but it suited him, she decided. Any other style would detract from his strong cheekbones, his square chin with just a hint of a cleft in it. His hair wasn't black, she realized, but a dark brown. His brows were straight and equally dark and set above eyes that, when open, were as deep and intense as the rich, mysterious earth she turned over each spring in her garden. His skin was bronze despite the time he'd spent in the hospital.

He should have looked completely out of place against her decidedly feminine decor, but instead she discovered that his masculinity was only intensified by his surroundings. Abigail reached out to touch his shoulder, hesitated, then let her arm drop to her side. She couldn't help wondering if it would be safe to put her hand on his shoulder even when he was asleep. Would she feel that incredible jolt while he was peacefully stretched out on her furniture with his eyes closed? Or had that tingle come not from the physical contact but from the glance he'd turned on her? Unwilling to find out, she turned and tiptoed back to the kitchen.

Taking down a big platter, she covered it with an assortment of goodies. She put the platter, two antique plates, two cups and saucers, and silver on an oversize wooden tray. She poured the coffee into an insulated carafe, tiptoed into the living room to put it on the coffee table, then slipped quietly back into the kitchen. After adding two flowered linen napkins to the tray, she entered the living room with the cups rattling and her smile firmly in place.

When she saw Rafe's eyes blink open, then snap to immediate wakefulness, she knew she'd been right to serve dessert in the living room. The intense gaze he turned on her was much too powerful to meet over a small table.

Rafe lowered his left leg to the floor next to his good one and struggled to sit up straight against the overstuffed pillows. "I told you I'd come into the kitchen."

"Oh, I don't mind serving in here. Besides, this way you can keep that leg elevated if you need to."

"It's fine."

"Oh, you don't have to put up a brave front for my sake." She set the tray on the table. "I'm not doing it for you." She smiled and looked down at her bare toes. "I'm not used to high heels, and I decided I wasn't going to suffer for another minute."

Rafe smiled back at her. "In that case..." He lifted his leg onto the ottoman and settled back in the chair.

Abigail lifted the platter from the tray. "I thought you might want to sample several desserts." She moved closer to Rafe, holding it before him. "I'll let you decide what you want."

"You know, I enjoyed everything the class sent me while I was on San Miguel and in the hospital, but the cookies and brownies were the best." He pointed to several different items on the platter. "Just give me a little of each."

Abigail set to work transferring the calories to his plate. "I was afraid they'd be like rocks by the time you got them."

"Even rocks taste better than MREs. Meals Ready to Eat," he explained. He took the napkin she offered and spread it across his lap, then eagerly accepted the plate. Abigail watched as he studied the contents. He took a bite of Eleanor's cake and savored the taste.

"The hospital food wasn't much better than the pre-packaged stuff." He took another bite. "But this . . . this is heaven."

Abigail poured the coffee. "You mentioned the food in your letters—the students got a real kick out of it. Do you take cream or sugar?"

"Black." She set the coffee on the table as he sampled another dessert. "I probably mentioned it in every letter just to keep the supply of cookies coming."

Abigail couldn't help smiling. "I do think there was a rush at Stafford's Market on sugar and flour after each of your letters. The first time, so many kids brought cookies that I had to work out a rotation system. Otherwise you would have had thirty-one dozen cookies in each package."

"That would have been okay by me," he said around a bite of trifle. "My biggest problem was saving some for myself once the guys in my outfit saw the package."

"Oh." Abigail's smile faded. "I wish you'd said something. I could have sent more."

Rafe raised his dark gaze and stared at her. Even across the room, she could feel the heat. "I didn't mean to imply you did anything wrong. Everything you did was perfect."

Abigail laughed as she spread her napkin across her skirt. She hoped she wasn't blushing. "I'm hardly ever described as perfect."

"Then people around here need to be set straight. What you did was perfect. The letters kept me going, but the goodies were like magic. It was more than I ever expected. More than I deserved."

Abigail shook her head so hard that she felt a stray curl or two fall free from her upswept hairdo. "It wasn't nearly enough." She looked down at her hands, folded primly over her napkin. "It didn't seem like nearly enough after you'd rescued all those children, but I didn't know what else to do. I thought about wiring flowers once you were sent to the hospital at Camp Lejeune." She looked up and smiled. "But I wasn't sure a marine would want pansies at his bedside."

"I would have loved pansies, but cookies were even better."

"I'm glad." Abigail cut herself a small piece of Eleanor's cake. "I hope we weren't pests."

"Pests? How could you possibly have been pests?"

"Well, after you saved those children, we saw you on the news and in the newspapers. You were in *People Magazine* and *Life*."

"My fifteen minutes of fame, you mean?"

"It was more than fifteen minutes, and you deserved it. It's just that I figured you were probably swamped with media. I tried to suggest that maybe we shouldn't send so many letters—or at least we shouldn't expect so many letters from you—but the students were so concerned. I think the mail output doubled instead of declining."

"I'd have been disappointed if it hadn't. I didn't want to talk to newsmen or generals or anything. I just wanted to hear from my pen pals."

"That's kind." Abigail took a bite of cake and chewed without really tasting it. She didn't know how to explain that he'd gone from being theirs—from being the pen pal for her class—to being a national hero. And that she'd felt bereft in many ways. She'd actually been afraid he wouldn't have time for them anymore.

She should have known he wouldn't turn his back. She should have had more faith in the man who'd written letters that had touched her in ways she couldn't even begin to explain. But she hadn't. She admitted now that it had been terribly selfish of her.

"There's something I've never admitted to anyone else," Rafe said softly.

Abigail laid her fork on her plate and stared into his somber eyes. "Yes?"

"If not for you and the students who wrote to me, I don't know if I would have ended up a hero."

Abigail shook her head. "I don't believe it."

"It's true." Rafe set his empty plate on the table. "When I saw those orphans in danger, all I could think about were the kids here in Pershing. I thought that if they were in the same situation, I'd want someone to save them." He picked up the delicate coffee cup and took a sip. His own hands felt big and awkward around the china. "The next thing I knew, I was in the middle of this big gun battle."

"That's not the way the press told it."

"Yeah, I know." He set the fragile cup back in its saucer. "You want to know the truth?"

Abby nodded. "If you want to tell me."

He did, he realized. He wanted her to know that he wasn't a hero, so she'd quit looking at him with those incredible green eyes. So he'd quit wanting to be a hero. Her hero.

"The missionary orphanage was several miles outside of town. We'd been stationed next to it the week before. One of my guys started visiting the kids. He took them food. Even some of your cookies," he admitted. "Ed was a nice kid from some little hick town in Tennessee. He'd come from a big family and he had a soft spot for the little ones. Anyway, after a week or so, the brass decided to move us away from the orphanage so there wouldn't be a chance of the kids getting hit by stray bullets."

Rafe picked up the coffee cup and stared down into it. "It sounded reasonable enough. Some of our patrols had been ambushed, and the encampment had been fired on a few times." He took a big gulp that practically drained the contents. "The problem was that once we moved out, the two wannabe dictators who were squabbling over the little island decided that they'd start throwing firepower all over the place."

He looked up in time to see her hand go to her heart. "Oh, no."

He nodded. "Oh, yeah. It wasn't as if they were aiming at the kids—they just weren't very good at what they were doing. So a few bombs accidentally fell on the grounds where the kids played."

"Couldn't you stop them?"

"We were supposed to be there to keep the peace. In order to fire upon anyone, we had to have permission from everyone from the cook to congress and the president. Those things take time."

He held out his coffee cup, needing a refill. This wasn't the kind of thing that could be told without help. He would have liked a beer; he settled for more black coffee.

"Early one morning, a ragtag band of kids came limping into camp. The nuns had sent as many of them as they could—as many as they thought might be able to make the hike—out in the middle of the night. The orphans told us that the nuns were still there, along with the babies and the kids too sick to walk." He took another drink of coffee and again wished for something stronger. "We all wanted to go back and get them, but the brass had to think about it. What if it was a trick? What if there was an ambush?" He set the cup down and ran a hand over his face. "We'd lost several men in an ambush just a couple days before, so the brass weren't anxious to have that happen again.

"A few hours later, I realized Ed was gone. And I discovered that one of our big trucks was missing, too. I put two and two together and came up with a guy who had more heart than brains. So I took a jeep and slipped off to look for him.

"It didn't take me long to find him. He was pinned down in a dry riverbed with a truck full of screaming kids and praying nuns. The two armies were firing at each other—and Ed was right in the middle. I radioed for help. They said to sit tight while they called in the attack helicopters.

"The only problem was that I could see Ed. He'd been hit—thrown clear across the cab of the truck. I could see blood all over him, and he was still struggling to get back behind the wheel. It was pretty obvious that if I sat tight, Ed wasn't going to make it. And neither were those kids."

"So you decided to save them?"

Rafe laughed. He couldn't help it. "I don't remember deciding anything. On minute I was sitting behind a ridge in my jeep and the next I was zigzagging across open land like a bad imitation of John Wayne. When the jeep hit a rock and turned over, I took off on foot. The only reason I can figure that they didn't kill me was that they couldn't believe their eyes. They couldn't believe anyone would really be that stupid."

He rubbed his leg; just the memory had it aching. "Anyway, I was lucky. About that time the helicopters came swarming across the sky. They kept the gunmen busy while I crawled up into the truck and drove it back to camp.

"A couple of the kids were wounded. One of the nuns was hit pretty bad. But it was too late for Ed." Rafe looked straight into Abby's eyes. He didn't want to miss the moment when her admiration turned to disappointment. "The medics tried, but there was nothing they could do."

"That must have been awful for you." She closed her eyes, but Rafe could see a couple of tears work their way from beneath her lashes.

He closed his own eyes. But that was the coward's way out, so after a few seconds he forced them open again. Forced himself to watch for the change in her expression. "So you see, Ed was the real hero."

Abby's eyes opened wide. "That's not true."

"Yeah. It was."

"I don't believe it."

"But Ed was dead. And the press . . . well, they like live heroes. Ones they can photograph and get quotes from." Rafe took another sip of coffee to cover the bitter taste of the truth. "So Ed was forgotten, while I was given credit for saving all those children."

"But you did save them!"

"No, Ed's the one who drove out to get them. He's the one who had them almost back to camp. I just turned up at the last minute to drive the truck. I would have told them so, too, only they rushed me into surgery and then kept me so doped up for the pain. By the time I came out of it, the brass had decided that a soldier saving orphans was a great story."

Abby rose. "It's not just a great story. It's an act of heroism."

"We'd been taking a beating from the media. We'd arrested the wrong people, been caught in ambushes, destroyed some of the homes of people we were supposed to be saving. Our information was so bad that we were at a disadvantage every day. Things had gone from bad to worse. So a marine saving orphans was great press, and

Washington decided to make the most of it.'' Wearily, Rafe closed his eyes and leaned back in the chair.

He was relieved to have the burden lifted from him, he told himself. Relieved that he wouldn't have to play hero anymore.

"Would you rather have died?" Abby whispered.

Rafe opened his eyes to find her kneeling beside his chair. He wondered if the tears swimming in her eyes were for Ed or for the death of the hero that had never been. "I don't know.''

"I do.''

He didn't think he could bear to look any longer, but neither could he drag his gaze from hers.

"The world would be a poorer place without you.'' Gently, she laid her hand on his arm. "My life would have been poorer without you.''

"Ed was the hero,'' he insisted.

Abby nodded. "And so were you. My guess is that there were lots of heroes on San Miguel that we'll never know about. That doesn't make what you did any less heroic. It doesn't make you any less brave.''

Before he realized what was happening, Abby's hand glided down his arm to snuggle within his grasp. As he savored the contact, she laid her cheek on his arm.

"I'm glad you didn't die,'' she whispered. "I'm glad you lived and came home to us.''

And for the first time, Rafe was glad he'd made it. Glad he'd endured the wounds and the pain and the self-doubts. It was worth it, to have just one evening like this. Just one evening when, despite everything, he felt like a real hero.

He could feel Abby's tears soaking into his sleeve, so when she raised her head, he was surprised to see that she was smiling. With his other hand he reached out to wipe away the drops that clung to her lower lashes. To have a woman like this cry for him...well, it was more than he'd ever expected from life.

Now, he found that it wasn't enough. He looked at the curls that lay draped over his arm and at the red dress pooled at his feet, and he felt a tightening in his stomach that had nothing to do with heroism. He wanted to kiss her, to drink the tears from her lips and hold her close to his heart. But he knew he couldn't because he was a guy brought up with the gangs and the *cholos* who hung out on the street corners and the hopelessness of big-city poverty, while she was a woman raised in small-town America. If not for The Crisis, they would never have met. Besides, he was leaving tomorrow, and he was afraid one kiss would make him want to stay. And that, he knew, would be the most dangerous thing he could do.

He gave her hand a gentle squeeze, then released his hold on it. "I think I'd better go. We've both had a very long day."

Abby sat back on her heels and swiped at the tears. "I didn't mean to get all emotional on you."

He fought the urge to reach out for her. "Don't apologize. If anyone should apologize, it's me. I came here and dumped all that hero stuff on you. I told you things I haven't told anyone else."

Her smile was quick and dazzling. "I'm glad you did."

"I'm not." He stood. "It doesn't seem like much of a thank-you for all the trouble you went to."

She started to rise but got tangled up in her skirt. Rafe caught her by the shoulders and held her steady.

"You okay?"

She looked up at him and nodded. "Thanks."

Only the distance between them kept him from taking her in his arms and kissing her—not the distance from his lips to hers, but the distance between their worlds. He backed away from her and walked to the door. He stopped with his hand on the knob and turned back to her.

"Thanks for everything. You'll never know how much it all meant to me."

Then he stepped out into the darkness and went back to his lonely hotel room.

Chapter Six

Someone cared about him, was Rafe's first thought the next morning. Someone really cared. No, not someone, Rafe realized. It was Abby. She cared about *him*. About his past and his future. And the fact that he was alive.

Rafe couldn't remember another person ever telling him that his life mattered, that his death would make the world a less-meaningful place. There'd been plenty of people in his life to tell him the opposite—that he was nothing but trouble. That he'd never amount to anything.

But even more important was the fact that Abby hadn't turned away from him when he'd told her the truth. When he'd left her house last night, she'd looked at him the way she had all day: like he mattered. He'd still seen respect in her eyes.

He didn't know what he would have done if she'd turned away from him. If she'd said he didn't deserve the respect of the kids. If she'd said she was sorry he'd ever come to Pershing.

He wasn't sure what had prompted him to tell her the truth. He supposed it had something to do with the kind of day it had been. He could probably put it down to dealing with cheering crowds or fighting back tears. He might even convince himself that it had something to do with his looming reenlistment date. After all, that was a big decision for a guy who'd invested ten years in military life.

If not for his time on San Miguel and the way the brass had handled Ed's death, he wouldn't even pause to think; he'd just sign those reenlistment papers. But Ed was dead, and Rafe had become a hot PR property, so Rafe was giving his reenlistment careful consideration. And while he considered it, he also had to admit that he didn't have one male relation who'd made a success of civilian life. The thought of ending up like his father and brothers made going to war seem like a walk in the park.

Rafe shook off the thought. All this introspection was dangerous. A guy who thought too long didn't react quickly enough to get out of the way of a bullet.

He shook that thought off, too. He wasn't at war now. The problem was that he'd felt like a fake from the moment he'd stepped into Pershing. And all the speeches and the songs and the cheering had only made him feel like more of a phony.

Then, sitting in Abby's kitchen last night, listening to her tell stories of how Kevin had talked her into including a rap song and how Rachael had been so scared the first time she was at the microphone that her knees shook . . . well, listening to all that as if he was a real part of this community had been more than his conscience could take.

He'd never believed he was a hero. Not when the reporters had wanted to interview him. Not when the president had called him in the hospital. Not even when the military brass had handed him the Bronze Star. None of that had been real. When he thought about it, it was almost like it had happened to someone else.

But the look in Abby's eyes... that had been real. Her voice saying that his death would have mattered to her... that was real. And this morning, for the first time in a very long time, he felt as if he *was* real. As if Rafael Calderon mattered in this world. He was actually whistling by the time he'd dressed in a pair of brand-new jeans, a black T-shirt and comfortable sneakers.

Not that he was a real hero, he told himself as he descended the stairs to the first floor of the old hotel. He knew that even if Abby didn't. He'd simply been in the right place at the right time. Or maybe it had been the wrong place at the wrong time. Not that it mattered now. What mattered was that when he stepped through the door into the bright sunlight, he could hold his head high. He could go see Kevin's baseball game without feeling like a phony. And when he left this afternoon, he wouldn't feel like he'd conned the kids. That was a helluva lot more than he'd expected when he drove into this town.

The desert community was already heating up when he stepped onto the sidewalk. He figured it would be in the nineties by this afternoon, but for now the sun felt pleasantly warm and the breeze was cool. There were actual birds in the trees. He'd just had the best night's sleep he'd had in a year and a half, and he was hungry. No, he was starved. Which was kind of hard to explain, since he'd eaten more yesterday than he'd eaten since he'd been shipped to San Miguel.

He glanced up and down the few blocks that made up downtown Pershing. About a block and a half down on the right-hand side was a big sign with a picture of a cup with steam rising out of it. The Koffee Kup, the sign said. Rafe started in that direction. By the time he was seated at the counter on a Naugahyde stool, he'd run into at least ten people from the night before and been greeted by others he didn't know from Adam. He could only assume that Pershing didn't get a lot of strangers, and that word about his presence had spread. However, he had to admit that it wasn't an altogether unpleasant situation.

He took the plastic-coated menu from behind the napkin holder and studied it. When a cup of steaming coffee appeared at his elbow, he took a long swallow.

"Good morning, Rafe."

He looked up into the eyes of Sherry Scott. "Morning." He remembered her saying that she worked the morning shift on Saturdays. "Kevin home getting ready for his game?"

"He and his sister were watching cartoons when I left, but something tells me he'll be doing a little batting practice before today's game."

He longed to ask her how Kevin was doing. Really doing. But there were people on the stools next to him, and he remembered Kevin saying his mother cried when she discussed his illness. So he settled for small talk and breakfast.

Sherry introduced him to others who came in. Regulars, she told him. A real-estate agent, a retired trucker and the owner of the hardware store down the block. They talked about the weather, and the retiree complained about the cost of things. They all agreed government was out of hand and kids today didn't have much respect for their elders. Rafe decided he could hear the same discussion back home in Los Angeles, in Wyoming and everywhere else in the country. But he enjoyed being part of it, being asked his opinion as though it mattered.

When he got ready to leave, Sherry informed him that the retiree was paying for his breakfast. Rafe felt bad about taking money from the old man, but when he tried to pay the bill himself, the cook stepped out from behind his griddle. A little, wiry guy, he crossed his arms and stared at the old man. "Bud, you old codger, you can't pay this boy's bill."

The retired trucker rolled his toothpick from the left side of his mouth to the right. "Don't know why not."

"'Cause I'm not charging him." The cook reached out and grabbed the bill from Bud's gnarled hands. "You don't think I'd have a war hero in here and actually charge him, do you?"

"You charge me," Bud pointed out.

"Jeez, Bud, that was a dozen wars ago."

Bud laughed, slapped a tip on the counter and stood. "Get your free breakfasts now," he advised Rafe. "They'll make you start paying for them soon enough."

Rafe thanked Bud for the offer and thanked the cook for breakfast, though both made him uneasy. He still wasn't used to being called a hero. He put a tip by his plate and rose.

"Put that money back in your pocket," Sherry told him softly. "Please."

Rafe pocketed the money and decided he could become a pushover for this "please" routine.

Sherry smiled. "Are you going to the park later?"

Rafe nodded. "The game's at fourteen hundred hours, right?"

"Two o'clock." She smiled, that sort of sad, slow smile he'd noticed last night. "I just wanted to be sure."

"I wouldn't go back on a promise I made to Kevin."

Sherry nodded. "Thanks."

"No need to thank me. I'm looking forward to it."

With almost three hours to kill and nothing to do, Rafe decided to wander through town—sort of window-shop, though he'd never been much for it before. But the town of Pershing fascinated him. As did the people. He discovered he could hardly get past two storefronts without having someone stop to talk to him. Store owners came out on the sidewalk and passersby stopped to chat. It took him an hour and a half to make it through half the town.

By then his leg was hurting, so he went back to the hotel to rest. When he asked in the lobby about directions to the park, the desk clerk drew him a map and told him he could check out after the game. It was heady stuff, this being treated like someone important. He reminded himself not to get used to it. He'd be back in L.A. tonight.

Rafe arrived at the park about thirty minutes early. The place was filled, and it seemed like most of the kids in Abby's class were there. He greeted them by name as he worked his way toward the baseball diamond.

The scene was like something out of an old movie. There were kids all over the place. Families were at the picnic tables, and old men played checkers under a covered patio. An ice-cream truck cruised around the area, its recorded music blending with the voices. Close to the baseball diamond were big, shady trees with bleachers under them. Parents sat comfortably on the benches, while knots of children played or sat on the grass. The field, where the two teams were warming up, took the full impact of the sun.

Rafe remembered the letter Rachael Nightwind had written to him about wanting to spend time with her friends instead of her family. He'd made up stories about going on picnics with his family. He'd told about playing baseball with his older brother and pushing his little sister on the swings. He'd written that those were the most memorable times of his life. But those had been dreams. No, they'd been lies. Here was everything he'd ever dreamed about but never experienced. It felt a little like coming home.

Kevin raced across the sun-washed open space to catch hold of the chain-link fence that served as a backstop.

"Rafe," he called. "Sit over there. My team's in this dugout."

Rafe nodded. "Sure thing." He would have said more if the coach hadn't called Kevin back onto the field.

He made his way to the bleachers between home plate and third base and found himself seated beside Eleanor Burton's family and the Staffords. Jeremy's younger brother was on the nearby playground equipment, while an even younger child sat at the very bottom of the bleachers next to a cardboard box.

The little girl, who had eyes like Jeremy's, turned to look up at him. "You're Rafe, aren't you?"

Rafe smiled. "Yes."

"I'm Wendy." She pointed into the box, where Rafe could see only a pink blanket and a ball of gray fur. "This is Fluffy. She's my new kitty."

Rafe peered into the box. "She's very pretty."

The little girl nodded her head, setting her blond ponytail swinging. "She's asleep now."

Rafe heard her father mutter, "Thank God," and saw his wife jab him with an elbow. Obviously the new pet was a point of some contention in the family.

Rafe smothered a smile. "It's important for kitties to get their rest."

"That's what Daddy said."

Rafe couldn't hide his smile this time. He was saved from making further comment on the Fluffy situation when people called and waved to him from the other side of the field. He glanced around, realized that he knew kids on both teams and decided right away that he couldn't be too partisan. He didn't want to hurt the feelings of the guys on the opposing team.

Before Wendy could think of something else to say, Eleanor started talking to him. Luckily, with Eleanor he didn't need to do much besides nod and murmur "uh-huh" once in a while as he watched the guys warm up. When the game started, Mr. Burton told his wife to keep it down so they could concentrate. He gave Rafe a wink when Eleanor wasn't looking. Rafe grinned and turned to watch the game.

Kevin's team was up first. They got three hits, no runs and left a man on third. Rafe found his attention caught by the third-base coach, so he missed the first batter for the opposing team. It was a girl coaching third, he realized. She was tiny, but he knew she wasn't any fifth grader. He didn't ever remember seeing a fifth grader with that kind of figure. She had on a baseball cap, pulled low with a ponytail hanging out the back, a blue tank top and cutoff jeans that hugged her bottom while they showed off great legs. Not long legs, of course, because she was such a compact package. But their shape was great. Rafe forced his gaze to home plate as the next batter stepped up. It wouldn't do to be caught ogling some kid's mother.

The batter smacked Jeremy's second pitch. The ball bounced over the shortstop's head and into left field. The runner was whizzing past first by the time the fielder had a firm grip on the ball.

"Throw it to third," the third-base coach yelled. "Throw it here."

Rafe didn't bother to keep his eye on the ball when the coach jumped up and down. That cute little coach with the shapely derriere and the great legs wasn't someone's mother, after all. It was Abby. Man, did she look different when she let her legs hang out. When Kevin caught the ball and tagged the runner out at third, she did a little jig.

"Great play," Rafe heard her tell Kevin. She patted the boy on the shoulders. "A good catch."

Rafe cupped his hands and yelled, "Great coaching."

Abby's head snapped around. She smiled when she saw him and executed a cute little bow. Rafe suddenly remembered how much he liked baseball and why third base was his favorite position.

During the next inning Rafe pumped Eleanor for enough information to discover that Abby's dad coached the team and that Abby was his assistant. It wasn't difficult. All he had to say was, "That's Abby coaching, isn't it?" and Eleanor did the rest.

By the time the second inning was over, he also knew that John, Abby's father, had started coaching when his oldest boy, who was now thirty-five, had started playing at the age of eight, and that he'd been coaching ever since. Much to his surprise, Rafe discovered that Abby had been the first girl in town to play on a boys' team and that she wasn't afraid of flying in the face of tradition when justice demanded it. It didn't sound much like the prim-and-proper schoolteacher he'd met yesterday, but it certainly did intrigue him. By the fourth inning, Rafe decided that whoever had dubbed baseball America's favorite pastime knew what they were talking about.

* * *

Abby told herself she was being ridiculous. There was no way she could actually feel Rafe's gaze on her. A gaze wasn't a physical thing. You couldn't touch it or taste it or measure it. Then why was she so certain that she could feel his eyes making a detailed survey of her? And why did she think the temperature had taken a sudden upswing? She had to force herself to concentrate on the game.

By the fifth inning, the score was tied. When they took a break, she turned to find Rafe just behind her. He stood right next to the fence with his fingers looped through the chain links about shoulder height. The first thing she noticed was that he looked overwhelming. He was so big that he blocked out the sun and saved her from squinting up at him. The second was that, without the uniform she didn't feel like she was looking at the class's pen pal. She knew she was looking at a man. A very handsome, intriguing man.

He grinned down at her. "You didn't tell me you coached."

"I just help Dad out. He's the real coach." Rafe was much too handsome, she suddenly decided. And much too intriguing. "My real forte is basketball."

His eyes glided up and down her full five feet. "You seem a little short for that."

"That's why I coach."

His gaze locked with hers and a puzzled look came into them. "What?"

"Girls' basketball. Fifth-and-sixth-grade team."

He was ready to spout some pick-up line about a little one-on-one or a quick skirmish. Then he remembered this wasn't some broad he'd just happened to run into. This was Abby. This was a teacher, for God's sake.

"I'll bet you're a tough coach."

Her smile was quick and surprised. "How did you know?" Most people assumed she'd be a softie; she wasn't.

"Could be something about the determined way you came after me that gave me a clue. Every time I said no, I wasn't going to visit the school, you came right back at me with another reason why I should. I figured you had to be one tough cookie." He gave her a quick grin. "I didn't realize you'd also be cute."

Abigail gave him her most withering scowl. "I hate being called cute."

"You've had a big problem with that, have you?"

"Cute is for babies and teddy bears and—"

"Look, Mrs. Dixon." Abigail glanced down to see Wendy Stafford with a ball of gray fur in her hands. "My kitty is awake now."

Rafe hunkered down so that he was on eye level with the little girl. With his index finger he rubbed the sleepy tabby's head.

Wendy looked adoringly at the animal. "Isn't she cute?"

"—And kittens," Abigail finished. Rafe's laughter wasn't exactly the reaction she was hoping for.

The umpire stepped up to the plate and yelled, "Play ball!"

Abigail resumed her position in the coach's box. When she threw Sergeant Rafael Calderon an exasperated look over her shoulder, he didn't even have the good grace to look apologetic. She heaved a sigh. That was the problem with being five feet nothing; she found that people didn't always take her seriously.

That was why she tried to exude a competent, professional image in the classroom—and why she tended to be

so darned competitive in everything else. Abigail sighed
again. Such was the burden of cuteness.

By the time the seventh and final inning came around,
the score was still tied, and Abigail had gotten over the
urge to turn around and see if Rafe was still there. She
knew he had to be, because she could hear Wendy keeping up a steady stream of childish prattle, and every once
in a while she heard Rafe's deep voice in soft reply. He
had obviously fallen under the spell of the cute kitten—
and the even-cuter child. Abigail refused to give him the
satisfaction of knowing she cared whether he was still
there.

Though the game was shortened from the standard nine
innings because of the players' youth, the final inning was
a dilly. Abigail's team scored three runs off of a homer hit
by Kevin. The crowd on their side went wild, though she
did hear the kitten's yowling protest. Abby wondered if
the animal objected to all the noise or whether Wendy had
squeezed the poor little thing too tightly.

In the bottom of the inning, the other team scored two
runs with only one out. All they needed was one more run
to tie the game again and two to win. Andrew Chang hit
a double. Matt Jackson hit a pop fly into right field that
was caught, but the throw to third was too late. The other
team had one out remaining, and the tying run was on
third. When Rachael Nightwind stepped up to the plate,
Abby knew they were goners.

Rafe didn't understand the collective moan from the
parents around him when Rachael appeared.

"That's it," Eleanor mumbled, starting to gather up the
things scattered around her on the bench.

Rafe turned to question the woman. "What do you
mean?"

Before Eleanor could answer, he heard the resounding smack of the bat connecting with the ball. He turned in time to see the ball sail over everyone's head and roll into the bushes and trees at the edge of the field. By the time the outfielder had found it, both Andrew and Rachael had crossed home plate and their team was celebrating. Rafe tried to think of encouraging things he could say to the losing team. He was certain they'd be heartbroken at having lost such a close game.

Only they didn't look heartbroken when they came off the field. They were mostly concerned with an after-game tradition that Rafe discovered had to do with large quantities of food for the individual teams and good-natured ribbing among the parents. The players themselves seemed to mingle without any concern over who wore the white uniforms and who wore the blue. Rafe found himself being offered food by both teams while he wandered through the crowd, talking to each of the players. He was congratulating Rachael on her home run when Kevin materialized beside him.

"She's the best player," Kevin said without rancor. "She's usually a pitcher, but they put her out in the field today so she could hit. Great game, Rach."

The girl smiled so that a dimple showed in each cheek. "You, too," she said before wandering off.

Rafe ruffled Kevin's hair. "You played great. Good hitting and heads-up play at third. I didn't know you were so athletic."

Kevin shrugged. "I played better than usual. Mrs. Dixon's been working with me some after school."

Rafe glanced to where Abby was talking to Eleanor Burton. When she looked up and gave him a grin, he felt something happen to his insides. He felt them tie up in knots that even sailors wouldn't be able to undo.

"That's great." He dragged his gaze back to Kevin. "She must be a good coach."

"The best. Of course, my mom also says that baseball is in my genes. Mickey Mantle was my great-uncle on my father's side of the family."

Rafe let out a low whistle. "Those are impressive genes. You ever meet him?"

Kevin looked over his shoulder, then back at Rafe. "When my dad was around, we used to visit Uncle Mickey. But now..." Kevin shrugged.

Whatever else he might have said was lost in the piercing scream that stopped everyone in their tracks.

"My kitty," Wendy wailed from where she stood beside the cardboard box. "Somebody stole my kitty."

Mary Stafford knelt beside her crying child. "No one stole Fluffy. She just wandered off."

"Nooo," the child cried. "She's been catnapped."

"Too much television," Wendy's father said with a meaningful glance at his wife.

Rafe would have found the situation amusing except for the obvious distress of the child. "Let's all fan out and start looking," he suggested.

There was general agreement, and everyone, players and parents, began to search the nearby bushes and flower beds. Several kids went to the playground to see if Fluffy had decided to use the sandbox.

"What color is it?" questioned a player who had pushed aside branches of a nearby bush and was peering behind it.

"Gr-gr-gray," Wendy sniffled.

The boy let the branches snap back into place. "That's not it." He resumed searching.

The other boys came running back from the playground empty-handed. People were about to give up,

when one of the fathers called out, "I think I found it."
All eyes focused on the man, then turned to look up into
the tree where his gaze was directed. There, from a branch
at least fifteen feet above the ground, the kitten gazed
down upon them with what Rafe could only describe as a
smirk.

Wendy raced over to stand beneath the tree. "Fluffy,"
she called. "Come down." She extended her arms in front
of her. "I'll catch you."

Jim Stafford knelt beside his daughter and put an arm
around her shoulders. "I don't think the kitty is going to
jump, sweetheart."

Mary knelt on the other side of the child. "Cats like to
climb trees, sweetie. We may have to wait until Fluffy is
ready to come down on her own."

Wendy ran to get the cardboard box Fluffy had escaped from. Placing it under the tree, the child plopped
down on the grass beside it and folded her pudgy little
arms. "I'll wait right here."

Her parents exchanged worried glances. Everyone else
became suddenly interested in what they were eating or in
cleaning up.

Jeremy rolled his eyes. "Oh, brother," he mumbled in
typical older-sibling fashion.

Jim blinked at his wife through Coke-bottle lenses. "I
could go home and get the extension ladder."

"You don't need a ladder," Kevin told them. "All you
need is someone to climb the tree."

Rafe looked down at the boy who stood beside him.
"That's too high for you to climb."

"I know." The boy nodded. "But you could do it, no
sweat."

"Me?" Rafe felt his eyes go wide as he stared down at
Kevin. He didn't know what was more frightening, the

idea of risking life and limb to save a cat that looked perfectly satisfied where it was or the look of absolute confidence on the boy's face.

"What makes you think I can do it?"

Kevin grinned. "You can do anything."

"Now, Kevin—" Abby began in her calm, rational voice, only to be cut off by Wendy's gleeful voice.

"Rafe! Rafe!," the child cried. She hopped up and ran to Rafe, throwing her arms around his good leg. "Will you save my kitty?"

When Rafe looked down into those tearful blue eyes, he knew he was a goner. He, Rafe Calderon—who should have a lot more sense—was going to save Fluffy.

This hero stuff was definitely getting out of hand.

Chapter Seven

Abigail couldn't believe it. Not only was everyone ignoring the fact that the kitten was perfectly happy just where it was, but they were willing to let Rafe climb up the tree to rescue it.

"Don't worry, Fluffy," Wendy called up to the animal, whose main concern seemed to be cleaning her left front paw. "Rafe is coming to save you."

Abigail rolled her eyes. She just couldn't help it; this had all the earmarks of a bad melodrama. She watched as Rafe stepped back and studied the tree; she assumed he was searching for the easiest route to his quarry. The cat spared him a mere flicker of a glance before switching her attention to the other paw. Shaking his head, Rafe walked around to the other side of the tree. A group of children followed him. Rafe crossed his arms and eyed the tree critically. Kevin and Jeremy did the same.

Jeremy pointed at a branch just above them. "That's the lowest branch. It might be a good place to start up."

Abigail shook her head. The tree was an old scrub oak, the kind native to the area. The trunk had to be four feet in diameter. If he started there, he'd have to work his way around the trunk to get near the cat. That could be tricky—and it might give the cat an opportunity to move to another branch.

"Nah," Kevin said after serious study. "He doesn't need to start on one of the low branches. He's tall enough to reach the others."

Jeremy nodded his agreement after a moment's consideration.

Rafe moved back around to the cat's side of the tree, recrossed his arms and studied things from that angle. The boys followed him, crossed their arms in a similar manner and fell to studying the tree again. The cat paused long enough to blink down at the trio, then returned to the matter of cleanliness.

"If he starts here—" Jeremy pointed to the branch directly beneath the cat's position "—he can go straight up."

Kevin scrunched up his face in thought. "It's better if you can climb kinda sideways. It's easier than pulling yourself straight up from branch to branch."

Jeremy nodded. "Yeah, I think you're right."

The cat blinked and shook her head, as if in disbelief that humans would even consider such a ridiculous undertaking. Rafe refolded his arms and moved about a quarter way around the tree. The boys followed him. Abigail was beginning to feel like she was watching a Three Stooges movie. She walked a little closer and gestured for Rafe to come talk to her.

"Wait here," he told the boys, then stepped to her side.

Abigail sighed. "What, exactly, are you doing?"

"Hoping the cat will take pity on me and come down on its own."

She laughed. She just couldn't help herself. "I don't think that's going to happen. The cat looks perfectly happy."

"I was afraid of that."

"Now what?"

Rafe shrugged. "I guess I'm going to have to figure out how to climb a tree."

"What do you mean, figure out? Didn't you climb trees when you were a kid?"

"There weren't many trees in the part of L.A. where I grew up. And certainly none like this."

"Are you trying to tell me that you've never climbed a tree before?"

"Shh." He glanced back to where the boys were deep in conversation. "I have my pride, you know."

"You're going to have a broken neck if you're not careful."

"I'm open to suggestions."

"Don't do it."

Rafe looked at little Wendy, where she sat beside Fluffy's empty box, and then at Kevin and Jeremy, who were watching him expectantly. "That isn't an option."

She looked him in the eye and realized he meant it.

"Besides," he continued, "this has to be easier than giving a speech."

She shook her head. "You're never going to let me forget that, are you?"

"Nope."

She looked him straight in his serious brown eyes and realized there was no talking him out of this. "Will you take some advice from someone who practically elevated tree climbing to an Olympic event?''

He frowned down at her. "Who would that be?"

"Me."

"You?"

Abigail nodded. "None of the boys could keep up with me."

"A lady of many talents, aren't you?"

"You have no idea."

Rafe nodded. "Maybe not. But I think I'd like to."

Abigail felt her mouth go dry when he looked down at her. How did he do that? she wondered—make her go from perfectly normal to fighting a blush with a few words and a look? "Do you want to know how to climb that tree or not?"

"More than you could possibly know." When she smiled up at him, he added, "Because otherwise I'm not going to be around to discover what your other talents are. And I'm really curious, Abby. More curious than I've been about anything in a very long time."

This time she couldn't fight the color, so she pulled the bill of her cap down to shade her cheeks.

"You do realize that once you get up there, that cat may not want to be rescued, don't you?"

"I've got that covered. You just show me how to get up there."

"Okay," she told him. "Then listen up. And listen good, 'cause I'm only going over this once."

"Yes, sir, General, sir." She was sure she could hear laughter in his voice.

Rafe rubbed his hands down the pair of brand-new jeans that now had a tear in the knee and, he strongly suspected, one in the seat. He'd followed the ascent Abby had mapped out for him, and he was relieved that, though it had been filled with rough bark and branches that snapped back when he least expected it, it hadn't tested the strength of his leg. He'd gained a whole new respect for Abby in the last few minutes; this tree climbing was not as easy as it looked. He wondered why parents let their children do it.

Too bad the stupid cat hadn't managed to take refuge on the top of a chain-link fence or cinder-block wall. Those he'd learned to scale when he was in first grade; it had been the only way out of school between the hours of eight and two-thirty.

Grasping the branch just above him, Rafe ducked his head and stepped onto the limb where the cat lay curled up about ten feet from the trunk. Fluffy raised her head from her paws, gave Rafe a look that asked what he was doing there disturbing her sleep, stretched just a bit and snuggled back into her comfortable napping pose. Rafe fought the urge to grab the limb and shake it.

"How'd you like to see if you can land on your feet from this far up?" he muttered. The cat didn't deign to respond.

When Wendy began calling her kitten's name, Rafe's common sense took over. He put his finger to his lips and signaled for her to be quiet; he certainly didn't want the cat to take it into her head to move to another branch. Fluffy, however, wasn't even fazed by the noise. Cats, he decided, were a lot like generals: too self-important and sure of themselves for his liking. Well, this one was about to get a surprise.

Rafe eased down to straddle the branch, then pulled his T-shirt off over his head. From his pants pocket he removed a package of cheese and crackers he'd lifted from one of the snack setups. They were a bit crushed now, but that didn't matter. He opened the package and made a trail of food, beginning as far out on the branch as he could reach and plopping the biggest pile right in front of him. Then he settled back against the rough tree trunk and waited for Fluffy to make her move.

It didn't take too long for the kitten's curiosity and appetite to take over. In no time, Fluffy was within three feet, then two. Rafe didn't make a move until the cat was right in front of him. Then he threw his shirt over the kitten to prevent Fluffy's claws and teeth from doing permanent damage. When Rafe had the hissing, struggling cat rolled up so that only her furious little face was showing, he began to work his way down.

When he dropped to the ground to find Wendy calling his name and the rest of the crowd applauding, he decided it had been worth it.

Wendy stretched her arms up toward the cat. "Fluffy."

But Fluffy was not at all happy about being "rescued," so Rafe passed the hissing cat, shirt and all, to Wendy's father. It wasn't until another parent called out for everyone to stand closer together and wave that Rafe realized his entire bout of insanity had been captured on videotape. Shirtless, and feeling like a fool, he stood with the Staffords and the furious cat and waved into the camera for posterity. If it hadn't been for that last drop to the ground, he didn't think his leg would have been much the worse for wear. As it was, he wanted some aspirin and the chance to rest it before he drove into L.A. tonight.

Once the Staffords whisked Wendy and Fluffy away, the rest of the group started to break up. Once again Rafe found himself saying goodbye to the kids, promising that he'd write if they did, wondering how to say thank-you to people who'd changed his life. How to say goodbye to Abby.

He wasn't good at speeches, he reminded himself. The best he could do was a simple thanks and goodbye. He'd barely managed to get through his farewell to Kevin when he heard Abby call his name. He turned to see her standing with the man who'd coached Kevin's team. Up close, Rafe could see that there was more to the man than his short, pudgy physique. He had a ready smile and a gleam in his eyes, which were much like his daughter's.

"Rafe, I'd like to introduce my father, John Alexander."

John pumped Rafe's hand like a man half his age. "Great show, Rafe. Really great. I don't think I've enjoyed anything quite this much in a long time. I especially liked the expression on Jim's face when you handed him that hissing, spitting cat." John laughed and slapped Rafe on the back. Rafe wondered how long it would take the handprint to fade from his skin. "I haven't seen Jim look like that since old Mrs. Purvis backed into his store through the plate-glass window."

Abby gave her Dad a gentle jab with her elbow. "Dad."

John Alexander ignored his daughter's warning. Rafe figured he was one of the few people who'd have the nerve. "I want to invite you to dinner tonight. My wife, Lisa, is fixing her famous pot roast. There's not a man in town who'd turn it down."

"Well, I'd love to, but I'd planned to drive to L.A. tonight."

"Have a good dinner, get a good night's sleep and get an early start tomorrow. What do you say?"

Rafe looked from father to daughter. Truth was, he didn't want to leave yet. Not until he'd satisfied his curiosity about Abby. The problem was that once he'd done that, he might not want to leave at all.

"I have to check with the hotel. I told them I'd be leaving this afternoon."

John smiled. "No problem then, since I own the hotel. Just tell them I said it's okay." John readjusted his baseball cap over his balding head. "Why don't you ride with Rafe, Abby? That way you can give him directions." John started to turn away, then thought better of it. "And you'd better pick up a shirt when you stop by the hotel. Lisa won't let you come to the table without one."

Rafe ran a hand down his bare chest. "I wouldn't dream of it, sir."

"Don't call me sir. I did a stint in the navy and hated it. Just John." He gave Abby a quick peck on the cheek. "Dinner's in forty-five minutes."

"Thank you, sir—John," Rafe corrected himself as the older man jogged toward the parking lot.

Rafe felt just a little embarrassed about his state of undress, though he knew that his chest was nothing to be ashamed of. While he'd been doing physical therapy for his leg, he'd also done enough weight lifting to keep his upper body in shape. He'd feel just a little better about it, though, if he thought Abby was having trouble keeping her eyes off of him. As it was, she looked perfectly at ease.

Rafe gestured toward the parking lot. "We should probably get moving if I'm going by the hotel." He found it necessary to shorten his stride so that Abby wouldn't have to run to keep up.

After taking a few steps, Abby raised her chin so she could see him without the brim of her hat being in the way. "You're sure this is okay? I know your family must be anxious to see you."

"The only thing I'd be doing at home tonight is sitting around the house, watching TV." There was nothing particularly appealing about watching his old man get drunk.

It was even worse when his brother came over to drink with him. "There wouldn't be any pot roast." Maybe some tacos from the corner stand or tamales from Martinez's Market. He shook those thoughts away.

Abby shrugged. "I was just wondering, is all."

"Wondering if I had a hot date or something?"

Abby pulled the brim of her hat down again so that he couldn't see her face. "Something like that."

Rafe stopped, caught her by the shoulders and turned her to face him. "Look at me." Her chin came up and he bent down a little so he could look directly into her eyes. He wasn't smiling. "I don't have any hot date waiting at home. I haven't been home in almost three years. No one's waiting."

"Oh." Abby nodded.

"And there's no one back at Camp Lejeune, either."

Abby nodded again. "Okay." When she would have turned away, he held her firmly in place.

"And I'm glad your dad gave me an excuse to stay another day. To spend more time with you. More time in Pershing." He was going to remember every minute of it. "If things were different, Abby, I wouldn't want to leave at all. There's nothing I'd rather do than stay here and satisfy my curiosity about you. About us."

Abby stood rooted to the spot. She didn't think she could have moved if her life had depended on it. She had to moisten her lips before she spoke. "If what things were different?"

"The way I was raised. The way you live."

"Those things don't matter. What really matters is the way people are on the inside."

He smiled at that, a sad smile that tore at Abigail's heart. "I wish I believed that." He released his hold on her and straightened to his full height. "I wish the rest of the world believed it, too." He shook his head. "But that's not the way it is out there. Trust me, I've looked."

But Abby didn't believe him. She knew the measure of a man was found in his heart and in the way he treated others. It was what her parents had taught her. And she thought that, for the most part, the people in Pershing took the measure of a man—or a woman—in much the same manner.

She wished there was some way she could make Rafe see himself through her eyes. Some way she could make him recognize himself for the miracle he was. Because somewhere along the way, someone had convinced him that he didn't deserve the good things in life. That he didn't deserve to have the kids look up to him. That he didn't deserve to be called a hero. If he could take anything with him when he left Pershing, she wanted it to be the knowledge that he was a hero.

And she wanted him to take memories of her, for she suspected his memory would linger with her for a very long time.

Rafe stopped gaping at the Alexander home and opened the car door for Abby. But not looking at the house didn't make his impression of it any less overwhelming. Now, instead of seeing the rambling house set in the foothills several miles outside of Pershing, he was looking at the long driveway shaded by big trees and set off by a split-rail fence. Roses climbed the fence, just as they did in Abby's little front yard.

"You didn't tell me your family lived in a mansion."

Abby sighed. She should have been prepared for Rafe's reaction, but she hadn't been. "This isn't a mansion. It's a ranch. Well, sort of a ranch."

"How can it be sort of a ranch?"

"It was a real working ranch in my grandfather's time. They ran cattle and raised horses. But that's not as lucrative these days, so Dad got rid of the cattle years ago and only has horses enough to ride for pleasure. He makes a living off the trucking firm and the minimall and the hotel."

Rafe nodded and slammed the car door. He ran a hand down the front of the polo shirt he'd put on with his other new pair of jeans. There were wrinkles in his shirt that hadn't come out when he'd hung it in the closet. "Are you sure I'm dressed okay for this?"

"Oh, for heaven's sake. This isn't Buckingham Palace. We don't 'dress' for dinner. Look what I'm wearing."

Rafe looked down. Abby was probably the one thing that could distract him from the house and its surroundings.

"Dad will still be wearing what he had on at the park, and Mom will probably be in jeans." She smiled up at him. "Your problem is that you're overdressed."

But Abby was wrong. Her mom was wearing a silk pants outfit when she opened the door, and her father came from the back of the house slicking down his thinning hair, which was still damp from a shower. He had on a pair of slacks with a neatly pressed shirt.

"Overdressed, huh?" Rafe whispered in her ear once they'd been ushered into the house. Lisa had gone into the kitchen to check on dinner and John was pouring a cold beer into a glass at the wet bar. "I'll bet you feel underdressed."

Abby hung her cap on one of the wooden hooks by the door and fluffed her bangs in the hallway mirror. "Don't be silly. I grew up here. I always dress like this."

Lisa returned and sat on the sofa. Rafe noticed that she was giving her daughter a critical once-over.

"It's a shame you didn't have time to change, dear."

"Oh, for heaven's sake." Abby plopped down in one of the chairs and took the glass of wine her father offered. "I dress like this every weekend."

"But we don't have guests every weekend," Lisa pointed out.

Abby slanted her mother an exasperated look. "Don't think of Rafe as a guest. Think of him as family."

Rafe wondered about the arched eyebrow and tilt of the head Lisa directed at her husband.

Dinner was going very well, Abigail decided. Once her family got over the idea that they were entertaining royalty, things settled down nicely. And Rafe was more comfortable, too.

Abigail didn't point out that her mother had brought out the antique Haviland china inherited from Grandmother Nicholson and the Waterford crystal that Abigail and her siblings had given their parents for their thirty-fifth anniversary. She decided that her mother meant the gesture to be very sweet rather than intimidating, but she knew it would make Rafe feel uncomfortable. So they sat down to dinner with fresh flowers on the table and her mother's exceptional cooking and wine from a southern California vineyard that her father had an interest in, and they had a wonderful time. Conversation was easy, and Abby got the definite impression that Rafe was feeling very much at home.

"Why don't you show Rafe around while I clear the table," Abigail's mother suggested. "There's enough light left, and the pie needs to cool a bit longer."

John rose. "I'll go along with you two."

Lisa smiled at her husband. "I don't think so, dear. I need your help in the kitchen."

"My help?" John stared at his wife. "In the kitchen?"

"A little problem with a leaking faucet," she explained to Rafe.

John tossed his napkin onto the table. "I'll fix that tomorrow."

Lisa skewered her husband with a look. "And the garbage disposal."

Abigail smothered a grin. Her father wasn't very good at picking up subtle hints, but he recognized *that* look.

"You two kids run along," he suggested. "I'll just take a look in the kitchen."

Rafe set his napkin beside his plate. "Is it anything I can help with?"

Lisa smiled at Rafe. "Oh, I don't think so."

Abigail rolled her eyes; men could be so dense.

"I'll make it a quick tour," she promised her mother.

"Oh, take your time, dear. Your father may be busy in the kitchen awhile."

Abigail held her laughter until they were out the door and around the corner.

"What was that all about?" Rafe asked.

Abigail just shook her head. "Mother wasn't very subtle, was she?"

"Subtle?" Rafe shook his head. "She must have been too subtle for me, because I don't understand what happened."

"Men." Abigail shook her head and led the way around the house. "That was mother's way of letting me know you have her seal of approval."

"Whoa!" Rafe grasped her arm and pulled her to a stop. "Seal of approval for what?"

"In case you have any, uh..." Abigail tried to decide how she could put this tactfully. "In case you have any designs on her daughter."

"She approves of *me?*" Rafe decided the woman had to have rocks in her head. He wouldn't approve of someone like himself for his own daughter, if he had one.

"Strictly honorable designs, of course."

"Of course."

Abby grabbed his hand and tugged him along. "Let's go back to the stables. Dad will be upset if I don't show you the horses."

"You don't have to do that."

"Of course I do. They're Dad's pride and joy, now that the kids are all grown."

Rafe couldn't resist her. Her smile was completely disarming and the sway of her hips incredibly appealing. The problem was that the closest he'd ever been to a horse was a John Wayne movie, and he wasn't absolutely certain he wanted a closer acquaintance with an animal that large. Not even if he got to follow the sway of Abby's hips all the way to the barn.

The sun was just above the horizon, and the breeze lifted the curls that had come loose around Abby's nape. He decided that she had one of the sexiest necks he'd ever seen. He didn't pay much attention to the garden or the gazebo that she pointed out, but as they approached the barn, he caught his first glimpse of the horses.

They were beautiful, powerful animals, just as he'd expected, but their grace surprised him. He followed Abby to the fence, where she climbed up onto the top rail. He stood beside her, almost shoulder to shoulder now, admiring both the horses and the world in which they lived. A world of fresh air and sunshine and lots of open space. A world where people weren't crowded in so that they had to struggle to survive. A man could get used to this, he decided. A man could get used to a woman who grew up in this kind of world.

Rafe studied Abby's curls, which fluttered in the wind, and her ponytail, which swayed with each move. He listened to the excitement in her voice as she pointed out each of the horses. He studied the sheen of her skin in the growing twilight. And he decided that a man would have to be a fool not to find out what she tasted like. Rafe had been called a great many things in his life, but he'd never been called a fool.

"Abby?"

"Yes?" Smiling, she turned to face him.

"Do you think your father has figured out why your mother wanted him in the kitchen?"

Abby's laughter had him smiling. "I'd say that once we were out the door, she didn't wait for him to figure it out. My guess is that she spelled it out for him."

"So, do you think that if he talked her into taking back that seal of approval, he would have found us by now?"

"He's had plenty of time."

He brushed a stray curl back from her face. "So if I decide to satisfy my curiosity, I can be fairly sure we won't be interrupted."

"If Dad had any objections, we would have heard them by now."

Rafe nodded once. "Good." His gaze never wavered as he brought his lips closer to hers. "What do you think your dad would say about this?"

Abby smiled. "I don't know what Dad would say, but Mom would say it's about time."

She was still smiling when his lips touched hers.

Chapter Eight

She tasted like sunshine and moonbeams. Just one gentle brush of his lips over hers and he was seeing stars. When he went back for the second kiss, sunlight exploded to cascade over him like liquid gold. He felt himself drowning in it. When her arms came around his neck, he knew he was a goner.

Abigail had known he was going to kiss her. She'd almost dared him to, but she hadn't been prepared for the way his kiss would consume her. The moment his lips touched hers, her whole body began to tingle. Not just her lips and the places his hands touched, but clear down to her fingers and toes. She wondered if her hair was standing on end or simply frizzing. When he came back for the second kiss, she realized she didn't care if it had caught on fire. She wondered if this was the kiss she'd been waiting all her life for. If this was the man she'd risk everything for. Reminding herself that she'd risked everything for

Robert Dixon and lost didn't bring the rush of good, hard logic she'd hoped for. Remembering how her ex-husband had left her with a broken heart and an empty pocketbook didn't even put a dent in the spell Rafe was weaving, though the sensible part of her knew it should. She only wanted the tingle and the heat to go on forever.

Rafe couldn't believe the sweetness. Couldn't believe that he could hold sunshine in his hands, feel moonbeams dance along his skin. He kissed her cheeks and her eyelids, murmured her name, pulled the band from her hair so that it tumbled around her shoulders in a riot of curls. His hands got lost in her hair and his lips returned to hers, first in gentle, persuasive kisses, then with an ardor even he found surprising. His hands fisted in her hair, holding her head still for the demands of his mouth. His tongue swept within, demanding that she surrender her sweetness.

And she did. Without qualm or hesitation, her tongue mated with his. Without fear or question, she surrendered her sweetness to him.

Her surrender was what finally had him pulling back. Her sweetness was what had him leaning his forehead on hers. His desire to pull her into a corner and make hot, delicious love with her was what had him gentling his hands, still caught in her hair.

"Dear God, Abby, do you have any idea what you do to me?"

He was relieved that her laugh was as shaky as his insides. "I think I have a pretty good idea."

No, he didn't think she did, or she wouldn't be smiling at him. She wouldn't be within an arm's length of him, let alone leaning against him with her wrists braced against his shoulders and her feet still on the bottom rail of the fence. If she had any idea of the emotions she'd set boiling within him, she'd be running for home.

Because he was afraid she'd glimpse the violence, Rafe closed his eyes. When he opened them again, he put his hands on her waist and swung her to the ground. The moment her feet touched the earth, he backed away. She swayed toward him, and he almost gave in to the need to hold her. He almost swept her into his arms for another kiss.

Then he remembered who she was. Remembered where he'd come from. Remembered that they had to go back to the house, and he had to make polite conversation with her parents. He didn't think he'd ever been in this situation before; he'd never been the kind of boy anyone brought home to Mama. And so he backed away a little farther and waited for her eyes to focus.

Abigail gripped the rough wood of the fence and willed herself not to reach out for him. Not now. Not yet. He wasn't ready. She could see it in his eyes. Could see the desire and the fear. The desire was like her own, but it was the fear that had her smiling up at him. It was the fear that proved she'd gotten to him in ways he hadn't expected. It was the fear that had her hoping he wouldn't run away. Only a coward would run from this intense emotion, she told herself. And Rafe was no coward.

Rafe plunged his hands deep in his pockets and cleared his throat before he attempted to speak. "I think we'd better get up to the house before your father comes looking for us."

Abby tossed her hair back over her shoulders and smiled up at him. "Do you think he won't take one look at us and know what happened?"

Rafe shrugged and turned to pace back and forth. "I don't know."

Abby's smile grew wider. "I think a blind man could see what's happened. And Dad might be dense, but he isn't blind. As for Mother—"

"Oh, God." Rafe passed a hand over his face. He'd be lucky to get out of here alive.

"As for Mother," Abby repeated, "she'd be disappointed if you *hadn't* kissed me. Why do you think she sent us out here?"

Rafe stopped and stared at her. "I don't have a clue. And I still don't understand why she gave me her seal of approval." He started to pace again. "Are you certain about this seal-of-approval stuff? Maybe your parents are plotting a way to get rid of me before dessert."

"Don't be ridiculous. If they wanted to be rid of you, Mom would have cut and served the pie before the other dishes were cleared."

"How do you know?"

"Because it's happened on one or two occasions."

"Really?" Rafe gave her a long look. "Anyone I know?"

"Uh-huh." She pushed the hair back from her face and eyed the ground around her. "Jim Stafford, actually."

Rafe stopped. "Jeremy's dad? The one who was going to get a ladder to rescue Fluffy?"

"Don't laugh like that. I was a teenager and in my poetic period. I spent long, lazy afternoons reading Keats and Swinburne. And Jim actually fancied himself something of a poet."

"He wrote you poetry?"

"He tried." She glanced up at him and shrugged. "In retrospect, it was pretty dreadful stuff."

"Your dad objected to the poetry?"

Abby shook her head, sending her hair flying again. "Dad objected to his lack of backbone. He said I'd 'run

roughshod over the boy till the end of his days.' And that's
a direct quote."

"Your dad's a pretty sharp guy."

"Yeah, it's just that it was tough to admit when I was
in my teens. All kids want to think they can outwit their
parents. I always knew I didn't stand a chance." Abby
pulled her hair away from her face again. "You haven't
seen my hair band, have you?"

He stepped closer. "Hold still," he commanded as he
used both hands to work something from the tangled mass
of curls. "Your hair band," he said as he presented it to
her.

"My hero," she said lightly as she took it from him.

Rafe knew he wasn't her hero. He wasn't anybody's
hero. But he found himself wishing he could be, if only for
a little while.

Rafe lay the fork on his empty plate and sighed. "I've
never tasted better pie."

Lisa smiled. "Would you like another piece?"

"Oh, no, ma'am. It seems like I've done nothing but eat
since I got to town. If I'm not careful, I won't fit into my
uniform when I report back to base."

John tossed his napkin on the table. "When is that?"

"Three weeks."

Lisa scooped a dainty portion of pie onto her fork.
"Then you won't be rushing away, I hope. It would be
wonderful if you could stay for Frontier Days and the
Fourth of July."

Rafe looked at Abby. "Frontier Days?"

"It's an annual event in Pershing. Everybody dresses up
in Western style. We have barbecues and a Western dance
and a big Fourth of July celebration."

Lisa smiled at her husband. "John's the grand marshal this year."

"Congratulations," Rafe said. "What does a grand marshal do?"

John scowled at his wife and daughter. "Sits on a damned float, that's what he does."

"Dad wants to ride his horse in the parade."

"I've been at the head of the equestrian riders for the last twenty-five years. Don't know why they won't let me ride my horse. Don't know why I have to be put on a float like some old-timer who can't sit a horse anymore."

Abby hid her smile behind her napkin and Lisa reached over to pat his hand.

"Now, dear, this is quite an honor."

Rafe was almost disappointed when the phone rang. He wanted to see John's reaction to that statement.

Lisa went into the kitchen to answer the phone. "It's for you, John. The trucking company."

The man let out a heavy sigh as he pushed away from the table. "Can only be trouble on a Saturday night," he muttered. "I'll take it in my office."

Abby waited until her father was out of earshot. "He goes into the office so he can cuss. He never uses that kind of language in front of us."

Rafe noticed the frown on Lisa's face when she came back to the table. "Your father's too old for this sort of thing," she told her daughter. To Rafe she said, "He promised me he'd turn the day-to-day operations over to someone else this year."

"He would, Mom, if he could find someone." She shook her head as she turned to Rafe. "He's gone through three different managers this year. When he finds someone who knows trucks, the man can't manage people. When he finds someone who has good management skills, he doesn't know anything about trucks. I don't know what—"

"Lisa?" John's voice preceded him down the hallway. "I'm gonna have to go in tomorrow, hon. Gonna have to take a look at a couple of the trucks." He sat heavily at the table. "I'm getting too old to be crawling around those big rigs."

"Perhaps I could help," Rafe offered. When all eyes were turned on him, he explained, "That's what I do in the military. If it runs on wheels or caterpillar track, I can fix it."

Abby was the first to find her voice. "But I thought you were leaving tomorrow."

"There isn't anything pressing I have to do. Another day or two won't matter."

Lisa smiled. "That would be wonderful."

John gave him a considering look. "You're sure it won't inconvenience you?"

"It seems like the least I could do after this wonderful meal."

John smiled. "That would be a big help. I'll pick you up at the hotel around ten."

"And you can come back for dinner." Before Rafe could decline Lisa's invitation, she added, "Abigail will be here."

"I'd love to."

"Good." Lisa slanted her husband a smile. "I think this is all going to work out wonderfully."

The silence driving back to Abby's wasn't at all uncomfortable, although Rafe did wonder if she was considering the possibilities of a good-night kiss. When he thought about what had passed between them at the barn, Rafe didn't think a kiss was out of line.

"I hope you don't mind that I'm coming to dinner tomorrow."

"Mind?" Abby turned to look at him. "Why would I mind?"

"Well, two days in a row might be too much."

"Nonsense. Besides, I really appreciate your volunteering to help Daddy. I was just thinking that it's time for him to retire. Or at least semiretire. He'll be sixty-five next year."

"I wouldn't have guessed it."

"It's time for Mom and Dad to have some time together. I know Mom's always wanted to travel. If they don't do it soon, it might be too late."

Rafe said nothing. The concept of spending old age with someone you love—someone who shared your worries and your joys—was so foreign to anything he'd ever experienced that he was still mulling it over when he stopped in front of Abby's house. When she reached for her door handle, Rafe reached across and stopped her.

"I'll be coming around to open your door."

"Don't be ridiculous. I'm perfectly capable of opening my own door. Besides, you've been massaging your left leg all the way home. It must be hurting."

"The ache in my leg is nothing compared to how much I want to kiss you. And I plan to do that on your doorstep." Just like he'd seen in old movies. He had the feeling that they did things like that in Pershing, and he wanted the memory to take with him when he left.

"Oh."

Rafe smiled to himself as he came around the car. He kind of liked it when he surprised Abby enough to keep her quiet. He only wished he knew what was going on in that head of hers.

Abigail wished she could form a coherent thought, but that ability seemed to have disappeared. She'd been doing just fine on the way home, but since Rafe mentioned kissing her, she just couldn't pull things together.

She looked up when he opened the car door. "Did you do that on purpose?"

He took her hand and helped her out. "What?"

"Throw me off balance?"

He slammed the door. "How'd I do that?"

"By saying that you were...you know, going to kiss me."

"You've got to give me a break here. I'm new at this."

She slanted him a look as they passed under the streetlight. He was over six feet of hard body and good looks and he wanted her to think that he wasn't used to dating. "Give *me* a break here, Sergeant. You don't expect me to believe that, do you?"

"I don't know." He shrugged. "Maybe I have an ulterior motive."

They were at her front steps. "What kind of ulterior motive?"

"Maybe I just want to be sure that you're concentrating on me." As soon as they were on the porch he initiated a quick little maneuver that had her trapped between the wall and him. "Is all your attention centered on me now?"

Her hands came up to circle his neck. She grinned up at him. "You bet."

His hands slipped around her waist and he nuzzled her neck. "You're sure?"

"Oh." She couldn't speak when his clever lips found a particularly vulnerable spot on her throat. She closed her eyes and leaned into him. "Oh."

She felt his smile as he trailed kisses up her neck and across her cheek. "Cat got your tongue?" he asked just before his swept into her mouth.

She couldn't believe a simple kiss could do this to her—turn her brain to mush and her body to molten liquid. But it had. She gave herself up to the sheer pleasure of it.

"Well?" he asked a moment later.

She tried to lift her eyelids, but they were too heavy. She shook her head almost imperceptibly. "I...I don't remember the question."

His laughter was a rich rumble against her throat. He gave her one last, hard kiss before stepping away from her.

"I'll see you tomorrow."

She just stood there, smiling at him. He decided she'd lost the ability to move. He smiled when he realized he'd done that to sensible Abby Dixon, schoolteacher.

"Where's your key, Abby?"

She fished it out of her pocket and held it up for him to see.

"Go inside, Abby."

"Okay." She turned and slipped the key into the keyhole on the first try. "Good night, Rafe."

"'Night, Abby. Sweet dreams."

She closed the door behind her, then stood back in the shadows without turning on her lights so she could watch him walk back to his car. He was bent over and limping.

She hoped that wasn't all due to his leg injury.

Rafe checked his watch as he climbed the stairs to his room. It wasn't quite ten-thirty. Still early enough to call Theresa, he decided. She was the only one who would worry about him. The only one who'd notice he wasn't home. He punched in the numbers on his bedside phone.

"Hello?"

There was a quick stab of relief when he heard her voice. "Hello, yourself."

"Rafe!" There was no mistaking her delight. "Where are you?"

"Still in Pershing."

"I thought you might be home already."

"Not yet." He massaged his leg.

"Is everything all right?"

"Sure." He kept rubbing the area where the scar tissue had formed. "Listen, sis, I'm not going to be home for a few days."

"There isn't a problem, is there?"

The fact that his little sister worried about him had Rafe smiling. God knew he'd worried about her enough. He'd practically raised her after their mother's death. She was probably the only person on earth who even cared where he was. Or at least she had been until he'd started writing to the kids here. Until he'd made the acquaintance, via the post office, of thirty-one little kids and one terrifically sexy teacher.

"No problems," Rafe assured her. "But I volunteered to help out a guy here, so I'm going to stick around for a few more days. I'll call you when I'm ready to start home."

"You haven't talked to Papa, have you?"

Rafe eased back on the bed and leaned up against the headboard. "Nah. I don't see much sense in calling him. Half the time he's too drunk to remember who I am. The rest of the time he doesn't give a damn. Did you tell him I was coming back?"

"Yes, of course. Want me to call him and tell him you won't be home right away?"

"If you want to." He shrugged. He'd placed one phone call to his old man from the hospital; the elder Calderon had told Rafe that he was a fool to have risked his life for some damn stupid kids. Kids were nothing but trouble anyway. Rafe hadn't bothered to call since, and the old man hadn't made any effort to contact him. "Call him if you want. I doubt he remembers I'm coming home." Or cares, Rafe added silently.

"I'll let him know."

"Fine."

"Rafe, I have some good news to share when you get here."

"What kind of good news?"

He heard her sigh. "Someone special I want you to meet."

Rafe went perfectly still. He didn't talk till he could trust his voice. "You want to tell me about him now?"

"No, I want you to meet him."

"He's not some *cholo,* is he?"

Theresa laughed. "No, he's not a gang member. I don't hang out with those kinds of people."

Rafe breathed a sigh of relief. "You better not. Does he have a job?"

"Yeah, he has a job."

"A good one?"

"Yeah, he has a good job. You're going to like him, I promise. Now, no more questions, Rafe. Just wait and meet him."

"Okay. I'll be home soon, and I want a good look at this guy. Okay?"

"Okay. See you then, big brother."

"Yeah. See ya."

Rafe cradled the phone and stared at the ceiling. His little sister was in love. He'd only been ten when she was born, but his mother, who'd died a year later, was never well after that. Rafe had been the one to take care of

Theresa and Frank, who'd been seven. He'd done the diapering and the cooking and the general child care. It still amazed him that Theresa had survived infancy. But because of it, they'd been close.

He hadn't joined the marines until he'd been able to move her in with an aunt and uncle, his mother's sister and her husband. They were good people, but they'd had children of their own and been so poor that he'd had to promise them money before they'd take Theresa. His father had been glad to get rid of her. Since good jobs and steady employment were hard to come by in his neighborhood, Rafe had joined the military. As he looked back at it now, it was one of the best moves he'd ever made. It had given him a skill and a sense of his own worth. But he often wondered if he would have joined up if Frank hadn't been killed.

Frank had started hanging with the *cholos,* the local gang members, when he'd been only twelve. Though Rafe had been in a few scrapes with the law, he'd been smart enough to avoid running with the gangs. Rafe had tried to reason with his younger brother, but the gangs had too firm a grip on the boy. Soon after his thirteenth birthday Frank was dead, the victim of a drive-by shooting. Rafe was still angry at the useless way he'd died, but if he was honest, he wasn't sure Frank's life would have been all that productive anyway. Maybe the best thing that could be said for his younger brother's life—and death—was that it had forced Rafe to take a long, hard look at what he wanted and to stress the importance of an education to Theresa.

And it had worked out just fine for his little sister. She had a good job as a paralegal, she'd moved out of the old neighborhood and now she was in love. Maybe getting married. He tried to imagine her as a bride, but could only see her in the diapers he could never get to stay on and later in the pigtails that he never got quite even.

He scrubbed his hands down his face and laughed. Thirty-two wasn't old, so why did the thought of his little sister getting married make him feel ancient?

Fluffing her freshly washed hair, Abby padded to the bed. She was twenty-eight years old, and she felt like she was eighteen. She didn't remember a kiss ever making her feel that way before. Of course, she'd never been kissed by Rafe before tonight.

Mixed with the heady euphoria was the knowledge that she was headed for heartache. Rafe was only going to be here for another day or two; the smart thing to do would be to avoid him. But when it came to a question of her head or her heart, Abby always chose her heart. And where Rafe was concerned, her heart was definitely involved.

She reminded herself that this was how she'd been fooled before. Robert Dixon had swept into town with a big grin and an even bigger story about having once owned his own trucking company. He'd told of being swindled by his partner and needing work. Abigail had believed him. She'd even talked her father into giving him work. Then he'd swept her off her feet. They'd run off to Vegas to marry. They'd been husband and wife less than three months when he disappeared—along with every cent she had in the bank and the jewelry that had been handed down from Grandmother Nicholson. She'd felt like the biggest fool in the world. She'd wondered how she would ever hold her head up in Pershing again.

Then her family and friends had rallied to her support, and she'd realized she was still one of the luckiest women in the world. But along with counting her blessings, she'd promised herself she'd never be duped again.

Abigail had always kept her promises, to others and to herself. So why was she falling under the spell of another handsome stranger?

Only this was no stranger, she reminded herself. This was Gunnery Sergeant Rafael Calderon. She'd known him for a year and a half, albeit by mail. No matter what had happened before, she was going to follow her heart with Rafe. And if she was perfectly honest, she had to admit that Rafe had held a spot in her heart for quite some time. When had that happened? she wondered. When, exactly, had she begun to succumb to his honor and his charm? It had all started so innocently that she couldn't pinpoint the moment he'd ceased to be the class's pen pal and become her hero.

Dear Sergeant Calderon,

My name is Abigail Dixon. Kevin Scott is my student. Kevin speaks highly of you, and I have been very impressed with the letters you have written to him. (I hope that you don't mind him sharing them with me.)

We have been trying to find something to do as a class project. Kevin has suggested that we adopt you as our official pen pal for the class. The other students have voted unanimously to do this.

In this box, you will find letters from all thirty-one of my students, along with some special gifts for you. I hope you won't take offense at the teddy bears, but the students said that if they had to go to a place that was scary, they would want to take their stuffed animals. Therefore, you will find several teddy bears in here. If you don't want them (and I have trouble picturing a marine needing one,) please donate them to a school or orphanage. You will also find several boxes of cookies. I hope they are edible by the time you get them. I assure you they were baked by the students with lots of love.

Mrs. Abigail Dixon
Teacher, Pershing Elementary School

Chapter Nine

Lisa Alexander looked up from the sauce she was mixing and gave her daughter an assessing look.

"Don't play coy with me, young lady. What, exactly, is going on with your soldier?"

"Well, I—"

"See if I have more cream in the refrigerator. You don't have to quit talking just because you're bending at the waist," she added as Abigail peered behind the milk and juice.

Abigail had heard that phrase enough times in her twenty-eight years for it to elicit a smile.

"I'm not sure what to say." She set the cream on the counter beside her mother and went back to the chopping block where she was slicing asparagus. "I don't know if you want the truth or something that will reassure you."

"If you were going to reassure me, what would you say?"

"That we're just friends. That I like him, and I'm glad he came to visit my students."

Lisa made a sound of thorough disgust. "Do you actually think I want to hear an old line like that? Let's have the truth."

Abigail stopped and looked at her mother. "I'm attracted to him."

"Ha! That's what I told your father." She wiped her hands on her apron and reached for the flour canister. "One look last night and I knew. Men can be so dense."

"Dad might have been better off remaining dense."

"How can you say that? You're his daughter."

"Because I don't see that this can lead to anything but heartache. And God knows we went through enough of that last time."

"He still has a right to know." Lisa picked up the whisk and stirred briskly. "How does Rafe feel?"

Abigail shrugged. "I'm not sure. He—"

"He's interested," Lisa interjected before her daughter could finish. "All I had to do was look at him looking at you to know that."

"Mom!"

"A mother knows these things." She smiled at her daughter. "A woman knows these things."

Abigail grinned. "You are such a romantic."

"A woman who's still in love with the man she married almost forty years ago is entitled."

Abigail popped a piece of raw vegetable into her mouth and chewed. "That's all I ever wanted, you know."

"Have you finished with that asparagus yet?" The older woman adjusted the flame on the burner and set the frying pan on it. "What's all you ever wanted?"

"To be happy like you and Dad." Abigail swiped another piece of vegetable as her mother got ready to toss it into the skillet. "I was never like Travis or Spence or Kate. I never wanted to set the world on fire or make piles of money. I just wanted to get married and have kids and live a normal life."

Lisa set the vegetables back on the counter, removed the pan from the stove and eyed her daughter. "Your father and I have insisted that each of you choose your own goals. I've been proud of each of you, but I've always thought you chose the most difficult path."

"Me? Why me?"

"Because your brothers and your sister chose goals that didn't depend on anyone else. They could become lawyers and doctors and architects all by themselves. But the goal you've set for yourself involves finding someone else who wants exactly what you want. Someone as wonderful as your father." Lisa smiled and reached for her daughter's hand. "I know how difficult that can be."

Abigail told herself she wasn't going to cry. "I've made a fine mess of it so far, haven't I? First I married a con artist, and now I'm attracted to a guy who's just passing through."

"You made a mistake. You weren't the first person to be fooled by Robert Dixon. But you know what I've always been proud of?"

Abigail shook her head. "I can't imagine."

Lisa took her daughter's face gently between her hands. "I've always been proud of the fact that you didn't let Robert Dixon change you. Oh, I know he hurt you and you cried, but you never let him change who you are, deep down inside. You became a bit more careful. A little more wary. But you never let him take away your basic sweetness or your faith in people."

"I tried to be bitter. Really I did." Abigail felt the tears gathering. She wouldn't be able to hold them back much longer. "I just didn't know how to hold on to it."

"That's what I mean, sweetie. You didn't let him destroy my Abigail."

"I have no talent whatsoever for holding grudges or remaining bitter."

Lisa smiled. "I know. That's why I know that whatever happens with Rafe, you'll come through it strong and intact. Your strength is in your heart, Abigail. It always has been." Lisa used her thumbs to wipe away her daughter's tears before turning back to the stove. "Don't ever be afraid to follow your heart."

"You about finished there?"

Rafe glanced down from the truck motor he was working on to where John Alexander stood. From this perspective John looked even shorter and pudgier.

Rafe smiled at the older man. "Just a couple more minutes."

"Make it snappy. We've got dinner waiting on us."

Rafe fought a smile. If there was one thing he'd discovered today it was that John liked his doughnuts and his lunch and his afternoon break. And now he wanted dinner. Rafe gave a final turn on the torque wrench and climbed down. He couldn't help wincing when he dropped to the ground.

John was immediately at his side. "You okay?"

"Yeah." Rafe flexed his leg, then couldn't help running his hand over the tight muscles. "It just got a little stiff while I was working."

"I don't want you reinjuring yourself. Abigail will have my scalp." He ran a hand over his thinning hair. "Not that there's much there to take."

Rafe laughed. It was hard to be around John and not laugh. He was quick with a joke, quick with a hand and quick to let you know just exactly what he thought. His daughter was a lot like him, Rafe decided.

"Put those coveralls in the laundry bin over there," John told him. "You can wash up in the back. I'll be in the office when you're ready."

Rafe took another survey of the place while he was cleaning up. From what he'd heard, he figured John ran a fleet of over two hundred trucks; that was big for an independent. The facility was large enough to take on outside jobs. However, as far as Rafe could tell, the company was having trouble just keeping its own vehicles on the road. Good management was the key, he knew, but he hadn't seen any indication of it today. Of course, Sunday might not be the best day of the week to judge these things.

He found John in the office, sifting through stacks of papers.

"I'm getting too old for this," the older man complained. "I'd always thought one of my boys would take over, but they've gone off to 'pursue other interests,' as they put it."

Rafe settled on the corner of John's desk. "You could sell."

"Don't want to. I built the place from the ground up, and I'm not ready to turn loose yet." He pushed the paperwork away. "But Lisa's after me to take more time off. She wants to travel, see the world." Placing his hands flat on the desk, John rose from his chair. "If I don't find a manager soon, I may have to sell."

Rafe followed him through the office, where a couple dispatchers still worked. John waved goodbye and headed toward his car, with Rafe behind him.

"What do your sons do?" Rafe asked once they were settled in the plush seats.

"Spence is a hotshot lawyer and Travis is an architect. They never had any desire to work with engines or haul goods from one side of the country to the other."

Men with clean hands, Rafe thought, and looked at his own. They'd been clean when he left the hospital, but today there were a few stains that hadn't come out.

"Nothing wrong with a man having a little grease under his fingernails," John said, as though reading Rafe's thoughts. "Just means he works hard and has a way with mechanical things."

"Do your sons live around here?"

John shook his head. "The only one who lives locally is Abigail. Unlike her brothers and sister, she never wanted to leave Pershing. Keeps telling us this is where she wants to stay." He shook his head and turned off the highway. "Too bad *she* never had the urge to run the trucking company, but truth to tell, she was never good with mechanical things. Her gift has always been working with people."

"She's a terrific teacher."

"The best," her father said without hesitation. "Just like her mother was before her. What she really needs to do is get married and have kids. Abigail would be a terrific mother." John looked over at Rafe. "I know all parents say that." He pulled his gaze back to the road. "But I really mean it. Besides, Lisa and I want to be grandparents, and Abigail seems like our best chance."

"Abby was married, wasn't she?"

John nodded. "To this no-good son of a—" He stopped and shrugged philosophically. "He broke her heart but not her spirit. Abigail may be little, but she's tough as nails."

"You don't have to convince me."

John turned into his driveway and pulled around to the back of the house. After switching off the ignition, he turned to look Rafe straight in the eye. "Just so you know. I wouldn't want you to be laboring under any misconceptions."

"No, sir." Rafe had to smile. "I would never mistake Abby for a shy, retiring violet."

Abigail was relieved that dinner was a more leisurely affair than the night before. She'd convinced her mother that since the men were coming straight from work, good china and crystal were out of place, so they barbecued steaks and ate on the patio. It seemed so right having Rafe share a beer with her dad over the grill and so comfortable having him help her mother carry out the food dishes that Abigail almost forgot that his presence was temporary. It seemed like he'd been there forever, like he'd still be there next Sunday for dinner.

"You two go for a walk. Your father and I can handle this," Lisa told the younger couple once dinner was finished. "We'll have dessert when you get back."

But Rafe insisted on carrying the dishes inside before he let Abigail take his hand and lead him down a little lane that cut back beside the paddocks. As soon as they were out of sight of the house, Rafe pulled her behind a tree and kissed her thoroughly.

"Admit it," he said when he came up for air. "You would have been disappointed if I hadn't done that."

"Disappointed?" She nipped at his neck. "I've been waiting all day." She used her teeth to tug at his earlobe. "If you'd asked for one more helping of asparagus, I was planning to drop the bowl."

"Just building the suspense," Rafe assured her. He paused for a more leisurely kiss, then straightened and looked around. "Where are we headed?"

"There's a little stream just ahead and the old oak where I had a tree house as a kid."

"Where you learned to climb trees?"

"Uh-huh."

"I've got to see that."

She took his hand and tugged. "Come on then."

The shadows were long by the time they reached the oak. The evening breeze rustled through the leaves and set the old rope swing in motion.

Abigail stared down into the creek bed, where only a trickle of water cut through the sandy bottom.

"You should see this in the spring, when the snowpack begins to melt. We used to play in the creek as kids. We would dam it up there." She pointed to the next bend. "And let this area fill. Mom would pack lunch and we'd all spend the day here."

She closed her eyes and remembered how simple life had been. How close she and her siblings had been then, and now she was the only one left in Pershing. She sometimes wondered if there was something wrong with her.

"When I was twelve I broke my arm trying to dive into the stream." She smiled, remembering how Travis had warned her it wasn't deep enough and then had cried all the way to the hospital, though she'd remained dry-eyed.

Rafe stepped up behind her and wrapped his arms around her. "Do you have any idea how lucky you were? Not many kids get to grow up like this."

"Where did you play as a kid?"

"In the streets and alleys." He pulled her closer, savoring her natural sweetness and the flowery smell of her shampoo. When he was thirteen he'd been diapering

Theresa and trying to keep Frank from shoplifting from the local market. He couldn't imagine a more startling contrast in life-styles.

"Daddy built the tree house just up there." She pointed to the juncture of the biggest limb. "The boys tried to say Kate and I couldn't use it, so we had this major confrontation. For a while Kate and I got the even days and the boys got the odd. Then I discovered this interesting thing about the calendar. There are six months that have thirty-one days in them, and every four years February has twenty-nine. That meant at least half the time the boys got two days in a row, the odd-numbered day at the end of the month and the first of the next month. I teased them terribly, telling them that Daddy had given them the odd days because they were odd. They insisted that Kate and I take the odd-numbered days the next month."

"You think you're pretty clever, don't you?"

"I laughed about that for years. All I have to do is mention it to get a rise out of them. Especially from Spence, who's this big-time attorney now. I always tell him that he needs to read the fine print." She twisted her head and looked up at him. "Tell me something about your brothers and sister."

Rafe nuzzled her neck, hoping to distract her. The kind of memories that came to mind weren't anything like hers.

"Cut that out," she told him. "That tickles."

Her laughter blended with the sounds of the breeze and the trickle of water. Rafe turned her in his arms and gave her a gentle but thorough kiss. He was just becoming serious when he heard someone call his name.

"Abigail! Rafe!"

Rafe looked up to see four people on horseback on the other side of the creek.

Abby smiled, even though her skin turned an interesting shade of pink, and raised a hand in greeting. "Hey, guys."

"Hey, yourself," Eleanor Burton called back. All four of the Burtons waved and Rafe felt obligated to release his hold on Abby and return the greeting.

"We're just on our way back from the falls," Eleanor volunteered. "There's still quite a bit of water there."

"Has the pool dried up yet?"

"It's above my waist," little Burt volunteered.

"That deep?" Abby asked, looking impressed for the benefit of the child.

Martin nodded. "You ought to take Rafe there."

She looked back over her shoulder. "You want to see our falls?"

"Well..."

"It's not Victoria Falls or anything. But it's pretty and peaceful. How long are you staying?"

"I promised to help your Dad through Tuesday. I'm not expected home until next weekend."

"How about Wednesday?"

Rafe shrugged. "Sounds good to me, but don't you have school?"

"Only two more days till summer," Martin shouted.

"Summer!" his little brother echoed. "Oh, boy!"

Rafe looked at Abby. "Really?"

She nodded. "It's settled then. I'll tell Dad we need the horses, and if we play our cards right, Mom will volunteer a picnic."

"Horses?" Rafe looked at her in much the same way he had when she'd told him he had to give a speech. "You didn't say anything about horses."

"It's too far to walk."

"How about four-wheel drive? I'm a marine. I understand jeeps." He shook his head. "I've never been on a horse."

"You've never been on a horse?" Martin was wide-eyed at the thought. "Wow. I'll come teach you."

"You will not," Eleanor told her son. "Let's go on home now."

Once they'd said goodbye, Rafe turned to Abby again. "I don't think I'll be any good at this horse thing."

"That's what you said about making speeches, and you were terrific."

"But this is different. I don't know anything about horses."

"You're a big, bad marine." She held his face in her hands and went on tiptoe to kiss him. "What horse would have the nerve to disobey an order you gave?"

He went back for another kiss. "Only for you, Abby. I wouldn't do this for anyone else."

She smiled. "You just remember that, okay?"

Chapter Ten

Abigail glanced at the clock. One forty-five. Thirty more minutes of school. What was she going to do with a roomful of antsy fifth graders until then?

The last two days of school were always the worst. There were books to be turned in, library fines to be collected, athletic equipment to be locked away—and worst of all, children whose minds were already on vacation but whose bodies were still in the classroom. She blew a wayward curl out of her eyes and prayed she could get through the day without yelling at her class.

"Okay, I want everyone to return to their assigned seats."

"Kevin took my chair," Doreen wailed. "Now I don't have one."

Abigail skewered the boy with an exasperated glance. "Kevin Scott, you put Doreen's chair back right this minute."

"I was using it to stand on to put the literature books on the top shelf."

"Very well." Abigail made the effort to keep her voice low and her hands relaxed at her side. "Please return it to Doreen. Now."

"Yes, Mrs. Dixon."

"Martin and Leo, pick up the crayons you've been throwing. Everyone else go to your seats." When they didn't move as quickly as they should, she began to count. "One. Two. Three." She had almost achieved calm when there was a knock on the door. "Don't move a muscle," she warned the class as she crossed the room. She opened the door and stuck her head into the hall.

"We finished up early and I thought you might need reinforcements." The smile on Rafe's face was almost as good as a kiss. Almost.

She looked past him into the hallway. "Did you bring the army?"

"Now, Abby, maybe I haven't explained this before, but when there's a job to be done, you either call up the army or you call in one marine. I'm the one marine who can help you."

Abigail laughed and opened the door wider. "I'm desperate, so I'll try your one-marine theory."

As it turned out, one marine—at least if that one marine was Rafe—was enough. In less than twenty minutes, he'd managed to line up the students in rows, teach them to salute, teach them to march in place and sing the "Marine Hymn"—four times. Abigail was so grateful when the bell rang that she didn't even make them wait for her dismissal. She simply said, "Everyone out of here," and stayed out of their way.

Once the door was closed behind the last student, she walked over to Rafe, put her arms around his waist and laid her head on his shoulder. "I don't think I could have survived the last few minutes on my own."

He placed a gentle kiss on her forehead. "That's interesting, because I don't think I could have survived another minute without seeing you."

She turned her face up to him. "Prove it," she said, though the idea of kissing in her classroom seemed slightly scandalous, and he did.

It seemed their lips had barely met when the door squeaked open. They glanced toward the doorway in time to see Martin give Kevin a quick jab in the ribs.

"See?" Martin whispered. "Didn't I tell you?"

Rafe frowned at the boys. "Didn't you tell him what?"

Martin grinned. "That I saw you two kissing by the stream."

"Mushy stuff," Kevin added, with a look of abject horror on his face.

It was obvious that the boys didn't consider kissing a very worthwhile activity—especially for a marine.

Abigail couldn't stop the blush but she tried not to grin. "Did you forget something?

Martin nodded. "Mom said to tell you she'll be here at twelve-thirty tomorrow for the end-of-the-year party. She wants to know if you have enough paper goods left from the Easter party or if she should bring more."

"I'll have to check in the supply room. Martin, you come with me. Kevin, why don't you stay with Rafe until we get back."

Rafe waited until he was alone with Kevin. "How are you feeling?" He'd been in Pershing four days now, and as far as he could tell, Kevin hadn't gotten any sicker. He wondered how long the effects from Kevin's treatments lasted.

"I feel fine." The boy looked at his feet and then back at Rafe. "You really like her, huh?"

"You mean Mrs. Dixon?"

The boy nodded. "Yeah."

"Yes. I like her very much." He supposed it wasn't a good idea to tell the boy that Abby was the best thing that had happened to him, at least not unless he was willing to tell the teacher.

"She's nice. Mom says I'm really lucky she moved up to fifth grade this year so I could have her again." Kevin studied his shoes and the books stacked in the corner. "Did I ever tell you that my dad was a war hero, too?"

"No, I don't remember you mentioning that. What war was he in?"

Kevin shrugged. "I don't know. It was before I was born."

"You must be proud of him."

"Yeah, I am."

Rafe knelt down so he could look Kevin in the eye. "I bet you miss him, don't you?"

"Yeah. I wish he would call sometimes. Just so I'd know where he is." There was a new brightness in the boy's eyes; Rafe didn't know what to do if Kevin cried. "I don't know why he doesn't call."

Rafe reached out and held the boy by the shoulders. "Do you remember what I wrote you in my letter?"

"About how adults make mistakes sometimes."

Rafe nodded. "And sometimes they're too scared to say they made a mistake."

"And you said I should think about all the people who do care about me and who are here for me."

"Like your mom and Mrs. Dixon and even your mom's aunt Lucy." Rafe had never forgotten about the old woman with hair growing out of her ears.

"And you?"

"Especially me. We're buddies."

"Best buddies?"

Rafe gave him a playful jab in the shoulder. "You bet."

"Even if—" Kevin looked up as Abby and Martin returned.

"Even if what?"

Kevin shook his head. "Nothin'."

"Let's go," Martin called.

"Remember to give your mom that list," Abby reminded Martin as the boys headed for the door. After their noisy exit, she perched on the corner of her desk. "I'll never get this room in shape by tomorrow."

"Sure you will. I'm here to help."

"You don't have to do that."

"I'm volunteering for the mission." He glanced around the room and wondered if it wouldn't be better just to blow the place up and start over. But knowing Abby as he did, he was sure there was a place for everything, and he was determined to help her put everything in its place. "Then I'm taking you to dinner."

"Really?"

"You bet. It's one of the conditions."

"Conditions?" She cocked her head to the side. "I didn't know there were conditions when you volunteer."

"This is marine-type volunteering. There are always restrictions in the military." He didn't bother to add that they were generally set by the brass. "I was thinking in terms of a few kisses during the evening."

"We have to wait till dark?"

Rafe took two steps forward, stopping so that he stood right in front of her. "Not if you don't want to."

"I think I could use one now. Just to tide me over until we can take care of this mess."

Rafe grinned. "Did I mention that we're having a 'twofer' sale today?"

"What's a 'twofer' sale?"

"Why, ma'am, that's two for the price of one."

Laughing, Abby stood on tiptoe and threw her arms around Rafe's neck. "Have I ever mentioned that I'm a sucker for a good sale?"

"No, you haven't." Rafe put his hands on her waist and pulled her closer. "But I was hoping."

It was almost six-thirty by the time Rafe and Abigail slipped into a back booth in Tony's Italian Restaurant. Abigail had chosen the restaurant because it was quiet, dimly lit and not usually frequented by her students and their families. Rafe's time in Pershing was quickly drawing to an end, despite his agreeing to stay a few extra days. Tonight she wanted him all to herself.

In only a matter of minutes they'd ordered dinner and were sharing a bottle of wine.

Abigail sipped from her glass. "So how'd it go with Dad today?"

"Great. Your dad's a terrific guy."

"We think so." She paused and took another sip of wine before asking, "So what condition do you think the trucking company is in?"

"Why are you asking me? I've only been there a couple of times."

"Because I value your opinion. And because Mom and I are worried."

"You don't need to worry that the place is falling apart...."

She looked at him over her glass. "But?"

"It's just my first impression, so I don't know how accurate it is."

"Go on."

"I think it needs a firmer hand. Some of the mechanics are taking advantage of your father. Cheating a little on their hours, taking longer to do a job than necessary."

Abigail's gaze narrowed as she looked into the distance. "He could fire them."

"I suppose. The other problem is that some of the guys work overtime without charging it. They're trying to make up for the guys who are goldbricking. My guess is that they're old-timers."

"Why is that a problem?"

"It causes friction between the two groups." Rafe topped off their glasses. "They don't get along, and that's bad for morale."

"This wouldn't have happened if Dad had been doing the hiring recently." She took a sip of wine. "He's a good judge of character, he has almost a sixth sense about these things. But he's too old to go in there and start cleaning house."

"I agree. That's why he offered me the job."

Abigail realized the glass was slipping from her fingers. She set it down. "He what?"

"He offered me the manager's position. That's one of the reasons I asked you to dinner. I want to know how you feel about it."

"You want to know how I feel about it?" She sighed. "I don't know what to say."

"How about the truth?"

If she told him the truth—that having him here with her was what she wanted most in the world—she was afraid it would scare him away. "Can you do that? I mean, what about the marines? You can't just quit, can you?"

"My enlistment is almost up. When I report back to base, it's time for me to re-up or try civilian life."

"Really?" She pushed the hair out of her face. "You'd really consider that? Moving here, I mean?"

"I already am considering it. But it depends on how you feel about it."

Abby folded her hands on the table before her so he wouldn't see them trembling. She had to be careful how she answered. Just because he was considering the job her father offered didn't mean he wanted a future with her.

"How do *you* feel about it?" She swallowed. "I mean, that's a big change in your life. When I have to make decisions, I usually make a list of the advantages and disadvantages. We could do that."

Rafe reached across and laid his big hand over her clasped ones before she could start hunting in her purse for pencil and paper.

"Abby, everything I'm interested in is in this town." His response came from his heart. Not from his head, which knew there were other considerations, and certainly not from his conscience, which said Abby would be better off without him. Just straight from the heart. "At this table, actually. But I can't make a decision until I know what you think."

She should choose her words carefully, she knew. She should frame her answer so that he'd feel free to make whatever decision was best for him.

"I can't think of anything that would make me happier," she told him despite her best intentions.

Rafe grinned. "That's what I wanted to hear."

"But I think you should wait at least forty-eight hours before you give Dad an answer."

"Why is that?"

Abigail grinned. "So I have a good excuse to try to persuade you."

* * *

Rafe got to the trucking company early the next day and worked through breaks and lunch so he could leave early with a clear conscience. He wanted to see what an end-of-the-year party was like, especially one put on by Eleanor Burton. When he told that to John, the older man had only laughed and shook his head. When he got to Abby's room at one-thirty things were in full swing.

Eleanor was wearing a blinding, flowered muumuu, the students all sported plastic leis and Hawaiian music was playing in the background. A buffet that included sandwiches, salads, pineapple, macadamia nuts and a coconut cake decorated with palm trees and hula girls was set out on grass mats that covered the art tables.

Eleanor was the first one to spot his entry. She started across the room with a hot pink lei. "Aloha."

Rafe was unable to dodge the lei or Eleanor's kiss on the cheek. "Hi."

Eleanor scowled at him. "Get into the spirit of things."

"Aloha." Rafe grinned as he scanned the room. "Did you do all this?"

"You bet. Help yourself to some food."

Rafe nodded. "Let me say hi to Abby first."

He looked around until he found her sitting at one of the desks in the back of the room. She didn't look much different from the students, except that she had a big plastic flower pinned in her hair.

"Are you hiding out back here?" he asked as he eased into the small chair beside her. His knees came up so high that he could barely see over them.

"Just enjoying the sight. By next week I'll actually be missing them. Then summer school will start, and they'll be driving me crazy again. We're expecting lots of kids since we're doing a special program integrating art, music and drama." She smiled at him. "Your timing is perfect. You managed to avoid Pin the Surfer on the Surfboard and Eleanor's hula instructions."

"Thank God."

"You will be able to participate in the Hawaiian singalong, however." She checked the clock. "It should start in about ten minutes."

"I may not be able to stay long."

"Don't even try to get out of it, buster. Eleanor has promised that by two-thirty we'll know all the words to 'Pearly Shells'—in English and Hawaiian."

"I think I'd better get food, then. I'm going to need all my strength."

"Bring an extra piece of that cake, will you? Eleanor really has a way with calories."

Rafe had eaten two heaping platefuls of food and the class was learning the hand gestures to go along with finding those pearly shells when John Alexander walked in. Rafe wasn't sure whose facial expression was more amusing—Abby's or John's. He didn't have to be told that John's appearance in the classroom was unusual.

John adjusted his baseball cap so that it came lower over his eyes, then sidled back to where Abby and Rafe sat.

"What the heck is going on here?" he demanded of his daughter.

"Another event by Eleanor." Abby grinned, obviously enjoying her father's discomfiture. "Frankly, I'm just grateful she didn't hire an Elvis impersonator to sing 'Blue Hawaii.' Want some punch?"

"No, thanks." He glanced around the room again, as though he couldn't believe his eyes. "I just came by to tell Rafe that the Frontier Days committee met this afternoon."

Rafe looked up from where he sat in his miniature chair. "Oh?"

"Seems they've reconsidered their choice of grand marshal for this year's event."

"Oh, Dad, that seems so unfair."

John cast his daughter an exasperated look. "Don't be ridiculous. I suggested it."

"You did?"

John stood tall and puffed out his chest. "You bet."

"Who'd they select?"

Rafe had a sinking feeling even before John spoke.

"None other than Gunnery Sergeant Rafael Calderon, that's who. What do you say, son? Think you can stick around for the Fourth of July? It's a real honor."

Rafe looked at Abby and back at her father. "I don't know."

"You'd be doing me a favor. A real big favor."

Rafe thought for a moment. "There aren't any speeches involved, are there?"

Abby rolled her eyes. "Oh, for heaven's sake."

"Nope. No speeches."

"Have you talked to Lisa about it? I wouldn't want her to be disappointed."

"Talked to her last night. I wouldn't do this if she didn't agree."

Rafe looked at Abby. "What do you think?"

"I think you'd be perfect."

Rafe looked back at John. "I'll do it, then."

"Thanks, Rafe." John reached down to pound him on the back. "You won't regret this, I promise. Why, it'll be the event of a lifetime. Something to tell your kids and grandkids about."

"Dad, you don't have to convince him. He's already said yes."

John turned and stomped his way to the front of the room, where Eleanor was just showing the kids the hand motion for "fishes swimming in the ocean." He spoke to her a moment. Her eyes went round.

"I wish I'd known earlier. I could have used a patriotic theme for the end-of-the-year party. A cake decorated like the American flag. Red-white-and-blue streamers."

John didn't waste any more time discussing party decor. He turned to face the class, which was watching with eager curiosity.

"I just thought you boys and girls would like to know the good news. Seems I've been replaced as grand marshal for this year's Frontier Days."

There was a chorus of disappointed ohs, especially from the boys on his team.

"Don't want to see any glum faces. Fact is, I'm pleased as punch about the decision, because they've decided to honor Sergeant Rafael Calderon."

Thirty-one little faces turned toward the back of the room. Rafe held his breath, hoping they wouldn't be disappointed. They weren't. They were still clapping and yelling when the bell rang to dismiss school for the summer.

By ten o'clock that night Abigail had showered, shampooed her hair and watched two boring sitcoms on television. Rafe had promised to call her when the Frontier Days committee meeting was over. She was beginning to wonder if he'd forgotten all about her when there was a knock at the door. She threw on her robe and ran to the living room.

"Who's there?"

"It's the marshal, ma'am."

She opened the door. "It's about time."

Rafe stepped in and closed the door behind him. "Miss me?"

"I had plenty to keep me busy."

"I missed you." He pulled her close for a quick kiss. "But I have to say that I'm disappointed in you."

"In me?"

"You pulled a fast one on me again."

Abigail was confused. "What do you mean?"

"Remember when I asked you if I'd have to give a speech?"

"I swear there's no speech. At least there never was before."

"There's still no speech."

Abigail breathed a sigh of relief. "So what's the problem?"

"You didn't mention that the grand marshal is supposed to lead off the dancing during the nighttime festivities."

"So?"

"Abby, I grew up in Los Angeles. I don't know anything about country dancing. I don't have any idea what a two-step is. I don't know how to waltz at all, let alone do a country waltz."

"Oh." She put her hand over her mouth to cover her smile.

"This isn't funny, Abby."

"I'll teach you."

"By Saturday?"

"Give me thirty minutes and I'll have you dancing like you were born in Texas."

"Abby, I don't know how to break this to you, but even if I'd been born in Texas I wouldn't have learned to country dance. I would have been more likely to dance the lambada."

Abigail reached up and laid a gentle hand over his mouth. "Country-and-western dancing was invented by cowboys. The men have the easy part—it's the women who have it tough. If you can walk and count to four, I can teach you to dance."

She took his hand and tugged him toward the kitchen. It was the biggest open space in the house. She tuned the kitchen radio to a local country-and-western station and pulled him to the center of the linoleum.

"You're going to start with your left foot. There are four basic steps. Slow. Slow. Quick, Quick. That's it. Then you do it all over again."

Rafe tried it. Left foot. Right foot. Left foot, right foot. "That's all there is to it?"

"You need a partner. That's where I come in."

He pulled her into his arms. "This is the part I like best." Rafe's lips descended toward hers.

When Abby could speak again, she said, "You're not supposed to stop and kiss me in the middle of the dance floor."

"I knew there'd be a catch."

"Come on. Just keep those feet moving like I showed you. I'll do the rest."

Thirty minutes later, Rafe was two-stepping around the kitchen. He was even keeping the basic step while Abigail initiated a few simple turns.

"See? You're a natural."

Rafe shook his head. "It just proves you're a great teacher."

"Are you ready for a waltz?"

Rafe moaned. "Have a heart here. I've got to get up in the morning and learn to ride a horse." He brightened. "Unless you think we should spend the day practicing the two-step instead of riding to the waterfall."

"No dice. Tomorrow you're going for the ride of your life."

"I was afraid of that." He stopped in the middle of the floor. "Give me a kiss, then. I'd better go get some rest before I try leading a horse. Something tells me the horse isn't as light on its feet as you are." He kissed her, then, with his arm still around her, walked to the door. "You know, this robe with the little rosebud buttons makes me wonder about what's under it."

Abigail blushed. "A matching nightgown with more rosebud buttons."

Rafe shook his head. "I'm thinking about what's under the nightgown, too." He kissed her again. It was the kind of kiss that made her head spin. "Sometime soon I'm not going to want to leave." He fanned kisses across her brow. "I'm going to want you beside me all night long, though sleeping isn't what I have in mind." He kissed the hollow of her throat, worked his way up to her lips again. "Think about that, Abby. Someday soon I'm going to ask you to decide."

Before Abigail could tell him she'd already made up her mind, Rafe was out the door and halfway to his car.

Chapter Eleven

"Abby, are you sure the waterfalls are worth all this trouble?"

Abigail looked over her shoulder to where Rafe sat on Aunt Polly, the gentle mare that John had selected for him.

"Try to relax. Sort of roll with the horse's movements."

"If I'd wanted to roll with the movement, I would have joined the navy. I joined the marines because I wanted to keep both feet on the ground."

Abigail turned her attention to the terrain ahead, more to keep Rafe from seeing her smile than from any concern about their progress. "Only another thirty minutes or so."

His moan spoke volumes.

She pointed to the right. "Where we are now, the water has gone underground into the water table. We're going to follow that ravine just ahead, so the going will get a little rockier, then you'll notice that the vegetation starts getting greener. Before you know it, you'll see a little stream and then you'll hear the falls. Just hang on a little longer."

"Hanging on is exactly what I'm doing."

When they cut up the ravine and he found himself holding on for dear life, Rafe faced a moment of truth. The moment when he admitted that a man wouldn't go through this for simple lust. The moment he had to admit that he might be falling in love—stark, raving mad in love, if his actions were any indication. If anyone had told him when he arrived in Pershing that he was going to learn to dance the two-step and ride a horse, he would have told them they were crazy. Yet he'd found himself dancing slow, slow, quick, quick around his hotel room this morning, and now here he was, clinging to Aunt Polly's saddle.

Rafe couldn't stop grinning. No one had ever told him that falling in love could be like this. But then, he'd never met anyone like Abby before.

It was funny how life had taken a one-eighty on him when he least expected it. Three weeks ago he'd been in rehab, thinking that he had only ten more years to go before he could take his military retirement. Now he was considering a return to civilian life with a good job and the possibility of a relationship with a woman who deserved better but for some reason seemed to want him. It was a lot to risk. He'd made a decent life for himself in the marines. Better than it could ever have been in L.A. Surely a return to civilian life didn't mean he'd turn out like his old man. Just the thought made his blood freeze. And the fear that Abby might see him like that was enough to have his heart stopping. He tried to shake those thoughts away. He wasn't like his father. He wasn't!

He thought about the life John and Lisa Alexander enjoyed. And the Burtons and Staffords. Could he see himself like that in a few years? Could he picture himself with a family and friends? Hell, who was he kidding? The real question was whether he could picture himself with Abby and a picket fence and a couple of kids. A real family. A real life. Yeah, it was definitely something to consider.

And he realized suddenly that if he should decide on the job and the woman, he was also going to have to two-step and ride a horse. She was worth it, he decided without hesitation. He let go of the pommel and concentrated on rolling with the horse's movements .

He was concentrating so hard that he was surprised when Aunt Polly came to a stop. He looked up and found Abby watching him.

Rafe looked around. "Are we there yet?"

"Almost." She smiled at him. "You're really getting the hang of it."

He grinned back. "The horse and I are bonding."

"You'll need a horse with more spirit next time."

That was something Rafe hadn't considered. "Let's not rush things. You wouldn't want to break up a wonderful relationship, would you?"

Abby shook her head. "We'll follow the stream from here." Rafe noticed the easy flow of water in the middle of the riverbed. "It's only a few more minutes."

He could see that the vegetation was becoming greener as the trickle of water got larger. Then they came around an outcrop of rocks and he got his first glimpse of the waterfall.

At first he wasn't certain it was real, for it was set back in the shadows. The falls themselves were coming from about forty feet up, falling in a silvery sheet that was wider than his arm span. The water looked like it was coming directly out of the rock, to cascade into a pool that wasn't even thirty feet across. The pool emptied into the stream they'd been following. It was nothing less than a miracle, he decided, sitting there in the middle of the scraggly brush and jagged rock. After a while he turned, wide-eyed, to look at Abby.

She was watching him intently. "Well, was it worth it?"

Rafe looked from Abby to the falls and back at her again. He grinned. "Yeah. Worth every minute and every saddle sore."

"Wimp," she said with a laugh. "You can't get saddle sores this quick."

"Tell that to my..." He caught himself before he finished the statement, but her smile proved that she knew exactly what he'd been about to say. "Didn't you mention that we have lunch in these saddlebags?"

Rafe set out the blanket at the edge of the pool and put the cans of soda in the stream to cool while Abby watered the horses, then tied them to a nearby bush.

"Now comes the best part," she informed him as she sat at the edge of the blanket.

He watched as she removed her boots and socks. Next she peeled off her denim shirt, to reveal a skimpy tank top. Just when he was wondering if she was going to slip out of her jeans, she bent to roll up the legs.

"Come on," she told him. "There's no sense having all this water if you can't wade in it."

Rafe slipped his T-shirt over his head, removed his sneakers and rolled up his pants. "Now what?"

"Now comes the sheer pleasure of feeling the cold, clear water." She waded in. "It feels great after the ride."

Rafe followed her in. "You didn't tell me it was freezing."

"It isn't. It's just the contrast with your heated skin that makes it feel that way." She turned to look at the falls. "If you think this is cold, you ought to go stand over there and let the water hit you."

"So you don't think this is cold, huh?"

Still gazing at the falls, she shook her head. That was when he threw the water at her back. She shrieked and turned toward him.

He grinned. "I thought you said it wasn't cold."

"So you want to play dirty, do you?"

"No, I want to play wet."

"Just remember, you're the one who started it." She scooped up water with both hands and flung it at him. It was a direct hit. As water streamed over his head onto his chest, Rafe returned the favor. Abby saw it coming, however, and turned her body so that it splattered all over her back. Before Rafe could bend down to scoop up more water, she turned and came in low and fast. Her arms were a blur as she hit him with handful after handful of the chilly liquid. Bending down to scoop up water only made him an easier target, so he waited until she was within reach.

With a quickness that obviously surprised her, he caught her arm, then pulled her close enough to grab around the waist. Before she could do more than scream, he had her turned upside down, her head only inches from the water. Her hair, which had come loose from its ponytail, floated on the surface and washed around his legs.

"Don't do it," she warned, though her laughter took the sting from her words.

He lowered her another inch.

"*Please* don't do it," she cried.

"That's better." Still he lowered her closer to the water.

"Please, please, please don't."

"What's it worth to you?"

She laughed. "What do you want?"

"An apology for the wimp remark."

"I'm sorry I called you a wimp. Now let me up."

"Nope. That was too easy. I'm trying to decide what else I want." He smacked her on the bottom when she tried to wiggle free. "Hold still."

"Hurry up, then. The blood's starting to rush to my head."

"Hmm." He thought a little longer. "I want a kiss."

"I'll give you a hundred kisses, just let me up."

Rafe set her on her feet. "Some tough bargainer you are," he said, leaning toward her for the first kiss.

He closed his eyes in anticipation, and that's when it hit him—strands of cold, wet hair across his face and chest. He grabbed her before she could take more than two steps away, then set her squirming bottom on the blanket. Before she could struggle free, he had her flat on her back, her hands pinned by his, her legs anchored beneath his body. She was laughing up at him.

He tried to keep from smiling. "Is that how you pay your debts?" He shook his head and watched in satisfaction as fat drops of cold water settled on her face and top.

She quit laughing when his lips touched hers. The contrast of warm lips and cold water made the kiss that much more appealing. He felt her body go lax, realized she'd laced her fingers with his. Because there was no hurry, he lifted his head and smiled down at her.

"Ninety-nine to go." He liked the way she looked at him, all soft and dreamy. He kissed her again. "Ninety-eight."

She worked her hands loose from his and raised them to his neck. With just a gentle tug, she pulled him down so their lips met again.

He kissed the corners of her mouth, sprinkled kisses across her cheek. Drawn by the pulse in her neck, he trailed warm kisses down her throat.

With his hand, he pulled her tank top from her jeans. Beneath the damp cloth, her skin was cold. He spread his palm over her stomach, then moved it upward to cup her breast through the lacy bra. Her nipple was already puckered, whether from the damp top or passion, he couldn't tell. He pushed the top up out of the way. With his mouth, he warmed the rosy peak of her breast. She sighed and arched her back. He moved to the other breast.

Her soft moans and her hands on his back drove him wild. He came back to her lips and swept inside so their tongues could mate; all the while his hands were busy with the fastening on her bra. When he felt the front closure slip free, he raised his head. With one gentle finger, he traced circles around her nipple. When it pebbled even more at his touch, he smiled.

"You're perfect." He kissed the turgid peak, then lifted his head so that he could look into her eyes. "Absolutely perfect."

She brought her hands around to brush across his chest. When she found his hard nipples, she smiled. "You're not so bad yourself." She explored the sweep of muscle, traced the hair that narrowed as it disappeared into the waistband of his jeans. "I wanted to do this Saturday at the ballpark."

"You're kidding." He couldn't help smiling. "I thought you hadn't even noticed my body."

"Not notice? The only thing that kept me from staring was the fear that ogling male bodies in a public park might get my teaching credentials revoked."

"You have my permission to ogle me at any time."

He brought his lips back to hers, and this time the need grew stronger. It was as though one taste had made him greedy, as though he could never get enough of her. His fingers edged beneath her waistband, only to encounter lacy silk. He came back to the snap, loosened it and tugged at the zipper. As his lips worked magic, his hand came to rest over the curls still hidden from his sight. Abby moved against his hand, inviting him without words. He eased his finger beneath the lace, felt the warmth of her desire.

His own obvious need was still restricted by denim, but it lay hot and hard against her. Her hand came down to touch him. He moaned and pressed into her palm. In another moment, he knew, it would be too late to stop. Too late to draw back and save her. With a strength he'd never guessed he possessed, he moved away from her. With his hand on her shoulder, he held her at a distance.

"What did I do wrong?" she asked.

"Nothing." He closed his eyes against a wave of desire that almost undermined his determination. "You're perfect. It's me." He opened his eyes again, to gaze into hers. "I'm not."

"I'm not perfect, Rafe. And heaven knows I'm not looking for perfection."

"There are things you don't know about me."

"I know everything I need to know." She reached for him. "I knew you before you arrived in Pershing. Last night when you told me I'd have to make a decision, I realized I'd made it a long time ago. I want to make love with you. With the man I met in your letters."

He took her hand in his much-larger one. "I want it, too—more than you could possibly know. But the time has to be right."

"It feels right to me."

Rafe levered himself to a sitting position. "There are some things I have to settle first. Some peace I have to make with my past. Some truths I have to tell you."

"Then tell me now." She ran a hand up his arm. "I've already seen into your heart—nothing else matters."

He shook his head and looked off into the distance. "This isn't the place. Not here in the open beneath the sky. I need to tell you where it's dark, where I can't see your anger and your disappointment."

"I won't be angry."

"I can't take that chance." He rose and walked a few feet away.

His future—his whole life—hinged on Abby. He hungered for her and all that she represented, but he couldn't take what she was offering until he could be completely truthful with her. He had to be certain that she saw him as he really was before she took him into her body and her heart, because he couldn't bear to live in fear of her discovering the truth and sending him away.

The real problem was that Rafe wasn't sure who he was anymore. A week ago, he'd known. He'd been Gunnery Sergeant Rafael Calderon of the U.S. Marine Corps, a man who'd taken the lousy life fate had dealt him and turned it into something to be proud of. Now he wondered if he could escape the man who'd fathered him, the man who embodied every weakness he despised. Somewhere inside him were the genes of a failure.

Which was stronger? The man Abby saw or the one Rafe feared? He knew that he couldn't be certain until he went home again—or at least journeyed to that place his family lived. Until he stood beside his father and compared himself to the old man, feature by feature, trait by trait. And he certainly couldn't allow Abby's life to become entangled with his until he was satisfied that what he was had nothing to do with where he'd come from or what his father had become.

And if he even suspected that he could turn out like his old man, he'd have to walk away. It was the only way he knew to protect Abby.

He knew she was behind him even before he felt her hand on his back.

"I'm a patient woman." She laid her cheek against his shoulder. "I'll wait as long as it takes."

Rafe turned and caught her face between his hands. "I don't deserve you."

"Too bad." She smiled up at him. "You've got me anyway."

"I'm going to hold you to that."

He kissed her tenderly, like the treasure she was.

After lunch, they stretched out on the blanket to listen to the music of the water and talk when the mood struck them. Though she would have liked Rafe to level with her then and there, she didn't push. He had some doubts and fears; Abigail decided she could best support him by being patient. When he'd made peace with his past, she'd be ready for them to make a future. And if he thought she was going to give up and go away, he was sadly mistaken.

She raised up on one elbow and looked at him. "Penny for your thoughts."

He opened one eye to look at her. "I'm thinking that the only drawback to this is that I have to get on that horse again."

"You'll hurt Aunt Polly's feelings."

"She's already hurt something else on me. And none of your 'wimp' comments, if you please."

"I wouldn't dream of it." She smiled. "Greenhorn."

He closed his eye. "I'd take exception to that, but I'm much too comfortable."

She looked at the lengthening shadows, then closed her eyes. "We're going to have to start home before too long."

He sighed in resignation and they drifted into that comfortable quiet that Abby found so peaceful.

"You're the best thing that's ever happened to me, Abby."

Her head came off the blanket and she turned to look at him. His eyes were wide open.

"What brought that on?"

"I want you to remember that, no matter what."

Abigail rolled onto her side and propped her head in her hand. "You're good for me, too." She grinned. "We're good for each other."

"It's ironic that it took a dying child to bring us together, isn't it?"

Abigail nodded. "And that they'd be thousands of miles away on a small island in the Atlantic."

"I mean Kevin."

"Kevin?" She shook her head. "I don't know what you're talking about."

"I know about Kevin's illness." He reached out and touched her cheek ever so gently. "I want you to know that you can talk to me about it if you need to."

"I'm glad you know, because I'm confused. What illness are you talking about?"

"Kevin wrote to me, Abby. He told me he was dying. If it hadn't been for that, I don't think I would ever have come to Pershing. That's what I meant about a dying child bringing us together."

"Hold it right there." She looked Rafe straight in the eye. "Are you telling me that Kevin Scott wrote to you and said he was sick?"

Rafe nodded. "That he was dying. That he didn't have more than a couple months left."

"Kevin Scott is healthy as a horse."

"Now, Abby, why would he make up something like that?"

"For the same reason he told the other kids that he's Larry Bird's cousin. To try to get their attention and acceptance."

"Larry Bird? He told me it was Mickey Mantle."

"Kevin has a little trouble with the truth sometimes."

"You mean he lies."

"I mean that after his father walked out and left him, he started making things up. Telling stories to make himself sound important. To impress the other kids. The school has provided counseling for him, and I thought it was starting to do some good."

"Then why would he tell me he's dying? How is that going to impress me?"

She thought a moment. "He told you that to get you here." She held out her hand when he would have spoken. "I'd tried to get you here. All the other kids had written and asked you to come. You said no every time. Then you wrote to Kevin and told him you'd come for a visit. Not only did that mean you cared enough about him to come to Pershing, it also meant that his status with the other kids went way up. He did what no one else had been able to do."

"Why, that little con artist."

Abigail nodded. "We can't let him get away with this."

"Every time I asked how he was feeling, he gave me some story about just having had a treatment."

"Keep in mind that he didn't do it to be mean."

Rafe slanted her a look. "Give me a little credit here."

"I'm not sure what to do about it."

"Let me handle it."

She thought about it. "Maybe we should have a professional handle it."

"I'm the one he conned. *I'll* handle it."

"I don't know."

He smoothed the frown from between her brows. "Trust me on this. Okay?"

"Okay." She sighed. "We'd better get back if we're going shopping for you this afternoon."

He pulled her down so that her cheek lay over his heart. "Have I ever mentioned that I hate shopping?"

"Think of this as part of your duties as grand marshal."

"I'd much rather stay here with you."

She gave him a quick kiss on the cheek. "So would I, but if you're going to lead off the dancing on Saturday night, you have to have the right wardrobe."

A couple of hours later Rafe stuffed his foot down into the cowboy boot, hitched up his pants and stepped out of the dressing room.

"I don't know about this, Abby."

She looked him over. "Turn around."

It was bad enough that he was buying clothes in the feed-and-grain store, but being told to turn around like some model was the final insult. He did it anyway.

She reached over to adjust his collar. "You look wonderful."

"You don't think the pants are too long?"

"They're supposed to bunch up around the boots."

"I don't know about this shirt. I don't ever remember seeing John Wayne wear pink and green."

"Teal."

"What?"

"Pink and teal. Those are the colors in your shirt."

"Fine. Pink and teal. But I don't ever remember the Duke wearing them."

She waved her hand as if to dismiss his comment. "How do those boots feel?"

"Like they have pointy toes and high heels."

"That's because they do." She turned to the store owner. "What do you think about a hat?"

"How about one of the summer straws?" He plunked several down on the counter. "Try these for size."

Rafe stared at them. "A cowboy hat? Abby, I think you've gone too far this time."

"Just try one."

He did. "I feel like a fool."

She cocked her head to one side and studied him. "You probably shouldn't wear that."

"See? I look like a fool, don't I?"

"No, but you look much too sexy for me to let you run around like that."

He looked in the mirror. "You think so?"

"Oh, absolutely."

Rafe turned to the man behind the counter. "I'll take the hat."

"And the rest of the outfit?"

Rafe looked down at the bright shirt. "What do you think?"

"I think that I'd lock my daughters up if they were over ten."

"In that case, I'll take the whole thing. Will you accept a check?"

The man laughed. "From you I'd take a handshake."

But when Rafe came out to settle the bill, he was informed that it had already been taken care of.

"Don't look at me," Abby protested when he turned a scowl on her. "Dad took care of it."

The store owner backed her up. "That's the truth. He called this morning and said to put it all on his tab. If you've got a problem with this, you take it up with John."

"I will," Rafe assured them both. He put on the hat, took the package and thanked the owner.

They were on their way back to the car when Rafe spotted Kevin. He handed Abby the package and the keys to the car.

"This won't take long," he assured her.

Abby gave him a confident smile. "I know you'll do the right thing."

Rafe caught up with Kevin in front of The Koffee Kup. "Hey, Kevin."

The boy turned at the sound of his name. "Rafe! Great hat."

Rafe adjusted the newest addition to his wardrobe. "Abby convinced me that I needed it for the dance. Have you got a minute? I'd like to talk to you."

The boy smiled up at him. "For you? Sure."

"Want a soda?" Rafe nodded toward the coffee shop. "My treat."

"Mom's not working now."

"That's okay. It'll just be us guys."

"I'm supposed to meet Jeremy at the park."

"This won't take long. I promise."

Rafe led Kevin to a booth in the back that was unoccupied, as was most of the little restaurant. They were seated and had their sodas in record time.

"I'd like to talk to you about your illness," Rafe began.

Kevin stared into his cola. "I don't like to talk about it."

"I'm concerned that you're not getting the right treatment."

"No. I mean, yes, I am. The doctor here is great. He specializes in this."

"What, exactly, do you have, Kevin? You never told me."

Kevin's gaze remained on the table. "I don't know the name of it." He shrugged. "It's some big, long, Latin name."

"Your mom would know, wouldn't she?"

"Don't ask her! I mean, it'll only upset her."

"But I'm worried about you, Kevin. I want to be sure the doctors are doing everything they can."

"You don't need to worry."

"But I do, Kevin. We're friends. Friends worry about each other."

"You don't need to worry because . . ."

"Yes?" Rafe prompted.

The boy looked up at him then. His blue eyes were bright with unshed tears. "Because there's nothing wrong with me."

"You mean you're not sick?"

The boy shook his head. "I'm hardly ever sick."

"You mean that I was worried for nothing?"

Kevin nodded. "I tried to tell you the other day in Mrs. Dixon's room, but then Martin came back. I'm sorry I made you worry. Really." He studied Rafe for a minute, then said, "You knew, didn't you?"

"Yes."

"Then why didn't you yell at me? Mom always yells at me when I tell lies. Then she cries."

"I don't think friends should yell at each other. Besides, I thought you'd feel better if you told me the truth yourself."

"Friends? You mean we're still friends?"

"Sure we're friends. You don't think we were friends just because I thought you were dying, do you?"

"I—I didn't know."

Rafe shook his head. "We became friends when you helped me through some tough times. You wrote to me when I was on San Miguel and when I was in the hospital. Were you my friend just because I was a soldier?"

"No. We were friends because I could write to you about stuff. Personal stuff. And you'd always write back. You cared."

"That's right. And I came to Pershing to help you through a bad time, just like you'd done for me. I came because we're buddies." Rafe hesitated a moment, choosing his words carefully. "The thing is, buddies should be able to trust each other. When one of my buddies in the unit tells me something, I've got to be able to trust him. My life could depend on it. Both our lives could depend on it. That's the thing with friends—they've got to be able to depend on each other. So do you know what happens when you lie to a buddy?"

Kevin scrunched his face up in thought. "You think you can't trust him anymore, right?"

"Right. And then pretty soon you find you aren't friends anymore. Lying to people doesn't make them friends, Kevin. Lying to people drives friends away."

Kevin swiped at the tears that he couldn't keep from falling. "Does this mean we aren't friends anymore?"

"No. It means we aren't going to lie to each other anymore."

Kevin used his sleeves to wipe away the telltale tracks. "I can't believe you're being so cool about this."

Rafe had to smile. "I'm being 'cool' because I've done the same thing a time or two."

"You?"

"I'm human, Kevin. I make mistakes, too. The important thing is to confess our mistakes and try not to make the same ones again. That's part of growing up."

"I promise I won't tell any more lies."

"I want you to keep that promise. Now, go on. I'll bet Jeremy is wondering where you are."

Rafe watched as Kevin left the restaurant and started up Main Street. The problem was that he had a few lies to confess to himself. He only hoped that Abby would be as understanding.

Chapter Twelve

Friday morning dawned warm and smoggy. Rafe was in his rental car headed toward L.A. by nine. He didn't begin to feel like the world was closing in on him until the Ninety-one Freeway veered west and headed toward downtown Los Angeles. There was no more open space, no more empty land on the side of the road, only houses and industrial buildings and too many people. He fought the urge to take the next off ramp and head right back to Abby. But he couldn't do that. Not until he'd confronted his past. Not until he could go back to her knowing that he was whole. Then he was going to have to tell her the truth. He hoped she would understand.

Not that he'd told big lies. He hadn't said he was a millionaire or that he could leap tall buildings in a single bound. But he'd lied about himself to Abby and the kids, letting them think he came from a close-knit, loving family with a father who loved him. He'd also led them to believe that his older brother Eduardo was a hardworking family man. He'd even let them believe that his little brother had been the innocent victim of a drive-by shooting rather than a gang member who'd been caught in a pattern of murder and retribution. During the time he'd been on San Miguel, the letters from the kids had been the highlight of his life. But he hadn't wanted their pity, so he'd created a family he could be proud of. The only truthful part of his letters had been about Theresa. He'd written about her often.

But now he was going to go back and face the truth: an alcoholic father and brother. He was going to take a long, hard look at them and see if there was anything of himself in them. If there was, Pershing would only be a pit stop on his way back to Camp Lejeune. If there wasn't, he still had the hurdle of telling Abby the truth. If she'd have him after that, the only thing he'd be doing at Camp Lejeune was picking up his stuff.

The thought of Abby made him smile. She'd been disappointed that he was leaving for the day, but she'd also understood he needed some time with his family. She'd even volunteered to come with him. That had wiped the smile from his face. He didn't ever want her to see where he'd come from. Luckily she'd been content with his promise to return in time for the Frontier Day parade.

It was midafternoon when he pulled into the old neighborhood. It hadn't improved any in the three years he'd been gone. Knots of boys hung out on the corner or in front yards. Few children were out on the streets; the frequency of drive-bys in the neighborhood forced most parents to keep their kids in the house or in the backyard. Old men and women hurried past the groups of young people, afraid to make eye contact. Graffiti scarred the walls and fences.

Occasionally there was a boarded-up house. Less often there was a neat home with a carefully tended yard. But for the most part, it was a landscape of broken dreams. Rafe could almost taste the bitterness and despair.

He pulled into the driveway and killed the engine. When he assessed the house from the outside, he supposed it wasn't any worse or any better than the others. In the years since his mother's death, his father had managed months at a time when he'd pull himself together, when he'd get a job and clean the place up and say he was going to make a fresh start. Those periods had become less frequent as the years passed.

The chain-link fence around the house had been put up during one of those times. The aluminum siding was proof that ten years ago the old man had held a job for almost a year. But then he'd hit the bottle again. He'd lost that job, and he'd worked only sporadically since then. Rafe was amazed that his father could keep up with the mortgage payments and the taxes, but then Jesse Calderon had a knack for just squeaking by.

Rafe was careful to lock the car when he got out, and he skirted the weeds on his way to the front door. It was wide open. Rafe waited as his eyes adjusted to the dark interior. Once they did, he saw a few pieces of broken furniture and a black-and-white TV tuned to a talk show. His father was sprawled on the couch, a beer in his hand. There was nothing here to necessitate a lock on the door or bars on the windows.

His father laughed. "If it isn't the hero." He took a swig of beer. "It certainly took you long enough to get here."

Rafe stepped across the threshold. "I didn't think you were all that anxious to see me."

The older man shrugged. "Makes no difference to me. But some of the people around here, they're anxious to see the hero they grew up with." He held up his beer. "Want one?"

"Why not?" Rafe hoped it would cover the taste of bitterness.

Jesse turned toward the back of the house and bellowed. "Eduardo, bring your brother a beer!"

"Ed's here?"

The old man nodded. "Moved in with me last month when his wife threw him out."

Good for her, was Rafe's first thought. But he held his tongue.

"She said he was a drunk just like his old man, so he might as well move in with me." He laughed like he'd said something clever. "Hurry up with that beer."

Rafe looked over when his brother shuffled into the room. Ed looked almost as old as their father.

"Hey, bro." Eduardo passed him the bottle. "What's happenin'?"

Rafe fought the urge to wipe the lip of the bottle before he took a drink. "Not much," he said once he'd swallowed a mouthful of the liquid. "What's with you?"

"Can't complain." Eduardo sprawled in a chair. "At least now that I don't have my old lady on my back."

Rafe gestured toward their father. "He told me."

"She said not to come back unless I got a job."

Rafe nodded. "You found anything yet?"

"Nah." Ed took a long swallow of his beer. "I haven't been looking."

"What about your kids?"

"She said they're better off without me." He hesitated with the bottle halfway to his mouth. "She said she didn't want them turning out like their old man. Or ours."

Jesse laughed at that. "She should have thought of that before she married you."

There were several moments of silence during which Rafe studied his father and brother. His father was right; Ed's wife should have thought of that before the marriage. Even then Ed had shown a weakness for beer. Even then he'd been unable to hold a job.

When Rafe had been fourteen and lying about being older so he could get a job at a local fast-food restaurant, Ed had been hanging around street corners. When Rafe had cracked the books so he could earn his high-school diploma, Ed had bragged that he didn't need a diploma to pick up his welfare check.

Rafe searched for similarities between himself and the two men. All he could find was a likeness in the shape of his forehead and the cleft in his chin. Their hands were the same, he noticed. The same square shape, the same blunt fingers. But Rafe used his hands to fix things. He studied their eyes. They were the same shade of brown. But he didn't see anything of himself in them. Not a spark of determination, not a glimmer of hope. Their eyes were a flat, lifeless brown. If there'd ever been anything there— any kind of purpose or ambition—it was gone now. He set the beer on a scarred table and turned to leave.

"Where you going?"

He looked over his shoulder at the pathetic old man who'd fathered him. "There's nothing for me here."

"What's that supposed to mean?"

"Just what I said." He sighed. "I won't be coming back again. If you should need me, Theresa will know where I am."

Laughter wasn't the reaction Rafe had expected. He turned back for a final look.

Beer dribbled down Jesse's stubbled chin. "You haven't seen her yet, have you?"

"No."

"You're in for a surprise, then. Isn't he, Eduardo?"

Rafe's older brother chuckled. "*Sí.* A big surprise."

Rafe's instincts told him to run, but he asked anyway. "What kind of surprise?"

"Got herself in the family way. The only problem is the proud papa already has a wife." The old man took a long pull on his beer. "Congratulate me. I'm gonna be a grandfather."

Rafe was across the floor before his father's eyes could refocus. He hauled the old man up by his dirty shirt and shook him. The bottle fell from his hands, hit the cracked linoleum and rolled into a corner.

"What do you mean?"

"She's pregnant." The old man laughed until Rafe tightened his hold around his neck. The laughter faded and fear took its place. "Tell him, Eduardo."

"It's the truth." His older brother rose as Rafe let the old man slump back onto the couch and turned to him. "She got herself knocked up by that fancy lawyer she works for." He glanced down at the fists Rafe wanted to use. "Go see for yourself, man. Go on."

Rafe didn't bother to say goodbye. He didn't even bother to take a final look at the house as he backed out of the driveway.

Rafe drove directly to his sister's apartment in Hollywood. It was only a few miles from the old neighborhood, but seemed as far removed from the despair as Pershing. She wasn't home when he pounded on the door. He looked at his watch, realized she wouldn't be back from work for another hour or so and went in search of a restaurant. He hadn't eaten since breakfast, and he suddenly discovered he was hungry. Besides, it would give him some time to sort things out.

By the time he returned to Theresa's, the sky had turned from gray to the dull auburn twilight that was a product of L.A.'s heat and smog. He climbed the stairs and knocked on his sister's door.

The joy in her eyes was the first thing he noticed.

"Rafe!" She threw her arms around his neck and hugged him. "I wasn't expecting you until this weekend."

The second thing he noticed was the fullness where there should have been a flat stomach and trim waist.

His glance went from her swollen belly to her eyes. "It's true, isn't it?" He stepped into the apartment and slammed the door. "You're pregnant."

Theresa smiled and nodded. "Yes."

"How'd it happen?"

Her quick laughter annoyed him. "In the usual way."

"Don't be cute, Theresa. This isn't funny."

She took his hand and tugged him toward the sofa. "Sit down." She sat beside him, still holding his hand. "I know this isn't funny. But it is wonderful." Her other hand rested over the child. "I'm deliriously happy to be having this baby. I love my baby's father. You're not going to spoil that for me."

"Who's the father?"

"Carlos Negrette. He's an attorney at the firm where I work."

"How does he feel about it?"

"He's thrilled." Her smile was spontaneous and brilliant. "He's going to be a proud papa. And he'll be good to this baby. Not like our father was. He's nothing like that."

Rafe glowered at her. "You're married, then?"

"Not yet." An expression moved over her face that had Rafe holding his breath. She placed his hand over her stomach. "Can you feel it? He's kicking. There. Did you feel it?"

Rafe did feel it—that little fluttering movement that made him realize they were talking about a real person. He pulled his hand away.

Theresa's glance softened. "That's your niece or nephew. My baby. I don't want you to talk about the baby like he's some kind of inconvenience. It's a miracle."

"No." Rafe refused to look at it that way. "It's a simple biological function. Women have babies every day. It's not a miracle."

"All life is a miracle."

"Right. Well, I just left the old man and Eduardo. Are they some kind of miracle? Because if they are, I must've missed it."

"This baby is going to be loved by his mama and papa. He's going to wake up every morning knowing that he's wanted. He's going to have it easier than you or I did."

"Why hasn't the proud papa married you?"

Theresa squared her shoulders. "He has to get a divorce first."

Rafe rubbed his hands down his face. He'd hoped it wasn't true. He'd hoped the words had only been his father's way of getting to him.

"Why'd you do it?" There was no heat in his voice now, only this deep, dark emptiness where before there'd been hope. "I thought you'd be smarter than that. How'd you get into this mess? How could you let this guy seduce you?"

"He didn't seduce me. He loves me."

"How could you believe that some rich lawyer was going to fall in love with you?

Theresa's voice was soft. "I believed it because of you."

"Me?"

Theresa nodded. "You always told me I was as good as—no, better than—most anyone else. Why wouldn't I believe Carlos would love me when you'd taught me that?" She placed a gentle hand on his arm. "Listen to me, will you? It's not like you think. Carlos and his wife have been separated for a year. She's living in their place in Malibu while he's kept their place in Beverly Hills."

"Sounds like he either inherited money or stole it."

"He's older." She licked her lips before continuing. "He worked hard for everything he's got."

"He must've worked fast, too."

"He just turned forty."

"Forty?" Rafe rose and began to pace the floor of the small apartment. "He's not only married, he's old enough to be your father!"

"He doesn't look forty." She laughed at herself. "And it wouldn't matter if he looked fifty. He's good to me and he makes me happy."

"When is he getting the divorce?"

"He's working on it."

"Oh, now there's a new line." He stopped pacing and turned to look at her. "You believe that?"

"It's true." She stood and faced her brother. "He's negotiating with his wife's attorney, but she's being unreasonable in her demands. She knows about me, about the baby. She's using it for leverage. Carlos wanted to give her what she asked for—the houses, the cars, everything—just so he could get his divorce and we could get married. But I told him not to."

"You? *You* told him not to?"

"It's not fair, Rafe. It just isn't. The reason they separated was because she was having affairs—with her ten-
nis coach, her next-door neighbor and God knows who
else. It's not right that she should walk off with two-thirds
of everything he's worked for. So I told him not to give in.
I told him the baby and I weren't going anywhere."

"That's great. Just great. Meanwhile she's sitting in
some big home in Malibu and you're in this crummy little apartment."

She waved her hand to indicate the room. "Not for
much longer."

Only then did Rafe notice the boxes stacked around the
walls, all the indications that Theresa was moving.

"Moving you into a nicer apartment, is he? That seems
like the least he could do."

"He's moving me..." She stopped and put her hand
over her stomach. "He's moving us into his home. Our
home."

"Without the benefit of a wedding band or a marriage
license."

"Those will come in time." Theresa walked to him and
took both his hands in hers. "I want you to meet him,
Rafe. Talk to Carlos. Get to know him. Then tell me how
you feel."

"Okay. I want to meet him." Rafe squeezed her hands
before he let go. "When can I see him?"

"I'll call him now." Turning, she rushed to the phone
and pressed the top number on her speed dial. "Carlos."
She smiled. Her voice took on a softness that made Rafe
want to hit something. "I'm packing as fast as I can. No,
you can't help." She glanced at her brother. "Rafe's in
town. Yes, he surprised me." She listened for a moment,
then looked at Rafe. "How long are you going to be
here?"

Rafe walked over and snatched the phone from his sister's hands. "Negrette, I want to talk to you."

The voice on the phone was friendly. "I'm anxious to meet you, as well. I suggested that the three of us might get together for dinner tomorrow night."

"Not the three of us. You and me."

"I see."

The change in the man's tone convinced Rafe that he did see. "I want to see you *now*."

The man sighed. Rafe figured he'd interfered with Carlos's plans for the evening. He didn't care.

"Where can we meet?"

"Why don't you come to my house?"

Rafe wrote the address and directions on a pad Theresa kept by the phone. "It should take me about twenty minutes."

"I'll be waiting."

Rafe slammed down the phone.

Theresa grabbed his arm. "I want to go with you."

"You can't." Rafe shook off her hand. "I want to talk to him alone."

"Why? What are you going to say that you can't say in front of me?"

"Get out of my way, Theresa."

"What are you going to do?"

Rafe tucked the directions into his shirt pocket. "I'm going to do what Papa would have done if he'd been any kind of man."

"Don't do anything stupid. Please."

Rafe set her out of his way. "You're the only good thing I ever had in my life." Until now, he thought. Until Abby. "I wasn't here to protect you, but that doesn't mean I'm going to let the bastard get away with this."

She grabbed his sleeve when he started toward the door. "He didn't have to get away with anything. I love him. Do you have any idea what that means?"

"Yes." If she'd asked a week ago, he wouldn't have, but he did now. "It means protecting the person you love. Not using them."

"He didn't use me. He—"

"Not another word, Theresa." He pried her hand from his sleeve. "I don't want to hear it."

Rafe made the trip in fifteen minutes. By the time he pulled into the circular driveway and killed the engine, he was more angry than he'd ever been. Angry that fate had made Theresa beautiful and vulnerable. Angry that he hadn't been around to protect her. And most of all, angry at the Carloses of the world who went around taking what they wanted without regard to whose life was ruined in the process.

When the attorney answered the door, it was all Rafe could do to keep his hands from knotting into fists. Rafe wasn't sure what he was going to say or do, all he knew was that if Carlos wasn't willing to take care of Theresa and the baby, Rafe was going to make him change his mind.

Before he left L.A., Rafe stopped at a pay phone and called Theresa. He got her answering machine.

"It's Rafe," he said after the beep. "I'm on my way out of town. I just wanted you to know that I settled things with Negrette. I'll be in touch when I can."

Then he turned the car toward Pershing. Any hopes he had of seeing Abby that night were destroyed when a jackknifed truck clogged the freeway till after midnight. Exhausted, Rafe pulled off in Corona and checked into a hotel. When he called Abby, he got another damn answering machine.

"My visit took longer than I expected," he explained. "So I'm staying in a hotel tonight. I'll be back in plenty of time for the parade tomorrow. See you then."

He hung up not knowing what else to say. He wanted to tell Abby that he loved her and felt empty without her, but that seemed like a stupid thing to say to a machine. Besides, he still wasn't sure if this trip had set him free of the past or ruined his chances for the future.

Chapter Thirteen

Rafe got an early start the next morning; he needed to be in his dress uniform and ready to start the parade at ten hundred hours. But he hadn't counted on the bumper-to-bumper traffic of people trying to get out of town for the Fourth of July weekend. He didn't arrive until oh-nine-thirty hours. He took a quick shower, put on his dress uniform and headed for the high-school parking lot. Abby had explained it was the only large open area near downtown.

He could hear the sounds of musical instruments, screaming people and yelping dogs long before he could see them. When he rounded the corner and actually saw the staging ground, it was a massive blur of bands and drill teams and clowns and horses. Yet, in all the excitement, he picked Abby out immediately.

She was standing serenely in the middle of all the activity. At least that was how it seemed to Rafe. She had her teacher smile on her face and her hands folded primly in front of her, while the rest of the world seemed to have gone crazy. He started across the football field, and as far as he was concerned, no one else existed. Only Abby.

"He'll be here, I tell you," Abigail assured the mayor. She only hoped that her voice sounded more confident than she felt.

She'd helped with the Fourth of July parade for the last six years. She was used to the cheerleaders, who walked around practicing their arm movements, looking like they were directing traffic in downtown New York. She wasn't even fazed by the fact that all five high-school bands, four from neighboring towns, insisted on practicing at the same time. She wasn't the least bit annoyed by the square-dancing seniors who complained each year about being behind Mrs. Purvis and her dancing poodles. Abby had promised that there would be someone with a pooper scooper and there would be, even if that someone was her.

But Mayor Driscoll, who insisted on pacing back and forth like a man anticipating triplets, was really starting to get on her nerves.

Abigail walked over to where her friend was just putting the finishing touches on her niece's Statue of Liberty costume. "Eleanor, if you don't settle your brother down, I swear I am going to strangle him with that hideous tie he's wearing."

Eleanor patted Abigail on the shoulder. "Let me see what I can do. Desmond?" She motioned for her brother to join her as she made a final inspection of the parade line.

That should keep him busy, Abigail decided. She knew everyone and everything was in place except for the grand marshal. Surely by the time Eleanor and her brother worked their way back to the front of the line, Rafe would show up.

Last night she'd had a horrible feeling, a sneaking suspicion that something was wrong. She'd spent most of the evening in the high-school gym working on the floats, and had been disappointed to arrive home after midnight and find Rafe's cryptic message on her answering machine. It wasn't the message that bothered her—not even the fact that he wasn't safely checked into the Pershing Hotel—so much as the sound of his voice. There had been pain in it and a hesitation she hadn't heard since his first day in Pershing. She hoped nothing was wrong with his family. To hell with his family, she thought. She hoped nothing had happened to him.

So he wasn't here yet. So what? Abigail checked her watch again; he still had ten minutes. He wasn't the kind of man who would let the kids or the town down. She was as certain of that as a woman could be.

Unless he'd had a car accident. Or been kidnapped at gunpoint or abducted by space aliens. Once she realized she was actually considering the space-aliens theory, she knew she was losing control.

Rafe was a responsible adult, for heaven's sake. He'd managed to get through a war without being killed. What could possibly go wrong back in the good old U.S.A.?

The worst part was that she had no idea how to contact him. She didn't know his home address or his father's first name, or even what part of L.A. they lived in. She forced herself to take a deep breath. And then another.

It wasn't like her to panic. She was her usual overprepared self. She had a list for everything, even a list of her lists. The whole thing would go off without a hitch, if Rafe would just get here.

It had been stupid of her to let him go off without any way to get in touch with him. What if there'd been an earthquake? Or a nuclear explosion? How would she contact him then?

She glanced down the noisy column and saw the mayor making his way back toward her. She checked her watch. Rafe was really cutting it close; he had only three minutes.

"Where are you, Rafe?" she muttered.

Turning, she glanced across the football field and saw him striding toward her. She waved and started in his direction. When they met, he caught her by the waist and spun her around. Her feet hadn't even touched the ground before his lips captured hers. She was so relieved to see him that she didn't even worry about everyone watching. Besides, in a town this small, there were no secrets.

"I missed you," he told her, then bent down for another kiss. He was just getting serious about what he was doing when he heard someone call his name.

"Sergeant Calderon."

Rafe glanced up to see the little mayor fairly dancing around behind Abby. "Yes, Mayor."

"It's time to start the parade. We were getting worried, weren't we, Eleanor?"

His sister raised one brow. "*You* were getting worried."

Abigail watched the exchange between brother and sister from the safety of Rafe's embrace. "I told you he'd be here."

"Yes, you did." The mayor smiled and bobbed his head like a little bird. "And you were right, but it's time to start the parade now." He took several steps toward the procession, then turned back when he realized neither Rafe nor Abigail were following him. He waved his hand toward the column. "It's time to go, Sergeant. Time to—"

Before he could finish his statement, his sister had him by the back of his collar. "You know the problem with you, Desmond? Well, do you?" she asked as she led him away.

"No, Eleanor, I don't."

"The problem with you is that you have no sense of romance. No wonder you're still single."

"I know, Eleanor. You've pointed that out before."

Abigail smiled as the two passed out of earshot. "They've been arguing for as long as I can remember. They got along well with their other siblings, but those two..." She shook her head. "I don't know what they'd do if they didn't have each other to pick on."

"Traffic was terrible," Rafe explained without being asked. "I'm sorry if I worried you."

Abigail hooked her arm around his waist and started toward the red-white-and-blue float that was to carry Rafe down Main Street. "Apologize to Mayor Driscoll if you want. I never lost faith in you."

The parade was like nothing Rafe had ever seen. It had kids on bikes and men on horses, along with clowns and jugglers and marching bands. And he got to ride on the float with the teenage finalists for Miss Frontier Days.

After the parade, Rafe went back to the hotel to change into more casual clothes, while Abby supervised the storage of parade equipment that wouldn't be needed again until next year.

Then they went to the carnival that had been set up at the elementary school. They rode all the rides and went through the house of mirrors and ate too much junk food. At the shooting gallery, Rafe knocked down fourteen plastic ducks and won Abby a huge teddy bear that she said would fit perfectly into her decor. They kissed on the Ferris wheel and in the tunnel of love, and behind the cutout figures of Uncle Sam and the Statue of Liberty when they were supposed to be sticking their faces through the holes for a photograph. All in all, it was the best day of Rafe's life.

At eighteen hundred hours Abby informed him that she was going home to get ready for the dance. She warned Rafe that he'd better go back to the hotel and rest his leg, because she planned to dance every dance that night.

At twenty hundred hours he arrived back at the park to discover that everyone in Pershing owned a cowboy hat and western wear—and that Abby owned a short little denim outfit that looked great with cowboy boots and a hat. Ten minutes later, as Garth Brooks sang about being shameless and fireworks burst in the nighttime sky, Rafe led Abby onto the basketball courts that served as a dance floor. He managed to make three turns around the floor before anyone else joined them.

After that, they were just two people in the crowd. Rafe liked it that way, because he could hold Abby real close for the slow dances. He wondered why he'd never discovered this partner-dancing stuff before; it was great.

It was almost midnight when Abby yawned and laid her head over his heart. They were playing Alabama's "Once Upon A Lifetime," and Rafe realized he was holding his very own queen of hearts close in his arms. She was definitely worth the gamble.

He dropped a kiss on her forehead. "Getting sleepy?"

"A little." She yawned again. "I was up late last night working on the floats and up early this morning getting the parade in order. I think the adrenaline is finally starting to wear off."

"My feelings won't be hurt if you want to go home."

Abby looked up at him. "You're sure?"

Rafe nodded. "In fact, my feet will be grateful. I didn't have time to break in these boots." But when Abby tried to push away from him, Rafe held her against him. "Let's finish this dance. I like the slow ones best."

Abby snuggled up against him until the song was over, then they walked hand in hand through the warm summer night until they stood on Abby's front porch.

She leaned her back against the door and gazed up at Rafe. "So how was your first Fourth of July parade?"

"Great." He removed her cowboy hat and tossed it onto the wicker chair. He worked the pins loose from her hair where she'd pulled the sides back. When the springy curls fell free around her face, he bent down to kiss her. "But the best part wasn't the parade or the carnival or the dance. The best part was you." He kissed her again. "The best part of everything I am or ever hope to be is you."

She looped her arms around his neck. "I've been to twenty-eight of these celebrations, and I want you to know that tonight was the best one ever."

He stooped to nibble at her ear. "Why do you suppose that is?"

"Because of you."

Fascinated by the pulse she saw beating in his throat, she pressed her lips to the spot. When the beat accelerated, she smiled into the darkness. Tonight, she decided, she wouldn't be satisfied to kiss him good-night. Tonight she wanted to be held in his arms and loved.

With her lips, she set out to tantalize and torture. She placed warm, wet kisses at the base of his neck. She moved up to nip at the tendons in his neck, then swept inside his mouth with a boldness that surprised her. His hands came around to cup her bottom. He pulled her tight against him and she could feel the solid ridge beneath his jeans.

"Come inside," she whispered. "Stay with me tonight."

All his life Rafe had been on the outside looking in. Passing houses where people lived and loved in the light. Now here was Abby asking him to come into her home, into her light. But to do that, he would have to tell her the truth. He knew it was a terrible risk to take. After she knew about him—about what he'd come from—she might take the light away. But a night in her arms would mean nothing if she didn't accept the dark places in his soul.

He held her face in his hands. "There's nothing I want more than to make love to you."

She smiled. "That's just what I wanted to hear."

"But you don't know what you're asking." He shook his head. That wasn't right. "You don't know *who* you're asking."

"Then tell me," she whispered. "Tell me who you think you are, so I can tell you what I see."

"Oh, Abby." He pulled her close so that her cheek nestled against his heart. "There are things about me you don't know."

She placed her hands against his chest and pushed far enough away so that she could look up at him. "Then tell me. Tell me whatever it is you're keeping buried. It's time to stop running from your past and start planning our future. If that's what you want."

Breaking free of his embrace, she turned and pushed open the door. "Come with me." She stepped across the threshold. "Trust me." She extended her arm toward him. "Trust in us."

Rafe looked at Abby's hand. It represented everything he'd ever dreamed of, everything he'd always wanted. He looked into her eyes. There he saw love. It was the one thing he'd never expected, but it made everything else worthwhile. He placed his hand in hers and followed her into the house. But when she reached down to turn on a lamp, he stopped her. If he was going to risk it all, he would do it in the dark.

"No lights," he whispered. "Not until you know what you'll see when you turn them on."

With the pale moonlight filtering in through the windows, Rafe led Abby to the sofa. He tossed his hat onto the table and they sat facing each other, though Rafe was careful to keep some distance between them. He hadn't expected the separation to feel so cold. The only warmth came from Abby's hand holding his.

"I told you before there are things you need to know. Things about me, about what I've been."

"It won't make any difference," she said before he could continue. She raised his hand and laid her cheek against the back. Her lips grazed the broken skin and bruised knuckles. She opened her eyes. "You're hurt. How did this happen?"

"A little run-in with my past."

"It should be bandaged."

"It's only skin and muscle. It will heal. Right now there are other wounds you need to know about—wounds that don't show because they're on the soul, but that matter more than anything you can see."

She let their hands fall back onto the sofa. "Okay. I'm listening. But I'll tell you again that it won't make any difference."

He closed his eyes and prayed she was right. When he opened them, he was ready.

"I lied about my family. I told you and the kids that we were close. That we had this wonderful, loving relationship. The truth is that my father was a drunk and my mother abandoned us. I don't mean that she ran off and left us. She died of bitterness and despair. That was her legacy to us. I was twelve at the time."

When Abby opened her mouth to speak, he blundered on, unwilling to stop now that he'd started. "My father continued to drink, though occasionally he would come out of his stupor and actually get straight for a while. There'd be food and money for clothes, and the utilities would be paid. And then one day I'd come home and he'd be passed out on the couch. It was a helluva way to live. My older brother learned to deal with it by becoming part of it. He drank too much, got into fights and generally turned out just like the old man.

"My younger brother joined a gang. He was a *cholo,* a hard-core gang member, by the time he was twelve. He was dead at thirteen, the victim of a drive-by by a rival gang.

"That left only my sister and me. She was ten years younger, so it fell to me to take care of her. I learned early to go through the old man's pants and find whatever money I could in order to feed Theresa and myself. I learned when to stay out of the old man's way and how to keep Theresa from bothering him.

"I was the kind of kid you wouldn't have talked to. We were the poorest of the poor. I made up my mind that I was going to get out of there as soon as I could, then I realized I couldn't go off and leave Theresa with our father. I was twenty-two before I found a relative who would take her in if I would help with money. I joined the marines because it would get me away from home and pay me decent wages at the same time."

Theresa had cried when he left. He remembered that it had been her twelfth birthday, and she'd sobbed like her heart was breaking. Until Abby, she'd been the only person who had ever cried for him.

"It was the best thing I ever did for Theresa or myself. She got to live her teen years in a normal home with decent people, and I got to turn my life around. I was a good marine. I thrived on the discipline. I worked hard and moved up through the ranks to gunnery sergeant. Theresa went to college and became a paralegal. I didn't think life could offer any more than that.

"Then I got Kevin's first letter. He was a lonely, confused kid. I understood loneliness, so I thought I'd write him back. Then your whole class wrote to me." He smiled at her. "I was mad as hell over that."

"Mad? Why were you mad?"

"Because I'd convinced myself that I didn't need anyone, and all of a sudden I was waiting for mail call, spending all my free time writing letters. The students actually worried about me—and I'd never had anyone do that before. So I made up a family that I wouldn't have to be ashamed of, because I was afraid if they knew the truth they would realize I wasn't worth caring about. And then I gave them all that advice about loving their family and being a good friend and being honest, when I didn't know what the hell I was talking about."

"And that's why you wouldn't come visit?"

Rafe nodded. "Because I couldn't take the chance that the kids would see through me."

"They did. Didn't you know?" She brought her hands up to cup his face. "They saw right through you straight into your heart, which is good and true and wonderful. They saw the man who cared about them and who risked his life to save a truckload of orphans, and who cared so much about his little sister that he took care of her even when he could have gotten out.''

Rafe couldn't look her in the eye. ''They saw a sham and a fake. They were just too young to know it.''

''They saw you, Rafe, as you really are. They saw a hero.'' Tears were clogging her throat and she had to struggle to speak. ''They saw the man I fell in love with.''

Rafe closed his eyes against the hope. ''Don't say the part about loving me unless you really mean it.''

''Turn on the light, Rafe. Turn it on and look at me.''

He opened his eyes and discovered that his hand was shaking as he groped for the switch. ''You're sure about this?''

''Turn it on.''

He did, and the light was so bright that he had to close his eyes against it. He was afraid to open them. Afraid of what he would see when he looked at her.

She cupped his face in her hands and turned him toward her. ''Open your eyes,'' she said softly. ''Open them and really look.''

He was unable to resist her. He supposed if he lived to be a hundred, he'd still be unable to resist her. He opened his eyes to see her smiling at him. To see love shining in her eyes and tears clinging to her lashes.

''I love you, Rafe. There isn't anything you've said that could make me love you less. If anything, I love you more. I know now why I sensed that strength in you. It was forged by pain and anger, but the real miracle is the love and goodness in your heart. Be proud of what you've made of yourself.''

He grasped her wrists and turned his head so he could kiss both palms. ''I love you, Abby. I think the real miracle is that you can love me back. If you'll marry me, I promise I'll spend my life making sure you never regret it.''

"What?" Her laughter was quick and rich. "Say that again."

"I said if you'll marry me, you won't regret it."

"Was that a proposal?"

He grinned. "I guess it was." He wished he could take it back. He wished he'd taken time to get champagne and roses and a ring. "I could get down on one knee if it would help."

Abby laughed through her tears. "It wouldn't help at all."

"Then tell me what to do."

"Love me." She stood and held out her hand. "All you need to do is love me."

He laced his fingers with hers. "I already do," he told her as she led him toward the bedroom.

He set about proving it with a gentleness that made her want to weep. She'd never dreamed it was possible to feel like this. His lips cherished her, his hands soothed. His voice, when he murmured her name, conjured up images of soft breezes and twilight.

He was dazzled by her. She was sunbeams and moon glow. Candlelight and fireworks. She was the warmth he'd always dreamed of and the sweetness he'd never known existed. She was a miracle, and she was in his arms.

Where he'd intended to seduce, he found himself seduced. Her kisses, instead of satisfying, made him want more. His hands, instead of rushing, lingered over each pearl button. When her blouse was finally unfastened, he nudged it off her shoulders to fall to the floor.

"So beautiful," he murmured, tracing the edge of the lacy bra first with his hands and then his tongue.

Abigail clutched the bright fabric of his shirt for support. She was sure that her bones had turned to water, certain every muscle in her body had gone weak. He shouldn't be able to do this to her, she thought. Not with a few kisses and the glorious touch of his hands. She was grateful that he was the only man who could.

"It's not fair," she murmured when he pushed the straps off her shoulders.

He paused in the act of unfastening her bra. "What's not fair?"

"That my body has turned to rubber while you're so unaffected."

He laughed and, cupping her derriere, pulled her hard against him. She smiled and moved seductively, happy to discover he was not unaffected. Delighted at her power to arouse, she pulled his shirt from his pants and set to work unbuttoning it. When the splash of pink and teal landed beside her dull denim shirt, she pressed a kiss to the solid warmth of Rafe's chest. She was just looking forward to her own lazy exploration when he muttered an oath.

He thrust his hands into her hair and tugged her head up. His lips came down to plunder hers. His hands lost their gentleness as they moved from her hair to her breasts. Where before she'd felt like she was floating on air, now she was caught in a hurricane. His lips devoured, his hands demanded. She answered with demands of her own. First her bra joined the puddle of clothes on the floor, then her skirt.

Rafe doubted there was a more arousing sight on earth than that of Abby in a scrap of lace and leather boots. The fact that it was his prim-and-proper Abby in lace and leather practically brought him to his knees. He scooped her up and set her on the side of the bed. Going down on his knees, he kissed the soft skin on the inside of her thigh before he removed her boots—first one delicate thigh, then the other. When he stood, she reached out to fumble with his belt buckle.

He placed his hands over hers. "Not yet," he told her. He sat down to remove his own boots and socks, then stood. "Now."

Eagerly her hands resumed their task, making quick work of buckle, snap and zipper. In one swift motion he disposed of his jeans and shorts, to stand naked before her.

Abigail's mouth went dry at the sight of Rafe's body. He was all planes and angles. She felt tiny beside him, but not vulnerable. Despite the blaze of desire that lit his eyes, she knew he would never hurt her. She knew this was a man who would shelter and protect her. Her eyes swept down him and came to rest on the scar that cut across his muscled thigh. It curved from the hip forward to end just inside the knee. "Does it hurt?"

Rafe laughed. "My leg isn't what's hurting right now."

Still, Abigail reached out with trembling fingers to trace the length of the wound. When he would have snatched her hand away, she went down on her knees before him. With her lips she traced it again, from the inside of his thigh to his hip.

When she looked up, Rafe could see her green eyes glittering in the pale light.

"Are you crying, Abby?"

She bowed her head.

"Yes."

"Because of the scar?"

She looked back up at him. "For all the scars. The ones that show and the ones that don't."

"Don't cry." He reached down and helped her to her feet. "Without the scars, I wouldn't be here with you.

Without the scars, I wouldn't know how blessed I am to have found you. I went home yesterday to make peace with my past, Abby. But when I looked, I couldn't find any part of myself there. Now I know I need to make my peace here, with you."

"I don't understand."

"All the pain I've endured was necessary to make me the man you love." He reached out to brush away a tear. "I would endure it a hundred times over if that was what it took to have you in my arms. The pain is a small price to pay for all the joy you bring me."

Gently he laid her upon the bed and removed the last barrier between them. He kissed her and treasured her, and when he finally moved within her, there was joy like he had never known.

Chapter Fourteen

They woke several times during the night to touch and be touched, to love and be loved. When the morning came, Abby searched out the nightgown she hadn't needed during the night and padded to the kitchen to put on coffee. When she came back to the bedroom, Rafe was awake.

He flipped back the covers and Abby slipped into bed beside him. It would take several minutes for the coffee to perk. There was no reason to waste that time, she told herself.

Rafe was just whispering an interesting suggestion in her ear when the doorbell rang. Abigail pulled on her robe on the way to the door. Before she opened it, she fluffed her hair and wiped the sleep from her eyes.

"Sheriff Jackson?" Abby couldn't hide her surprise at seeing the man on her doorstep early on Sunday morning. "Is something wrong?"

Sheriff Jackson looked uncomfortable. "I hope not, Abigail." He took off his hat and turned it around in his big hands. "I'm looking for Rafael Calderon. Is he by any chance here?"

"Why, Curtis Jackson! I don't know why that would be any business of yours."

She was glad to see that Curtis had the good manners to look embarrassed.

"These two men—" Curtis gestured behind him to where two men in jackets and ties waited at the bottom of her steps "—are looking for Sergeant Calderon."

Abigail stood on tiptoe and looked over the sheriff's shoulder. They might have on jackets and ties, but they looked a bit shifty to her.

She leaned closer to Curtis and lowered her voice. "And just who are they?"

"L.A. police," he whispered back. "I've already checked out their ID."

Abigail straightened. "And what do they want with Sergeant Calderon?"

One of the men stepped forward. "Rafael Calderon is wanted for questioning concerning an attempted homicide."

"A homicide?" For a moment she couldn't even form a coherent thought. "Well...I can't imagine..." She sputtered and stood there, staring at the two men.

"Abby."

Abigail turned to see Rafe standing in her living room. He'd put on his jeans and the wrinkled shirt, which he was just buttoning. She wondered what Curtis and the two policemen would think about Rafe being at her house half-dressed at this hour, then blushed when she realized that what they were undoubtedly thinking was exactly what had happened.

"Abby, why don't you let them in? I don't think leaving them out on your porch is going to settle this."

"Oh." She looked around the living room to see if there was anything out of place. Rafe's hat was on the coffee table, but since he was in the living room big as life, there didn't seem much point in trying to hide it. She stepped aside. "Won't you come in?"

Rafe watched the three men enter Abby's little house. He nodded at Curtis Jackson. Curtis was Matt's father; Rafe had spent some time talking with the sheriff at the carnival yesterday. The other two men were obviously big-city cops. He remembered how the cops had come to the house when he was younger. Sometimes they were looking for Eduardo and sometimes for Frank. On a few occasions they'd even been after him. These two looked tough and cynical, and he didn't like the speculative glances they were giving Abby. He concentrated on keeping his hands from balling into fists.

"Were you in Los Angeles on July third of this year?" the shorter of the cops asked. Rafe noticed that they didn't even bother with the amenities. No introductions, no polite conversation. Just straight to the point.

"The day before yesterday?" He waited until the man nodded. "Yes. I was visiting family."

"According to your sister you also visited with Carlos Negrette at his house in Beverly Hills."

Rafe nodded. "Why do you need to know?"

"We'll ask the questions, if you don't mind. Would you tell us why you were at Mr. Negrette's house?"

"I might, but first I'd like to know what this is about."

The two L.A. cops looked at each other. The second one spoke up. "There was an attempt on Mr. Negrette's life."

Abby gasped and stepped close enough for Rafe to pull her to his side. The way the man looked at Abby had Rafe fighting the urge to tell him to go to hell.

"What did Mr. Negrette say we were discussing?"

"Mr. Negrette is unable to tell us anything. He's in a coma at Cedar Sinai Medical Center."

Rafe couldn't say anything for a minute. He stood there still as stone, trying to make sense of what these men were telling him.

"Carlos Negrette was conscious when I left him. We talked. We had a drink. Then I left."

"We'd like to know what you discussed."

"It was personal."

"Would you have been discussing your sister, Theresa Calderon, who claims to be pregnant by Carlos Negrette?"

Rafe ignored the way Abby turned astonished eyes up toward him. "She doesn't claim to be pregnant by Carlos Negrette. She *is* pregnant by him. Carlos admitted he's the father."

"Unfortunately, Mr. Negrette is unable to confirm that."

"I'm sure there are medical tests—"

"If it becomes necessary, we'll ask that those tests be performed. At the moment we're more concerned with what happened between you and Mr. Negrette."

Rafe didn't try to hide his bitterness. "Of course."

"Mr. Negrette had several facial lacerations and bruises. Lab reports show that some of the blood on his face and shirt are the same type as yours, according to military records."

"That could be true." Rafe looked down at Abby. "I went to see him when I found out he was the father of Theresa's baby. I was mad. We got into a scuffle, then I figured you'd give me holy hell if you ever found out.'' He brushed the hair back from her face. "We talked after that. I had a drink with him. He said he was going to marry Theresa as soon as he got a divorce. He even asked me to give the bride away when they had the wedding." He glanced back at the cops. "That's all I know."

"We want you to come into L.A. for questioning."

"Like I said, that's all I know."

"We still need to question you."

"Can't we do it in Pershing? I'm sure the sheriff will let you use his office."

"No problem," Curtis Jackson told them. "You can use it as long as you like."

The short cop took a step toward Rafe. "Mr. Calderon—"

"*Sergeant* Calderon," Rafe corrected him. "Gunnery Sergeant Calderon."

"Very well. Sergeant Calderon, we can do this the easy way or we can get a warrant. What will it be?"

Rafe looked down at Abby. Her eyes were big as saucers and he could see she was scared. "We'll do it the easy way. When do you want me to come in?"

"We'd like you to come with us now."

"Am I under arrest then?"

"No, you're not."

"Then I'll drive my own car. You can follow me if you like, but I'm not about to ride into L.A. with you and not have a way back here."

The policeman nodded. "We'll wait for you while you get dressed."

Rafe had been intimidated by cops in his youth, but he was older now. And he hadn't tried to kill anyone.

"You won't be waiting in Abby's house, and I won't be leaving right away." Before the cop could say anything,

Rafe continued. "I'm going to spend a little time here—Abby and I need to talk. Then I'm going back to my hotel to shower and change. I'll check out of the hotel and drive back to L.A.

"Now we can either do this the hard way, which is where you follow me all over Pershing and shadow me on the drive into town. Or we can do this the easy way, which means you set a time this afternoon and I'll meet you at the police station. It doesn't make much difference to me."

The two cops exchanged glances before the shorter one pulled a business card from his inside jacket pocket. "Three o'clock this afternoon. If you aren't there, a warrant will be issued."

"Oh, I'll be there—" Rafe glanced at the card "—Detective Weaver. You can count on it."

He walked to the front door and opened it. Without a word, the two city cops exited. Sheriff Jackson was a little slower.

He stopped at the door and turned his hat in his hands. "I'm sorry, Rafe. I didn't have any choice."

"I know that, Curtis." Rafe extended his hand. "You were only doing your job."

"If there's anything I can do, just let me know."

Rafe smiled. "We will."

The second he closed the door behind the sheriff, Abby was in his arms.

"What's happening?"

Rafe could feel her trembling. He led her to the big chair and sat down with her on his lap. "I'm not real sure. I probably won't know until I get into town."

What he did know was that the L.A.P.D. wouldn't be sending two detectives out to Pershing unless they were after big fish. Like someone they suspected of murder, but didn't have enough proof to arrest. Yet.

Rafe rested his cheek against the top of her head. "I hit the guy a couple times, Abby. But I didn't try to kill him."

"I know that."

"When he comes out of the coma, Carlos will be able to tell them." *If* he came out of the coma.

"Does your sister love him?"

Leave it to Abby to ask that question. "Yes, she does. And he loves her. He wants to marry her."

"How far along is your sister?"

"What?"

"When is the baby due?"

"I don't know." Rafe tried to remember how big she'd been. "Maybe in the fall. I don't want you to worry." He dropped a kiss on the crown of her head. "It's going to be okay."

"Couldn't we just tell them you were with me?"

"What?"

Abby levered herself away from his chest and looked at him. "Couldn't we just say you were here?"

"No, Abby, we couldn't. First of all, I wasn't here."

"If we both say you were, who's to say different?"

"Secondly, you were helping build the floats that night. The whole town probably saw you. And lastly, you're a terrible liar. It wouldn't work."

"Okay." She nestled back under his chin.

"Okay, just like that?"

"Uh-huh." She was silent for a moment. Rafe was working up the nerve to say goodbye when she spoke. "I guess I'd better take a shower if I'm going with you."

"You aren't coming with me, Abby."

"Of course I am."

He caught her by the shoulders and held her where he could look her in the eye. "You are *not* coming with me. You are not going into L.A., and you are not going to the police station. You are not going to get anywhere near this, do you hear me?" He especially didn't want her anywhere near his father and brother, and there was a very good chance the police would haul them in for questioning as well.

Her face took on that stubborn look, and her eyes narrowed. "We're going to be married. My place is with you."

"And you aren't going to tell anyone about that."

"Why?"

"I don't want you dragged into this."

"I'm already dragged in because you're dragged into it."

"You aren't to tell your mother or father or Eleanor or anyone. Promise me, Abby. Please."

"I'm not ashamed of it."

He gave her a little shake. "Promise me!"

"Okay." He let out a sigh of relief. "As long as you promise to keep me informed."

He nodded. "I will." He brushed the hair back from her forehead, then held her face in his big hands. "I'll call every night."

"How long do you think you'll be gone?"

"I don't know." It depended on whether they arrested him. He didn't tell her that. "Theresa may need me."

She smiled. "How selfish. I didn't even think of that."

"I have less than two weeks left of my leave."

"I hadn't thought of that, either. I guess I've just been living from day to day since you came into my life. I'm usually a lot more organized."

Rafe smiled. Only Abby would think she could get organized for a murder investigation. "We haven't had a chance to talk about our future, but I was serious about wanting to get married. I'd like to take that job your dad offered. I'd like us to live in Pershing, if that's okay with you."

Her smile was radiant. "I'd like that, too. But if you want to stay in the marines, I'll move back east with you. I'll go anywhere as long as we're together."

He kissed her then. He tried to keep the desperation out of it, but he didn't know how successful he was. He would have gone on kissing her if he hadn't seen that the cops were still parked in front of her house. He went to get his boots and tucked in his shirt. Her neighbors had enough to talk about without adding that he'd been half-dressed when he left.

He kissed her once more at the door. Since he knew it was going to have to last for a long time, he made it good. Then he wrenched open the door and stepped outside.

"Phone me tonight," she called after him. "And let me know where I can reach you."

Rafe nodded without looking at her. If he glanced back, there was a very good chance he'd turn around and head right back to her arms.

It was after six o'clock by the time the detectives finished questioning Rafe. Though he wasn't under arrest, he knew that he was their prime suspect. He had motive and opportunity, and his blood had been found at the scene. Even the message he'd left on Theresa's answering machine sounded incriminating when the police replayed it. Rafe figured the only thing preventing them from arresting him that minute was the fact that they didn't have a gun with his fingerprints on it—and the fact that he was a hero of the San Miguel Crisis. He didn't know how long that would keep them from coming after him.

The only other possible suspect was Laurie Negrette, but since she had wealth and influential friends, Rafe didn't hold much hope that the police would question her very closely.

He went straight from the police station to the hospital, where he found Theresa sitting in the waiting room. She threw herself into his arms and cried so hard he became worried about her and the baby. From a purely selfish standpoint, it was better than having her accuse him of trying to kill her lover. But she hadn't; Rafe held on tight to that fact.

"How is Carlos?" Rafe asked once the tears had passed.

"I'm not sure."

"Haven't the doctors talked to you?"

This caused a fresh bout of weeping, which had him patting her back and making soothing noises for thirty more minutes.

"They wo-wo-won't let me in," she finally told him. "His wi-wi-wife has had me barred from his room. She told the doctors not to talk to me."

"Can she do that?"

Theresa nodded. "They're still legally married, so she has all the rights of a spouse. And I have none."

When she started crying again, Rafe got worried about the baby.

"Carlos wouldn't want you to carry on so." He rubbed her back gently. "He'd want you to take better care of the baby."

"I know." She dabbed at her eyes with a mushy tissue. "What happened when you went to see him?"

"We talked."

"That's all?"

Rafe swallowed. "By the time I left, we'd come to an understanding."

Theresa's watery smile was smug. "I'm glad." With a sigh, she leaned her head against his shoulder.

When he'd been told it was Theresa who'd discovered Carlos lying on the floor in a pool of blood, Rafe had been worried. Now, seeing how pale and drawn she looked, he was even more concerned. When she admitted she didn't remember when she'd last eaten, he insisted that they go home. He fixed her soup and a sandwich and then tucked her into bed. In a strange way it reminded him of when Theresa had been little. He'd been the one to take care of her then. It seemed like things had come full circle.

He called Abby once Theresa was asleep. There was little he could tell her that she didn't already know. He gave her Theresa's phone number and told her he loved her. When he hung up, he settled down on Theresa's couch for the night.

The next day Rafe woke to the smell of coffee and the sound of Theresa crying. When he looked at the newspaper, he discovered Carlos was front-page news—not the banner headlines, but the lower right-hand corner, with pictures and more story on A18. According to the newspaper account, doctors estimated there was a seventy-percent chance that Carlos would come out of the coma. Of course, the longer it lasted, the greater were the odds against his recovery. There was a wedding photo of Carlos and his wife, as well as the story of their lengthy separation. There was mention of a pregnant girlfriend, but Theresa wasn't identified. Rafe hoped their luck would hold.

During the day there were more questions by the cops and a warning that Rafe shouldn't leave town without letting the authorities know. The rest of the time he spent at the hospital. He called Abby that night and told her the newspaper reporters knew more than he did. Again, he said he loved her. Again, she wanted to come to L.A. He told her to stay in Pershing. That night when he went to bed, he prayed that the reporters wouldn't discover the connection between himself and Pershing. He wanted to keep Abby out of it.

By the third day, the reporters had identified Theresa through one of Carlos's co-workers and the fact that he'd made Theresa's child the beneficiary of a large insurance policy. Rafe was mentioned as having been questioned by the police and released. The implication was that he was the prime suspect. Theresa was furious, but Rafe was philosophical. He'd expected it.

He and Theresa put in another long day in the hospital waiting room, trying to glean information about Carlos's condition. Despite Laurie Negrette's instructions, a few of the nurses felt sorry for Theresa and fed her bits and pieces of information. Theresa was grateful for every little crumb.

That night Abby was even more insistent that she was coming to L.A. Rafe didn't think he could stand it if she was dragged through the mud, so he told her she would only be in the way. Abby was crying when they said goodbye. He spent the night wondering what kind of hero would drag Abby into this sordid mess and what kind of bastard would make her cry.

The next day, Rafe's world fell apart. The newspapers delved into the story of the troubled Calderon family. The story included his mother's death, his father's lack of steady employment and dependence on state disability. It dredged up the troubles Eduardo had gotten into and the drive-by murder of his brother Frank, as well as his sister's pregnancy and accusations by Laurie Negrette that Theresa had tried to blackmail the Negrettes for a large sum of money. The grieving wife even hinted that the baby might not be her husband's. The Calderon legacy, Rafe realized. Inescapable and never-ending.

The article ended with one of the detectives stating that Rafe was their most likely suspect and that he would probably have been arrested by now except for his role as a hero on San Miguel. Prosecutors, the detective suggested, were reluctant to issue an arrest warrant for the military hero. If Rafe had ever believed he could escape from the past, the article proved him wrong. He could feel the noose tightening around his neck already—and there wasn't a damn thing he could do about it.

When he and Theresa arrived at the hospital, they discovered reporters waiting for them. Rafe declared the hospital off-limits to his sister. Theresa, he decided, would have to stay in her apartment and get news by phone. Thwarted at the hospital, the media staked out her apartment building and even phoned her. Rafe began screening phone calls, and Theresa got her first offer for a television movie. The vultures were circling.

The only good thing about the situation was that Rafe and Theresa had time to talk. They hadn't spent much time together since Rafe had joined the marines, so there was lots to catch up on.

"Do you ever wonder how things could fall apart so quickly?" Rafe asked as he used the remote to zip through cartoons and talk shows. "Just five days ago the world was our oyster. You were getting ready to move into Carlos's house, anticipating your marriage and the birth of your child. I was basking in the glow of being a hero, contemplating marriage and planning to leave the military." Those were big plans for a Calderon. Evidently fate thought they were too big. "How'd it all go so wrong?"

"Whoa! What do you mean, 'contemplating marriage'? Are you in love?"

He slanted a look toward where she was sitting in the recliner chair. "Did I neglect to mention that?"

"Yes, you did. I know I would have remembered if you'd told me that. Who's the lucky woman?"

"Abigail Dixon. That schoolteacher in Pershing."

Theresa laughed at that. It was the first laugh he'd heard since he'd found her sitting in the hospital waiting room several days ago. "You and a schoolteacher. That's rich." She stretched for a moment and tried to find a more comfortable position. "So why won't you be marrying her now?"

"For starters, I think there's a good chance they're going to railroad me into jail."

"Don't say that. When Carlos comes out of the coma, he'll be able to identify his assailant."

"I'd forgotten that." Rafe could have kicked himself for saying differently. Just because he was losing hope that Carlos would pull through didn't mean he should take hope away from Theresa.

"More importantly, I doubt the town of Pershing is going to want me around. I told some lies. When they read the article in this morning's paper, I don't think they're going to want me back." He scrubbed a hand down his face. "Then there's Abby. Why would she want a loser and a liar?"

"What could you have lied about that would be so bad?"

Rafe explained about the letters he'd written to the kids, about the family he'd created for their benefit.

Theresa had tears in her eyes by the time he'd finished.

"Hormones," she explained, wiping at the tears. "It's funny, I never knew you felt that way. You always seemed so self-assured, like you could take on the world. I was the one who was scared of my shadow.

"I made up all kinds of stories when I went to live with Aunt Sophia. About how my family had all died in an avalanche or a plane crash. My personal favorite was the one about how the family all went down in our private plane. You crawled through snow and ice to get help, but by the time you got back they were all dead. Eaten by hungry wolves, I believe. I had been too sick to go on the trip, therefore I'd been spared the terrible ordeal. It was quite dramatic." She gave him a tearful smile. "You were the hero of every story."

"We have some family, don't we?" Rafe couldn't believe he'd actually considered dragging Abby into it. "You don't suppose there's a curse on us or something."

"I don't think we're important enough to rate a curse."

"You're probably right." It was undoubtedly some defect in the genetic code, Rafe decided upon reflection. Something inescapable in the Calderon chromosomes. God knew he'd spent ten years running from it. He'd made a career in the military and had fallen in love with a terrific woman. He'd stayed as far away from home as he could, and still he found he couldn't escape his heritage. He knew it was only a matter of time until they arrested him for the attempted murder of Carlos Negrette. If Carlos didn't come out of his coma soon, it might even be murder. All the running and all the hard work had been for nothing. Rafe could feel himself being sucked right back into the hopelessness he thought he'd left behind.

The thing that worried him most was Abby. She was an innocent. She didn't deserve to be dragged into this. If he let her, she'd stand beside him throughout the entire ordeal. He could just imagine her sitting through the trial, visiting him in prison. He couldn't let that happen. Not to Abby. He had to cut her loose now.

He didn't call her that night, hoping she'd get the hint. She didn't. Not that night or the next or the next.

Abby's messages on the answering machine became more desperate each day. Theresa's silence each time Rafe listened but wouldn't pick up the receiver became more profound.

Friday night, Theresa broke her silence on the matter. "What are you punishing Abby for?" she asked her brother.

"I'm not punishing her."

"Then what are you doing?"

"I'm saving her."

Theresa's laughter held no joy. "I never figured you for a coward, Rafe."

He had the urge to strangle his sister; anything to keep her from discussing Abby. "I'm not a coward." If he was a coward, he would have asked her to come to him. He would let her hold him in her arms and assure him that everything would be all right. He knew that just holding her, touching her, would help him through this. Instead he was saving her.

"There's no sin in needing someone."

Rafe didn't know when his sister had gotten up and come to stand beside him. She laid a hand on his arm.

"You've always been the strong one. You took care of me when I was little and here you are doing it again. Who do you get to lean on?"

"I don't need to lean on anyone."

"Oh, Rafe." Theresa put her arms around his waist and hugged him closely. "Don't let them do this to you. Don't give up without a fight."

"I'm not giving up." His arms came around Theresa and he held her tightly. "I'm just not dragging Abby through it with me."

They stood there for several minutes—just the two of them against the world, Rafe thought. Just like when they were younger. Only this time the stakes were a lot higher. It was so quiet that the ringing of the phone made them jump. When the caller left a message, he started to curse.

"This is Abby. Rafe, if you're there you'd better pick up the phone. Because I'm coming to see you tomorrow, whether you like it or not."

Theresa grinned up at him. "I think this is one message you're going to have to take."

Chapter Fifteen

Rafe snatched up the receiver. "Abby. It's me."

"Rafe." There was an audible sigh of relief. "I was so worried."

"You don't need to be. I'm fine." He tried to keep his tone even. Tried not to let her know how good it was to hear her voice. "You promised you wouldn't come to L.A."

"You promised you'd call every night."

Stubborn woman, he thought. Aloud, he said, "I've been busy."

"So I gathered. That won't be a problem any longer. I'll be there tomorrow morning."

"I don't want you here."

"I see." There was a hitch in her voice. Rafe knew she was fighting tears. If she started crying, he didn't know what he'd do.

"I don't want you involved with this."

"Too bad. I was involved the minute you were in-volved."

"I don't want the reporters hounding you. It's awful here. It would be even worse in Pershing."

"Too late to worry about that, too."

"What do you mean, 'too late'?"

"The mayor decided you were losing the media war by default, so he and Eleanor arranged a little event here for the press."

"Cancel it."

"Too late for that, too. It's already happened."

Rafe couldn't help the string of curses he let loose. "Why didn't you ask me first?"

"Because you weren't returning my messages."

God, why did she have an answer for everything? "You didn't have the right to do that . . . whatever it was."

"You're wrong. We have every right—we're your friends. I don't know how it works in the big city, but in Pershing friends stand up for friends."

"Well, it doesn't work that way around here."

"If you'd returned my calls, you could have explained that to me. As it is, it's just too damn bad. You can't do anything about it now, though you might want to watch the eleven o'clock news."

Rafe couldn't help grinning. Hearing his Abby say "damn" was just too funny. Not *his* Abby, he corrected himself. Just Abby. Abigail Dixon.

"Now, are you going to give me directions to your sis-ter's place or do I walk back downtown and talk to the reporters who are still milling around Pershing?"

"I don't want you here."

"I know that, but I'm coming anyway. Just give me the address."

He did so reluctantly.

* * *

Rafe was in front of the TV by ten-thirty. As he used the remote to flip through the channels, he found the lead-ins all said the same thing: "New sources reveal heretofore unknown information regarding Gunnery Sergeant Rafael Calderon, the man police say is the prime suspect in the attempted murder of Beverly Hills attorney Carlos Negrette. Film at eleven."

By eleven o'clock even Rafe was anxious to see what the new information was.

"Pick one channel and stick with it," Theresa commanded. "This channel surfing is driving me crazy. Besides, if you keep changing channels, we might miss it. Oh, wait a minute." She struggled out of the recliner. "Let's record it."

She'd just slipped a cassette into the VCR when the anchorman began.

"Today reporters were invited to a press conference in the picturesque desert community of Pershing, California, as the town came out in support of their adopted citizen, Gunnery Sergeant Rafael Calderon," the man intoned as the screen showed footage of the community. Rafe got homesick just looking at it.

"This small community wanted the media to see another side of Gunnery Sergeant Calderon, who had been writing to Mrs. Abigail Dixon's fifth-grade class at Pershing Elementary." When the camera panned on Abby and the students, Rafe felt his heart stop. She looked great. Something twisted in his gut when she smiled into the camera.

The students who surrounded her carried signs. Kevin's hand-lettered sign read We Love Rafe. Jeremy's said Rafe's Our Man. The other signs had variations on that theme, except for the one Abby held up. It said When Are You Coming Back?

Theresa studied the screen. "A smart man would keep a woman like that. She looks like she'd be hard to forget."

Rafe didn't bother to respond.

"Mayor Desmond Driscoll started the press conference by showing videos of Sergeant Calderon's heroic welcome at the grade school." Film of the kids cheering and Abby standing up at the microphone with him filled the screen.

"Then the press conference, which one local resident termed 'a media event,' was turned over to the kids. The students each shared their memories of the man they call hero and friend, right down to four-year-old Wendy Stafford, who described Sergeant Calderon's rescue of her cat, Fluffy." There was film of Rafe in the tree and then standing with the Staffords, waving into the video camera.

Theresa laughed. "You don't even like cats."

"I like the kid."

"Gunnery Sergeant Calderon also served as grand marshal for the city's annual Frontier Days parade." The screen showed him riding on the float with the Miss Frontier Days finalists and leading off the dancing with Abby in his arms.

"Is that you in the cowboy hat?" Theresa howled as she watched him dance around the screen. "Yes, sir, a smart man would snap her right up."

Rafe wanted to smile, just to prove he wasn't affected, but he couldn't get around the pain in his heart. "Be quiet, Theresa. I'm about to forget your delicate condition and tell you what I think."

"The mayor concluded the event by reading a statement of support from Calderon's commanding officer, who characterized the soldier as a credit to the nation at large and the marines in particular, and the text of a speech in which the model marine was awarded the Bronze Star for heroic achievement during a military operation." They flashed up a still picture of Rafe in his dress uniform, with the medal pinned to his jacket.

"You may remember that Gunnery Sergeant Calderon received the medal for saving a group of orphans and nuns during the San Miguel Crisis. Another soldier was killed during the daring rescue in which Calderon was gravely injured."

The camera segued to a close-up of the newsman and then moved back to reveal another man at the desk with him. "And now here's Wally with the weather."

Wally gave the silly grin for which he was famous. "That's quite a different picture of that marine than we've been given by the authorities, isn't it?"

The anchorman turned his serious face to the camera. "Indeed, it is."

"I was also told by the camera crew that the ladies of Pershing served home-baked goodies to the media at the conclusion of the press conference. Of course, their appetites would have been better if the mayor hadn't been wearing that tie." Wally gave a small shake of his head and his trademark grin again. "Meanwhile, folks, I'm here to make sense of the weather for you. We're going to have a mild Santa Ana condi—"

With a flick of his thumb, Rafe silenced the TV. But in his mind he could still see it: Pershing. The mayor with another ugly tie. Eleanor directing the operation like a four-star general. The kids. Abby. *Home.* He closed his eyes against the emotions.

It wasn't fair to have had it all within his grasp and lose it. But where had Rafe ever gotten the foolish idea that life was supposed to be fair?

Abigail arrived in Los Angeles before noon on Saturday. She stopped at a corner phone booth a couple of blocks away from where Rafe's sister lived to tell him she was there. When she parked in front of Theresa's apartment and started up the walkway, several reporters recognized her. They asked questions, but she said nothing. The door opened just as she stepped up on the stoop and shut firmly on her heels.

She didn't even bother to remove her sunglasses before throwing her arms around Rafe. It took her a moment to realize that he wasn't returning the embrace. She sighed. So that was how it was going to be. She backed away from him and looked up at his expressionless face.

This was not the time to give in to tears and emotional outbursts. She'd come here for more than the need to see Rafe, to touch him and hold him. She'd also come because Spencer had suggested it. Spencer wasn't only her brother, he was a top-notch attorney. When he gave professional advice, she listened.

Abigail didn't smile. "Hello, Rafe."

"I told you not to come."

Before she could decide how to answer that, Rafe's sister stepped forward. "I'm Theresa, and I'm glad you're here. Maybe you can talk some sense into this stubborn brother of mine. Lord knows I've almost given up."

"Hi." Abigail could see that recent events had taken a toll on the other woman. Her eyes had dark circles around them and her skin was pale. "How are you feeling?"

"I'm doing fine, thanks. I'll be better when Carlos comes out of the coma."

"How is he?"

The smiled faded. "All I know is what I read in the papers. His wife has had me barred from his room."

Abigail had read that in one of the newspaper accounts. "That must be very difficult for you."

She nodded. "I'm going into the bedroom to lie down." The look she gave her brother was both affectionate and exasperated. "Rafe's making me take care of myself. Just remember that the walls are thin, and anything you say above a whisper I can hear."

Abigail waited until she was out of the room before saying, "You didn't tell me your sister is gorgeous."

Rafe shrugged. "It never came up. Can we forget the preliminaries and cut right to the chase? Why are you here?"

"Does there need to be something besides the obvious reason—that I want to be with my fiancé during a difficult time?"

"If that's the only reason, then let me help you out. I've decided that I don't love you. I don't want to marry you." He put his hand on the doorknob. "Now you can leave."

Despite the fact that she'd told herself Rafe was trying to push her away, the pain was so intense that she almost looked down to see if she was bleeding.

"Why are you doing this?" The question was out before she could stop it, even though she'd promised herself she wouldn't ask it. "Why are you acting like this?"

"Like what?"

"Like you don't want to see me."

"Because I don't. I don't want you here, and I don't want you involved in this. There, is that clear enough?"

"Did you watch the news last night?"

"Yeah." He glanced toward the blank television. "Tell the mayor and Eleanor and everyone I said thanks." He looked back at her, and she was relieved to see the coldness had left his eyes. Even the pain was better than the bitter cold. "How are the kids taking all this?"

"You saw them. They don't care anything about who your family is or isn't. To them you're a hero." She reached in her purse and drew out a stack of letters tied with yellow ribbon. "These are for you."

He stepped back as though she'd drawn a weapon on him. "Oh, God."

"Take them. Go on, take them! You can be as cruel to me as you want, but you can't treat the kids that way." When he didn't reach for them, she threw the packet at him, then whirled away to wrap her arms around herself and cry. She'd promised herself she wouldn't do this, and yet here she was, sobbing as though someone had died.

"Abby."

She heard the despair in his voice, but she couldn't turn around to comfort him. She was dying herself, and she didn't have the strength to deal with his pain, too.

"Don't do this, Abby." She felt his hands on her shoulders, felt him gently turn her around, but she refused to look up at him. She knew that if she looked at him, he'd be able to read everything she was feeling in her eyes. When his arms went around her and he held her next to his heart, she gave up her pride.

"Don't do this," she begged him. "Please don't send me away." Her arms held him tightly; her tears soaked into his shirt. "Let me stay here with you."

"No." She felt his hands skim over her back, felt his lips on her hair. "If you love me, you'll go home. I'd rather die than have you see me in prison."

"Prison?" She looked up at him. Her vision was watery, but she was certain she saw tears in Rafe's eyes before his mouth descended to hers.

His kiss was angry and desperate. He barely let her come up for air before he took her deeper. His hunger took her breath away. His needs and his emotions were almost primitive. But overriding everything was the unmistakable despair and finality. Abigail knew, without being told, that he would send her away. She also knew that she would go; she understood Rafe well enough to know that her presence would only make it more difficult for him. But she gave in to the kiss, putting all her love and hope into it. If this was the end, she'd at least take this memory with her.

It was Rafe who finally pushed her away. He grabbed her by the shoulders and held her at arm's length. She saw love in his eyes, as well as hope and desire, just before he shuttered them. Then there was only bleak despair.

"Damn you," she whispered. "Damn you for giving up. For throwing it all away."

But there was no answering fire in his eyes. They were the cold, flat color of obsidian.

"I'm a realist, Abby. At least I was until I met you." He didn't mean that to be an accusation, but it came out that way. She'd made him feel and believe, and now he was suffering because of it. "The reality of the situation is that the authorities need to punish someone. I'm going to be that someone."

"But you didn't do it."

"Are you sure?"

"Yes." She shook off his hands. "You know it and I know it. Obviously your sister knows it, or she wouldn't have you here. And if you give up, whoever did this is going to get away with it."

Rafe slipped his hands into his pockets. "You know why they have that blindfold on the statue of justice?"

"No, why?"

"So she can't see the way the system works. In my experience, it has little to do with what's right or wrong. It has to do with who has pull and who knows how to use the system."

"I don't believe that."

He shrugged and turned to pick up the letters. He held them against his chest and struggled for the strength to face Abby without tears. "Maybe it doesn't work that way in Pershing. But let me tell you a little something about how it works in the big city.

"People with money, high-powered lawyers and influential friends get by with murder. Literally." He turned back to her. "People who come from the ghettos or the barrios or the wrong side of the tracks get plowed under by the system. They're just so much fodder to keep the wheels of justice grinding."

"We can get you a good attorney. The best."

"Money's no object, right?"

"That's right. I have the money. I can—"

"No." The violence in his eyes frightened her. "I won't take your money. It would be wasted on a useless cause."

"I don't think it would be a waste. I can't think of anything I'd rather spend it on."

"Save your money, Abby. There aren't any happy endings for people like me and Theresa. The prosecution doesn't have the smoking gun, but they have my fingerprints on a glass and my blood on the victim. That's enough for most people to convict me right there.

"If that's not enough, they'll bring my father up to the stand. They'll point out to the jury that he's a drunk. That he can't hold a job for more than six weeks. That he's a drain on society. Then they'll parade Eduardo, who's so much like the old man he could be a clone. If they don't feel they've convinced the jury by that time, they'll drag out the pictures of Frank in his gang clothes. Pictures of Frank dead on the sidewalk with the bullet holes in him.''

"Those people aren't *you!*"

"I look like them, Abby. You put me next to them and you can see the family resemblance. Then the prosecution brings in psychiatrists who talk about the vicious cycle of poverty and violence. They point to me and say that no matter how hard I tried, I couldn't break free of it. By that time the jury's thinking, 'Oh, the fruit never falls far from the tree,' and the next thing you know, I'm doing ten to twenty in some prison, while Carlos's wife—who had a hell of a lot more to gain than I did—is walking around free in her designer clothes. That's the way the system really works, Abby. That's reality.''

She was looking at him dry-eyed and angry. It wasn't the reaction he'd expected.

"It only works that way if you let it." She drew herself up to her full five feet as she said it. If it wasn't so ridiculous, he would have sworn she was looking down her nose at him. "It only works that way if you won't stand up and say, 'Look at me. Judge me by who I am. By what I've done.'

"And do you know who they'll see if you do that? They'll see the man I fell in love with. They'll see a hero. Not because you saved those children on San Miguel, although that's part of it. They'll see a hero because of the way you've pulled yourself out of that cycle of poverty and violence. Because of the way you struggled to take care of your sister when your family and society let you down. They'll see a hero because that's what you've always been deep down inside. It's what you'll always be— as long as you believe it."

She wasn't dry-eyed anymore. Big, silent tears were coursing down her cheeks. She wiped them away with the back of her hand. "If you don't stand up and make them see it, they'll bury you. And they'll bury the next guy like you and the next."

She reached into her purse, pulled out a slip of paper and laid it on the table. "I called my brother Spencer to get the names of some top-notch attorneys. Spence practices up north, but he's on a state bar committee with some people from this area. These are the attorneys he recommends. If you decide to fight for yourself—or for us—call one of them."

She crossed to the door, then turned back to face Rafe. "There are two more things you should know. The first is that I love you. I always will. The second is that I've shed all the tears I'm going to over you. If you decide to fight, call me. I'll stand toe-to-toe with you and take on the entire justice system if necessary. If you want someone to weep over poor, disadvantaged Rafael Calderon, don't bother."

Then she turned and was gone, leaving him holding the packet of letters and his broken dreams.

Rafe told himself he didn't need her. He didn't need anyone. He was smart enough to know how the system worked, and he wasn't going to give anyone the satisfaction of watching him squirm. He wasn't going to struggle and hope and still end up on the losing side anyway. He even convinced himself that they—whoever *they* were— couldn't hurt him any more than they already had.

Then he thought about Abby and all the days and years they could have had. About raising children and growing old together. And the pain was so intense that he wanted to die. Death would be easier than the long empty years ahead.

That's when he knew Abby was right. He was being a coward. And it occurred to him that if he didn't fight, if he didn't put up the biggest damn struggle the justice system had ever seen, then he was as good as dead. No, it was worse than that. It would be as if Rafe, the man Abby loved, had never existed.

On Sunday morning, Rafe dialed the home number of one of the attorneys Spencer Alexander had recommended. He made an appointment for Monday morning. That afternoon, he went out and bought an engagement ring. It was a symbol of everything he wanted out of life—and of his belief that he deserved it.

He was going to ask Abby to marry him again. Only this time he'd do it right. This time he'd have champagne and roses and the ring. Though Theresa urged him to call Abby then, he refused. He wanted Abby to see him standing up for himself. He wanted her to see that he was fighting as hard as he knew how. He wanted her to see him as a hero again. Then he'd call.

Sunday evening, he sat down with Theresa to go over everything she knew about Laurie Negrette that might prove useful to his attorney. Not only did he need the information, but it kept Theresa's mind busy. Carlos had been in a coma for ten days now. With each passing day, doctors said it became less likely he'd come out of it.

It was late in the evening when the call came. Rafe, who was watching TV, answered it.

"This is Mrs. Walker," a soft voice said. "I'm one of Mr. Negrette's nurses."

"Yes?" He remembered her vaguely: mid-forties, very considerate of Theresa and her condition.

"I shouldn't be calling, but I thought your sister would want to know. Mr. Negrette is beginning to show signs that he's coming out of the coma. Don't mention my name, please.'' Then she hung up.

Rafe woke Theresa, who'd gone to bed early. She dressed and they arrived at the hospital around twenty-four hundred hours. They took up their vigil in the waiting room as they had before.

Rafe could tell that something was going on. Hospital personnel were rushing in and out of Carlos's room. The two detectives arrived thirty minutes later. When Mrs. Walker brought a pillow and blanket for Theresa, Rafe asked if Laurie Negrette was in the room. The nurse informed him that though the doctor himself had called her, she hadn't shown up.

Once Theresa had drifted off to sleep, Rafe bought vending-machine coffee and stationed himself at the end of the hallway, where he could watch who came and went. At one hundred hours Mrs. Walker went in. When she came out only moments later, it was to motion Rafe toward the room.

"Get your sister,'' the nurse told him. ''Mr. Negrette is asking for her.''

Rafe woke Theresa and escorted her down the hall. She swayed when they first stepped into the room. If Rafe hadn't had an arm around her shoulders, she might have stumbled. Someone should have warned them about the bandages and the tubes, Rafe thought angrily. Then Carlos opened his eyes.

"Theresa.'' His voice was weak, but he smiled when he saw her.

She was at his side immediately. ''You had me worried.''

"Sorry.'' He swallowed with effort. ''How's the baby?''

"Fine.'' Theresa was crying and smiling at the same time. ''Rafe's been taking care of us.''

Carlos looked back to where Rafe stood by the door. "I told them you didn't do it. They didn't want to believe me at first." He eyes slid back to Theresa. "It was Laurie. She didn't want to divide community property in a divorce settlement. She wanted it all. Any policeman with half a brain should have realized that she had the most to gain."

"Shh." Theresa reached out a gentle hand to caress his cheek. "I love you."

"I know. I'm a very lucky man."

Rafe stepped out of the shadows. "Does that mean you're going to marry my sister?"

"Just as soon as it can be arranged. I don't want to wait another minute."

Mrs. Walker bustled in. "Too much company isn't good for the patient." She glared at the cops.

What was it Rafe had said to Abby about there not being any happy endings for people like him and Theresa? Well, his sister certainly seemed to have happily ever after within her grasp. It was time for Rafe to see if he could arrange a fairy-tale ending of his own. And, like Carlos, he didn't want to wait any longer than necessary. There was a good chance Abby would make him eat crow in the process. But what did a little crow matter if he could spend the rest of his life with Abby?

He made arrangements with the cops to take Theresa home, promised his sister that he would return to give the bride away and was on the freeway by four in the morning. He pulled off in Riverside to look for a twenty-four-hour market that sold flowers and champagne, then hit Monday-morning rush-hour traffic. He didn't pull into Abby's driveway until eight-thirty. When she didn't answer the front door, he ran around to the back. Determined to talk to her, he came back around to beat on the front door.

"Abby, open up." He knocked again and rang the doorbell. "Let me in. Please."

His voice was getting hoarse by the time the neighbor came over.

"You can make as much racket as you want, but it won't do any good."

"Why? Where is she?"

"First day of summer school. That's where she is."

That put a whole different spin on things, Rafe decided. It was one thing to go down on bended knee in the privacy of her house. It was another to do it in front of her class. He could wait until school was over, but that was hours away. Besides, it seemed fitting. After all, it was the students who had brought them together.

Abby checked her watch again. Ten more minutes and the bell would ring to begin summer school. She had her lesson plans ready and the books stacked neatly on the table at the front of the room. This was going to be good for her, she assured herself for the thousandth time. It would keep her mind off Rafe. If would give her something to do other than fret about him.

Although she hadn't been able to stop worrying, true to her word, she hadn't shed another tear. Since he'd left town, she'd reorganized the garage, weeded and watered the flowers in the front of the house and cleaned out the closets. When she returned from L.A. she'd started refinishing that little desk she'd bought at a garage sale. She'd been so tired at night that she'd collapsed into bed, only to lie there staring at the ceiling. But she hadn't cried. That was a point of pride for her.

And she wasn't going to cry if the students asked about him. She would tell them what she knew and encourage them to write to him. But she would not cry.

"Martin, Leo, quit teasing Doreen." She spoke absently as she walked past the trio. "Morning," she said to Kevin. Abby put her arm around Rachael's shoulder when she came skipping up to her. But before she could find out what the dark-eyed girl had on her mind, there was a commotion at the other side of the playground.

Abigail turned to see students streaming across the yard. Even those around her ran to join the procession. Abigail blinked. That couldn't be Rafe at the head of the group, could it? She was speechless as the students followed him across the blacktop like some modern Pied Piper. He was grinning when he stopped in front of her. He was also carrying a bouquet of roses.

"I thought you'd like to know that Carlos came out of his coma. He told the cops that it was his wife who'd put the bullet in him."

"That's wonderful. About him coming out of the coma, not about his wife trying to kill him."

"I kind of figured that was what you meant. He and Theresa are going to get married."

So were we, she thought. "I hope they'll be very happy."

"They will be. I'm sure of it. Of course, that destroys my theory about there not being any happy endings."

Abigail rocked back on her heels and smiled. "I guess it does."

"Don't get smug on me," Rafe warned. "This isn't easy, you know."

"Admitting you're wrong rarely is."

"I'd already called one of the attorneys your brother recommended. I was supposed to meet with him this morning."

Abigail went completely still. "Does that mean you were going to fight? That you were going to go in there and beat the system?"

"We'll never know if I could have beaten it, but I can guarantee I was going to fight."

She felt the moisture gathering in her eyes. "I swore I wasn't going to cry anymore."

"I don't want to make you cry, Abby. I want to make you happy."

"Is this going to get mushy?" Martin asked.

Abigail laughed. "Oh, I hope so."

"I promised myself I was going to do this right." Rafe handed her the roses. "I have champagne, but I left it in the car. I thought there might be some law against having liquor on school grounds."

"There is." She brought the bouquet to her face and inhaled the sweet scent of roses. "These are beautiful."

"There's more," he assured her as he searched through his pockets. When he brought out the ring, Abby gave in to the tears. Rafe went down on one knee.

"You don't have to do that," she told him.

"Yep, it's the mushy stuff," Kevin complained.

Rachael elbowed him in the ribs. "I think it's cool."

"Girls," Martin and Kevin said in unison, shaking their heads.

Rafe smiled up at her. "I want to do it, Abby. You deserve it." He glanced to where Kevin and Martin stood. "You'd better take notes, guys, because one day you're going to have to do this."

Rafe looked back at Abigail. "I'd recite a poem for you, only I don't know any. But I do know a miracle when I see one. You're a miracle, Abby. You took a man who didn't believe in friends and gave him a whole town full. You took a man who didn't believe in family and made him want one. You took a man who didn't believe in love and taught him how empty life is without it.

"If that wasn't enough, you taught me to believe in happy endings. You made me believe that the measure of a man—or woman—is found in the heart. And when I would have thrown everything away, you made me believe in myself. You changed my life."

"*Really* mushy stuff." Martin shuddered.

Rafe and Abby slanted him a warning glance.

Rafe slipped the diamond over the very tip of Abigail's ring finger. "Will you marry me, Abby? Will you make the miracle complete?"

Abby looked from the man at her feet to the ring he was ready to slip on her finger. It was everything she'd ever wanted, and since it was never going to happen again, she wanted to savor the moment and lock it in her heart forever.

"Say yes," Rachael advised in a whisper.

Doreen looked at her Mickey Mouse watch. "And you'd better hurry. The bell is gonna ring."

Abigail laughed. "Yes," she said, before anyone else could offer advice.

Rafe slipped the ring into place and stood. Taking the bouquet from her, he handed it to Martin.

"Ooh, yucky roses," the boy complained. "I don't want to hold these." He pushed them into Rachael's outstretched arms. "You take them."

Rafe looked into Abby's eyes. They were bright with tears, though he couldn't tell if they were tears of joy or laughter.

"I suppose I could have picked a more romantic setting."

Abby glanced at Rachael's rapt expression. "You couldn't have found a more memorable one," she assured him.

Rafe tasted tears and laughter when his lips touched Abby's. But what else could he expect when he held a miracle in his arms?

* * * * *

Silhouette

SPECIAL EDITION

COMING NEXT MONTH

#919 MAIL ORDER COWBOY—Patricia Coughlin
That Special Woman!

Allie Halston swore she'd conquer rigorous ranch life, even if it meant taking on all of Texas! Then she faced sexy Burn Monroe—who was more than just a cowboy with an attitude....

#920 B IS FOR BABY—Lisa Jackson
Love Letters

Beth Crandall's single passionate night with Jenner McKee had changed her life forever. Years later, an unexpected letter drew her back home, and to the man she'd never forgotten....

#921 THE GREATEST GIFT OF ALL—Penny Richards

Baron Montgomery knew determined Mallory Ryan would sacrifice anything for her young child. But when her boundless mother's love was tested, could Mallory accept his help and his promise of everlasting devotion?

#922 WHEN MORNING COMES—Christine Flynn

Driven and dedicated, Travis McCloud had sacrificed his marriage for career. Now a chance reunion with Brooke compelled him to open his heart…and to take a second chance at love.

#923 COWBOY'S KIN—Victoria Pade
A Ranching Family

Linc Heller's wild, hell-raising ways were legendary. Yet Kansas Daye wondered if becoming a father had tempered Linc—and if he was ready to step into her waiting arms.

#924 LET'S MAKE IT LEGAL—Trisha Alexander

John Appleton gave up the fast track to become Mr. Mom. Then high-powered lawyer Sydney Scott Wells stormed into his life, and John knew he'd show her the best of both worlds!

MILLION DOLLAR SWEEPSTAKES (III)

Dark secrets, dangerous desire...

Lovers DARK AND DANGEROUS

Three spine-tingling tales from the dark side of love.

This October, enter the world of shadowy romance as Silhouette presents the third in their annual tradition of thrilling love stories and chilling story lines. Written by three of Silhouette's top names:

LINDSAY McKENNA
LEE KARR
RACHEL LEE

Haunting a store near you this October.

Only from ▼ *Silhouette*®
™

...where passion lives.

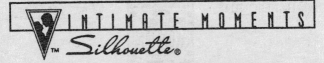

INTIMATE MOMENTS
Silhouette ®

NIGHT SHIFT, NIGHT SHADOW, NIGHTSHADE...
Now Nora Roberts brings you the latest
in her *Night Tales* series

NIGHT SMOKE
Intimate Moments #595

The fire was under control when American Hero Ryan Piasecki got there. But he was an arson inspector, so the end of the fire was the beginning of his job. He scanned the crowd, looking for that one face that might give him a clue, a lead. Then he saw her.

She was beautiful, elegant, cool—an exotic flower amid the ashes. She was an unlikely candidate as an arsonist, but as a woman...

As a woman she probably wouldn't even give him the time of day.

Look for Ryan Piasecki and Natalie Fletcher's story in NIGHT SMOKE, coming in October to your favorite retail outlet. It's hot!

NIGHT94

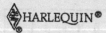 HARLEQUIN®   Silhouette®

The movie event of the season can be the reading event of the year!

Lights... The lights go on in October when CBS presents Harlequin/Silhouette Sunday Matinee Movies. These four movies are based on bestselling Harlequin and Silhouette novels.

Camera... As the cameras roll, be the first to read the original novels the movies are based on!

Action... Through this offer, you can have these books sent directly to you! Just fill in the order form below and you could be reading the books...before the movie!

48288-4	Treacherous Beauties by Cheryl Emerson	
	$3.99 U.S./$4.50 CAN.	☐
83305-9	Fantasy Man by Sharon Green	
	$3.99 U.S./$4.50 CAN.	☐
48289-2	A Change of Place by Tracy Sinclair	
	$3.99 U.S./$4.50CAN.	☐
83306-7	Another Woman by Margot Dalton	
	$3.99 U.S./$4.50 CAN.	☐

TOTAL AMOUNT	$	
POSTAGE & HANDLING	$	
($1.00 for one book, 50¢ for each additional)		
APPLICABLE TAXES*	$	_____
TOTAL PAYABLE	$	_____
(check or money order—please do not send cash)		

To order, complete this form and send it, along with a check or money order for the total above, payable to Harlequin Books, to: **In the U.S.:** 3010 Walden Avenue, P.O. Box 9047, Buffalo, NY 14269-9047; **In Canada:** P.O. Box 613, Fort Erie, Ontario, L2A 5X3.

Name: _____

Address: _____ City: _____

State/Prov.: _____ Zip/Postal Code: _____

*New York residents remit applicable sales taxes.
Canadian residents remit applicable GST and provincial taxes.

CBSPR

"HOORAY FOR HOLLYWOOD" SWEEPSTAKES

HERE'S HOW THE SWEEPSTAKES WORKS

OFFICIAL RULES — NO PURCHASE NECESSARY

To enter, complete an Official Entry Form or hand print on a 3" x 5" card the words "HOORAY FOR HOLLYWOOD", your name and address and mail your entry in the pre-addressed envelope (if provided) or to: "Hooray for Hollywood" Sweepstakes, P.O. Box 9076, Buffalo, NY 14269-9076 or "Hooray for Hollywood" Sweepstakes, P.O. Box 637, Fort Erie, Ontario L2A 5X3. Entries must be sent via First Class Mail and be received no later than 12/31/94. No liability is assumed for lost, late or misdirected mail.

Winners will be selected in random drawings to be conducted no later than January 31, 1995 from all eligible entries received.

Grand Prize: A 7-day/6-night trip for 2 to Los Angeles, CA including round trip air transportation from commercial airport nearest winner's residence, accommodations at the Regent Beverly Wilshire Hotel, free rental car, and $1,000 spending money. (Approximate prize value which will vary dependent upon winner's residence: $5,400.00 U.S.); 500 Second Prizes: A pair of "Hollywood Star" sunglasses (prize value: $9.95 U.S. each). Winner selection is under the supervision of D.L. Blair, Inc., an independent judging organization, whose decisions are final. Grand Prize travelers must sign and return a release of liability prior to traveling. Trip must be taken by 2/1/96 and is subject to airline schedules and accommodations availability.

Sweepstakes offer is open to residents of the U.S. (except Puerto Rico) and Canada who are 18 years of age or older, except employees and immediate family members of Harlequin Enterprises, Ltd., its affiliates, subsidiaries, and all agencies, entities or persons connected with the use, marketing or conduct of this sweepstakes. All federal, state, provincial, municipal and local laws apply. Offer void wherever prohibited by law. Taxes and/or duties are the sole responsibility of the winners. Any litigation within the province of Quebec respecting the conduct and awarding of prizes may be submitted to the Regie des loteries et courses du Quebec. All prizes will be awarded; winners will be notified by mail. No substitution of prizes are permitted. Odds of winning are dependent upon the number of eligible entries received.

Potential grand prize winner must sign and return an Affidavit of Eligibility within 30 days of notification. In the event of non-compliance within this time period, prize may be awarded to an alternate winner. Prize notification returned as undeliverable may result in the awarding of prize to an alternate winner. By acceptance of their prize, winners consent to use of their names, photographs, or likenesses for purpose of advertising, trade and promotion on behalf of Harlequin Enterprises, Ltd., without further compensation unless prohibited by law. A Canadian winner must correctly answer an arithmetical skill-testing question in order to be awarded the prize.

For a list of winners (available after 2/28/95), send a separate stamped, self-addressed envelope to: Hooray for Hollywood Sweepstakes 3252 Winners, P.O. Box 4200, Blair, NE 68009.

CBSRLS

OFFICIAL ENTRY COUPON

"Hooray for Hollywood"
SWEEPSTAKES!

Yes, I'd love to win the Grand Prize — a vacation in Hollywood —
or one of 500 pairs of "sunglasses of the stars"! Please enter me
in the sweepstakes!

**This entry must be received by December 31, 1994.
Winners will be notified by January 31, 1995.**

Name _____

Address _____ Apt. _____

City _____

State/Prov. _____ Zip/Postal Code _____

Daytime phone number _____
                            (area code)

Mail all entries to: Hooray for Hollywood Sweepstakes,
P.O. Box 9076, Buffalo, NY 14269-9076.
In Canada, mail to: Hooray for Hollywood Sweepstakes,
P.O. Box 637, Fort Erie, ON L2A 5X3.

KCH

OFFICIAL ENTRY COUPON

"Hooray for Hollywood"
SWEEPSTAKES!

Yes, I'd love to win the Grand Prize — a vacation in Hollywood —
or one of 500 pairs of "sunglasses of the stars"! Please enter me
in the sweepstakes!

**This entry must be received by December 31, 1994.
Winners will be notified by January 31, 1995.**

Name _____

Address _____ Apt. _____

City _____

State/Prov. _____ Zip/Postal Code _____

Daytime phone number _____
                            (area code)

Mail all entries to: Hooray for Hollywood Sweepstakes,
P.O. Box 9076, Buffalo, NY 14269-9076.
In Canada, mail to: Hooray for Hollywood Sweepstakes,
P.O. Box 637, Fort Erie, ON L2A 5X3.

KCH